CABIN 187

DAN B. FIERCE

FIERCE Imagination

COPYRIGHT

Cover art by Sheryl Hammontree
Illustrations by Dan B. Fierce
Edited by James G. Carlson

DEDICATION

This book is dedicated to my friends and family, especially my sister Vicky. (The younger one. Long story.) Without your help, these stories wouldn't look nearly as polished as they are. You were tantamount in the making of this book.

Now stop nagging me to get it out, for crying out loud.

Thank you, and I love you.

TRIGGER WARNING:

This is Horror.

Some of the themes in this book may upset sensitive readers. Those themes include but are not limited to child endangerment and murder, suicide, abuse, animal abuse, mental illness, violence, gore, and many other extremes.

This is not the book for those looking for feel-good stories. While there may be some wholesome and satisfying endings, make no mistake that the genre is built to frighten and make the reader think. No one is safe from life's horrors, not adults, children, or animals. That may be a brash way to see it, but it is, unfortunately, reality.

Also, note that these stories are works of fiction. Any similarities between real people, places, or events are coincidental.

As the author, I try to limit the scope of these experiences because I know the trauma involved can be very impactful. That said, buyer beware. Go into this book knowing that there are unsettling things contained herein.

You have been warned.

This. Is. Horror

Oh, and one final trigger warning: I am a proud member of the LGBTQIA+ community. If reading my book would be considered a form of support in the reader's mind or go against their beliefs, then they should take note and skip over it. I refuse to apologize for being who I am.

Never again.

CONTENTS

THE BANE OF NEW MADRID 7

THE CLAWFOOT TUB 43

THE ROSE-TINTED MIRROR 61

THE FOREST GUARDIAN 81

CRICKET SONG...92

THE NORTH SIDE OF THE TREES...........112

CURSE OF THE PIASA 140

WHEN THE WIND CHIMES STOP........... 168

LOCKED...177

DESECRATION: THE WET STONES 206

THE SOUVENIR 224

HAUNTED MEMORIES............................248

FERAL 269

ABOUT THE AUTHOR 293

OTHER STORIES 294

BY DAN B. FIERCE: 294

THE BANE OF NEW MADRID

Zeke awoke with a start on the floor of his newly erected cabin as it rocked violently in the middle of the night. Thunder seemed to rumble all around him, not from the sky above but from the ground below. Red hot coals danced in the fireplace, giving the carved male face in the center of the mantle an even more sinister appearance as it silently screamed a warning. The logs in his home groaned inhumanly from the pressure.

The fog in his sleepy brain barely beginning to clear, he attempted to stand, only to get pitched back to the earth. A feeling of nausea overtook him, emptying what little contents he had in his stomach. Fearing that his house might collapse on him, he clambered toward the front door to escape.

Once outside, the pitch black of the night gave little indication of his surroundings. Even the moon had retreated, hiding its face from the world, adding no helpful light. As his eyes adjusted, he stood in his long john underwear and watched in horror, paying no mind to the December chill enveloping him. Trees whiplashed back and forth, touching the soil on all sides. Some snapped, surrendering to whatever violent tantrum the earth was throwing. Streaks of lightning blossomed with an electrical crack from the ground, illuminating the awful racket. The air became heavy with dust and grit, choking him and causing him to cover his mouth.

He heard his horse scream in panic from the barn as it pitched much in the same fashion as everything else. He listened as the animal kicked its stall door down and fled the structure, running for its life.

"It's okay, Zeke."

The voice startled him, prompting him to spin his attention back to his home. It was Levi, the young man who had helped him build his log cabin. He stood in the doorway, seemingly unaffected by the temblor.

"The cabin will keep you safe."

His words sounded reassuring, but Zeke had a difficult time trusting that snake oil salesman's smile on his face, even in these circumstances. Still, the man beckoned him back inside.

Had he been there last night? Zeke just couldn't recall.

Water crashed somewhere in the distance, drawing closer from the sound of it. Explosions emanated from the bowels of the earth, spewing geysers of sand and lightning. Zeke clutched handfuls of crabgrass in terror. Balls of light floated into the air, dancing almost hypnotically in the night. One of the glowing orbs appeared to turn an angry red and zipped at him as if to attack. He yowled in terror as it struck him, and he hit the ground, knocking himself out cold.

The early morning sun did little to sate the chill in his bones as he shook himself awake, every inch of him covered in the dust from last night's quake. In the dim morning light, he looked at his cabin. It appeared as if nothing had happened at all. All around were the signs of a great and awful event. Trees were broken and uprooted. Water had filled a hole in a small clearing to the southeast where there hadn't been one before.

"Explains the water I heard last night," Zeke muttered in gap-jawed wonder at the destruction all around him.

The barn leaned at a severe angle. Huge crevices had opened, running north to south. Mounds of sand dotted the landscape like gigantic anthills.

Slowly, he walked toward the cabin, unsure of whether to trust the very ground beneath his feet. Peering inside his house, he witnessed that it wasn't only standing but devoid of any other human company. He rushed in, dressing hastily, distrustful of the deceptively sound building, before gathering his gun, a canteen, and some food. He then vacated the house as soon as he could.

Outside, his horse knickered nervously, having returned from its fright-induced retreat. Zeke stepped up to the mare, petting and patting her reassuringly. She was covered in silt, too. He tried leading her back to the barn to saddle her up, but she wasn't moving. Pulling with all of his might, he yanked the skewed door ajar. The entire outbuilding shifted ominously from the sudden movement. Zeke kept a cautious eye on the bones of the building as he gathered the saddle and bridle. Wood creaked in protest as he hastened back to the outdoors. He couldn't help but look at his cabin while he slung the harness into place. It was an oasis of serenity in a sea of devastation. And it didn't belong.

Snatching up a couple of pails, Zeke hurried down to the newly formed pond to gather some water for his horse. Bending down, he filled the buckets.

"That's as warm as bathwater!" he remarked.

He raised the container to his face, sniffing the steam. It had the faint, putrid smell of rotten eggs. Carrying the liquid back to his home, he offered it to the mare. She turned away with a wild look in her eyes.

"Ya gotta drink somethin', Spitfire."

He sighed and placed it on the ground in the chance she changed her mind.

"Might just be that it's warm."

He left her to graze as he surveyed any other damage.

The sun was finally above the horizon, but it did little to ease the devastation he saw. Approaching the threshold as if something inside might tear him apart, he peered into the cabin. It was as if nothing had shifted at all, despite what he'd experienced only mere hours ago.

"When I build something, I build it to last," Zeke recalled Levi saying as his cabin was being constructed. The funny thing was, he could barely recall the young man's appearance, as if it were deliberately made hazy in his mind. All he could remember was that Levi barely looked like he was in his twenties and had hair as black as a crow's feathers. "You'll die long before this cabin ever falls."

Zeke shuddered at that last statement. It seemed more of a sales pitch then. Now, it felt more akin to prophesy. Again, Spitfire whinnied nervously as she had in the wee hours, snapping him from his daze. He made his way back outside. The horse bucked, attempting to release herself from the reins. He unhitched her to prevent injury, and she raced off as soon as she was free. Zeke started to give chase, but the sound of cloudless thunder returned.

The earth pitched again, knocking him flat. It echoed through the valley, a snapping he'd only heard while trapping in the snow-covered mountains when an avalanche loosened thick rivers of snow. He got to his hands and knees just in time to see the hills make waves as if made of water themselves. Trees shook as violently as they had the night before; only now, he could watch as they whipped and bent, with some snapping from the strain.

Zeke's heart raced as he watched the earth throw another fit. Geysers of sand blew up into the air, clogging the wind with silt and sulfur. The field he had plowed for a small spring garden was riddled with belching spouts, rendering most of it useless. The gaping crevices that had formed the night before opened and closed like hungry mouths daring anything to feed them.

His newly relocated pond below seemed to boil from the tremor. It didn't feel as strong as the one in the night, but Zeke still watched as hillsides crumbled and reformed from the cataclysm. As the ground shook beneath him, he slowly spun his head back to the cabin. While everything around it shimmied and tossed, the house remained still and in place.

Nausea overtook him from the vision, and he dry heaved. Most men in his position may have considered it a lucky thing that their house had survived the wreckage. He was beginning to think that the townsfolk were right—he should never have built on this land. He'd made a deal with the devil to homestead his property and had gotten more than he'd ever bargained for.

Finally, the quakes subsided. Zeke cautiously got to his feet, fully expecting to be thrown back down in defiance. He glanced at his cabin. It still stood. When it was first erected, he was filled with excitement, pride, and a sense of accomplishment. He'd been a traveling fur trapper for twenty-some years. Now, he could settle down and make a family. He'd even thought about asking the New Madrid Madame, Maddie, to marry him. She'd probably say no since she didn't seem the settling type, but it couldn't hurt to make sure.

After the ground finished trembling beneath him and his abode appeared untouched, he had new feelings. "It ain't natural. I should be grateful, I suppose, but there weren't so much as a crack in the walls."

Just as she had the night before, Spitfire returned, her head bowed in what looked like shame. Zeke patted her comfortingly, reassuringly, while checking her reins and saddle. "I know you're spooked, old girl, but we need to get to town. Maybe we'll stop along the way to make sure no one needs any help."

His mind wandered through the trail that led to New Madrid. There were several homesteaders like him. He wondered if they were safe and if their cabins were also untouched. He already knew the answer before he ever threw his leg over the mare and mounted her. Still, he felt the obligation to check. It was a good hour's ride to the city, and from the looks of things, it might be a rough trip.

"Let's get a-going, Spitfire." He gently slapped the reins, prodding her forward. "We need to find Levi. He's got some explaining to do. And Maddie. Hope she's safe." The animal trotted down the path to town, slowly and carefully working up to a full gallop once Zeke was sure of the earth beneath them.

By the time he reached the bluffs overlooking the path to town, Zeke's heart was heavy from the catastrophe. Neighbor after neighbor, home after home, as he made his way to New Madrid, the scene was pretty much the same: collapsed cabins, ruined farmscapes, broken and mournful people comforting each other and praying for answers. Thankfully, no one had lost their lives so far, but the completeness of the devastation rang surreal, unearthly.

Spitfire came to a complete stop, nickering nervously, snapping Zeke's attention from his thoughts.

"Easy, girl." Looking forward to where the trail led, he could see why the animal had halted. In front of him, portions of the bluff had vanished, having collapsed to the river below. Other parts of the trail had upheaved into towering obstacles where there once was a flat pathway. "Dear God!" Zeke watched the flow of the river. It seemed to boil with anger. Trees, wrecked boats, displaced trees, and debris of all types clogged the channel. Then he saw the death. Farm animals floated in the water with no more life in them than the uprooted shrubbery.

Was that a person?

To his horror, as he looked closer, he discerned humans in the mix as well, many of them dressed like one of the local Indian tribes, as well as boatmen. His hand flew to his mouth, tears involuntarily falling.

Once again, the mare neighed in a growing panic. Twisting her head back, the horse nabbed Zeke's left arm, yanking him from the saddle and depositing him on the ground with an unceremonious thud. Zeke thought he might have felt something snap in the limb she had grabbed, but he still had use of it. White-hot flashes of anger rose in him, making him internally argue the merits of punching an animal. Spitfire reared up, causing the fur trapper to shield himself from twelve hundred pounds of stomping fury. When the attack never came, he peeked up to see his horse had, for the third time in less than a day, vanished on him.

Feeling a slight rumble under him, Zeke scrambled to his feet, wide-eyed in fear. His heart racing, he scattered back the way he'd come. The ground beneath him felt like it turned to liquid while making it to the top of the hill. He ran as if being chased by the devil himself until he thought he might be safe in the middle of the plateau above. As he watched, the terrain he had just been on plummeted into the river, just as the section he had been gawking at undoubtedly had, causing the river to roil angrily again.

Spitfire clopped up behind him and nudged him with her snout.

Zeke spun, grimacing hate at the animal. "You leave me again, and I'll have you boiled down for glue!"

The horse blubbered an apology at him, calming his ire.

He patted her to reassure her that he wasn't upset. "You could've just taken me with you, you know." He watched as yet another section of the bluff removed itself, carving a divot into the hillside toward them. "We're gonna have to find a new way to town."

The journey took twice as long, but Zeke managed to locate another safer roadway toward New Madrid. The horrific scene that awaited wasn't any more pleasant than the trip he'd made to get there. Buildings were cracked and crumbled. No chimney stood. No windows were left whole. People clambered about, gathering anything they could in preparation to abandon the city as quickly as possible. Women and children wailed as men prayed to God for forgiveness for unknown sins.

A cartful of Amish folk hastily hauled goods from inside the local grocer; an older man with hair as gray as a winter sky sat in the front seat, muttering what sounded like a prayer in German as three women and several small children of varying ages listened in. The heaviness in their eyes weighed down his soul. He slowly guided his horse by, garnering baleful glares from the passengers and elders alike. Two men popped out from the store, carrying bags of flour, sugar, and feed, plopping them down into the bed of the cart before returning inside. An older teen boy heaved a burlap sack of canned goods with a metallic clunk. Another child, this one about to be a teen himself, struggled with a bag of potatoes, gaining some assistance from one of the younger women inside the transport.

"Thou art the one who brung this upon us!"

The voice startled Zeke, nearly causing him to fall off of his mare. He slung his head so fast to the source that he thought he'd given himself whiplash. Another Amish man, this one about thirty to forty at a guess, scowled at him while carrying a sack of animal feed on each shoulder.

"Thou were warned to not build upon thine land, that thee would set upon us a curse," he said with ominous accusation before spitting at the ground by Zeke's feet three times.

The trapper's ire boiling over, he snatched the man up by his shirt and brought him nose-to-nose. Speaking through gritted teeth, he drew back a fist, causing Hezekiah to pale and shrink in his grasp. The women in the wagon shrieked, covering as many of the little ones' eyes as they could.

"I'm fixin' to forget we're both God-fearing men," Zeke growled. "Now, where's Levi?"

"Wh-who?"

Seeing the lack of recognition in the man's expression, he loosened his grip. He took in a deep breath and released the Amish "Young man. Late teens or early twenties. Black hair and pale complexion."

The elder in the front began shouting at them in German with such fervor that he looked like he might have a stroke. Zeke and Hezekiah listened for a bit; then, the trapper looked at the Amish for a translation. "My father says the whoreson died in the fire alongside his mother. He says if you're seeing him now, it means that his name was spelt wrong. Levi is evil."

Now it was Zeke's turn to lose the color in his face. His knees felt like they would give out on him at the news. "Maddie's dead? Her boy, too?"

Hezekiah straightened himself out, turning away to hide the fear in his face from the womenfolk. "Stay clear of him, trapper. He'll damn your soul."

"I'm afraid it's a might late for that." Zeke's breathing calmed, and his legs steadied. "Now, where can I find him?"

Hezekiah thought on it but came up empty. He turned to the elder and spoke, getting a still-fevered reply in German. "He says to try where it started," the Amish instructed Zeke, unable to gaze into his eyes. "Now, if you'll excuse me, I have a family to care for."

Zeke backed away with his hands held high. He knew he probably wouldn't get any more information from them. The men and boys finished loading while he watched. The eldest teen boy glared at Zeke, hopping into the back of the wagon, daring him to touch his family again as they drove away.

"Try where it started?" Zeke muttered to himself.

He pondered the cryptic message for a bit, then got an idea: *Maybe it was that burned building I saw when I came back to town.*

He had to be sure. Striding into the grocer's as the clerk finished ringing up a customer's items, Zeke stepped aside, allowing a woman out. She looked him up and down, her scowl heavy with judgment. Just as the Amish man had, she spat wordlessly at his feet and stomped out of the entry. The clerk regarded the trapper suspiciously. Zeke ignored the look.

"You know where Maddie's place is?"

"You mean the whore?"

Zeke flew at the clerk, taking his collar as he had the religious man's. "You call her a whore again, and I'll beat you 'till we both bleed! Now, where's her place?"

"Sh-she had a saloon on the southwest outskirts of town, close to the river. It burnt to the ground several years ago. She perished in the fire. Her son, too."

"Thank ye." Zeke snorted and let the man go. He then marched out of the store without so much as a backward glance.

That was *her place*!

Zeke crossed the dusty street, unhitched Spitfire, turned toward the southwest, and sped off. Arriving at the charred remains of a wooden building, he marveled at the leaning wall that still stood, even after the quake, but barely. The fireplace was in ruins, scarcely a pile of blackened stones, some cracked and broken by either the heat of the conflagration or gravity's grasp when the structure fell. No one was there.

"Oh, Maddie." Zeke's heart weighed down as he dismounted his mare. He shuffled over to the remnants, kicking the dust in his shame. As he scoured the long-dead embers, the sun caught something just right. He bent down, collecting a chain of silver with a heart-shaped locket from an inch of dirt. The heat and elements had caked the bauble with soot and discoloration. Knocking the dust off as best he could, it spun from his hand hypnotically. It was, indeed, the one he had given her those many years ago. "Oh, Maddie," he repeated. "I'm so sorry."

"Sorry isn't good enough anymore."

The sudden voice from behind the still-standing wall gave Zeke a start, and he jumped back. "Levi?"

The young man he sought was staring at the wreckage, a deep sadness in his eyes. Then he spun on the trapper, a damning fire in his glare. "You should've been here for her! For us!" He strode toward Zeke, baleful intent on his face. "You don't get to be sorry. You don't know regret! But I'll show you!" With unnatural speed, Levi closed the gap between them, placing a hand on Zeke's forehead.

Levi's voice washed over Zeke, growing distant and tinny, as he faded into memories that weren't his, his body jerking and spasming in an uncontrollable fit.

"Now you'll see! You'll feel her life and mine. You'll know why this town is damned."

Zeke watched his sixteen-year-old self facing a slightly younger Maddie as if observing from the outside.

"You said you loved me, Ezekiel Bane!" Maddie sobbed, looking down at her stomach. "My baby is gonna need a father."

The upset and frightened young man turned from the girl. "Maddie, I can't provide for you by staying here in New Madrid. I have to learn to trap. There's money in fur, and it's steady work. It's all there is around here." He turned to her, pleading in his eyes, and gently wiped a tear from her cheek.

Maddie started to speak when a knock came on the door. A grizzled older man covered in various furs peeked through the door. His face was stern and impatient, but there was a hint of empathy in his eyes. "You 'bout ready, Zeke? We're gonna have to catch the next boat up to Iowa, and it's fixin' to leave soon."

She watched the boy nod silently and heard the door quietly snap shut. She threw her back to him, clamping her eyes closed in an attempt to stop the flow of tears. "Just go then!"

She watched through squinted eyes as Zeke stumbled to say something, anything to comfort her. After a long silence, he hung his head, faced the door, and left, slump-shouldered, toward his future without her.

The next few months of Maddie's life flew by in Zeke's mind like flipping through pages in a journal. He watched as she desperately searched for a suitor to take her hand, but the more pronounced her condition was, despite her youth and enchanting looks, the less interested any man seemed to be in her. The townsfolk spat obscenities at her, the words clinging to her heart like tar. Even her church offered her no respite from the cruelty, banishing her to solitude. She could no longer take part in their holy rituals. It was all she could do to get the midwife to help her as she birthed her baby boy. The labor was long and not without complications, the recovery even more so. Still, she emerged a proud mother, steel protecting her soul from being an outcast in society. She scrimped and saved where she could, picking crops in the fields, even as she cared for her child in one hand. The final memory from Maddie's perspective was her clasping a deed of land as surveyors plotted the foundation of her saloon on the city's outskirts, close to the river.

Before Zeke's eyes, Levi grew from an infant to a toddler. He'd attempt to make friends with other kids his age, only for their parents to sweep them away from him as he looked on in innocent confusion. As he grew of school age, he quickly learned to fight, growing bitter from the name-calling and constant, unnecessary treatment. Flashes of awful, judgmental faces of all ages flashed into view. They spat venomous words at him: "Bastard!" and "Whoreson!" He was always the one to get into trouble, the harsh schoolmarm refusing to believe him over any "legitimate" children. She'd gone so far as telling him so on many occasions, treating him as a criminal for merely being born. Even age didn't bring understanding as he began to blossom into a young man. No father would allow his daughter to be seen with Levi. Zeke felt every pang of this horrible cruelty as it stained Levi's heart black and resentful.

The trapper, feeling black, palpable hate well up inside, witnessed as Levi observed his mother write letter after letter to her lover yet never send them off for fear of them coming back rejected. He listened to endless nights of Maddie crying when she thought her child was asleep, the sorrow sagging his soul.

A priest knocked on Maddie's door, smiling radiantly upon her weathered and tired face as she answered. It had been nearly thirteen years since she'd last seen this man. A pre-teen Levi peeked around them as they conversed. The feelings he felt emanating from his mother confused him. Loathing. Relief. Happiness that someone, anyone, would treat her as though she were human. The holy man was charming and grinned wide as he referred to Levi as "son."

The man began to visit them more as the boy's thirteenth birthday approached. Levi watched as his mother became smitten by the stranger, drinking in the priest's every word as it filled a deep need. They would go into the woods, all three of them, where they held hands and performed strange rites in preparation for something Levi was to be a part of on his birthday.

The next memory was particular in the time frame yet very obscured in content. Everything was hazy and blurred as if viewed by someone drunk. The world spun under Zeke's feet like he'd been on an all-night bender. He looked to his right and saw the most beautiful naked woman in his life. Madeline "Maddie" Johnson was holding his hand as they skipped under the light of the full moon on January 5th, 1806. To his left was a man clothed only in a leather strap with a sheathed dagger, his body in perfect shape, yet his face fuzzy from drink. Zeke couldn't see to tell, but the fact that every part of him felt a breeze as he relived this memory suggested that Levi may have also been in his birthday suit. Their speech was muffled, their conveyances only partly discernible.

"How does it feel, birthday boy?" Maddie grinned wide as they left the forest behind them, heading back toward their saloon and home.

"He is no longer a boy," corrected the nude priest. "He is now a full-fledged man."

He indeed felt as if things had changed. He felt the power that had surged through and into Levi that night. His nerves buzzed with it. His soul rang like a spinning silver coin from it. Still, it felt unfocused and new.

The preacher felt the delight and happiness in Levi's heart as it suddenly turned into cold, black terror.

"There they are!"

The three spun to the sound of the voice leading an agitated crowd on the near horizon. He couldn't yet make out faces, only silhouettes, briefly lit by flickering torches, brandishing weapons and heading their way. Looking at Maddie, he saw the sheer horror in her eyes as she screamed. When he turned his gaze to the priest, the man looked at him as he uttered a single word: "Run!"

"There!" The word echoed in the silence of the night.

"Get them!" answered a chorus of the gathering.

The three scrambled as fast as they could through the field, hearts racing, eyes darting back and forth from the mob to the safety of the saloon doors. The battle for their lives would be close. They were nearer than the crowd was and a bit faster. The trio leaped into the building, latching and barring the heavy oak door securely behind them, barely getting the portal shut before the thrall of voices surrounded the entrance. Fists pounded the door, shaking it in its jamb.

"Leave us alone!" Maddie screamed to the obstinate mob.

"Upstairs. Quickly," ordered the priest.

They clambered up the flight of stairs and into the main bedroom, slamming the door to add another layer of respite. The small windows of the living quarters offered little visibility to see what the crowd was planning. Finally, the drumming on the door ceased. The voices were too far away, and too many walls stood between them to hear the scheming. They didn't have to wait for long.

Plumes of smoke arose, first outside the building, then inside, and fire engulfed the structure. Flames licked up the outer walls, peeking into the windows, taunting the three to approach. Instead, they backed away, throwing the bedroom door wide to find a means of escape. Smoke and flame belched in every direction; everything was alight. There was no way out. Coughing from the dense fog of ruin, they hurried back down the stairs. The mob was still there, cheering on the purifying will of the fire.

The priest looked around quickly. He snatched up a splintered timber with a pained hiss—it still burned—and began scribbling on the wooden floor at the center of the room. His skin began to blister as he held the wood. Still, he continued his spell, chanting and muttering as the main crossbeam above them rained sparks. He could hear the wood creak and groan while the holy man continued his work. He completed the circle, still chanting as he approached Levi. Without explanation, he tossed the young man within the bounds of the sigil. He reached for Maddie to do the same, but a thunderous crack echoed above them as the main beam succumbed to the flames.

A sharp, white light flashed.

Suddenly, Zeke found himself transported back to the distant safety of the forest, watching the structure burn. Hiding behind a tree, racked by agony, blisters appeared on all parts of his body. His right arm felt broken. Fear drummed in his heart as if trying to push through his ribcage. He stifled his coughs as his lungs cleared themselves of the inhaled smoke so that he wouldn't be discovered. Tears ran over his cheeks as he watched the townsfolk celebrate their awful deed.

"Mom," Zeke felt himself whisper. Not "Maddie" but "Mom." The notion caught him off guard, staggering him. The grief of monumental loss hit him like a ton of stones, causing his legs to go limp. Quietly bawling through the injuries and loss, the hours passed. Mourning emptied his heart of the love for his mother and even the man who had become like a father to him in the last year, replacing it with palpable darkness. The sun rose on his skin that morning yet set on his soul.

Outside, the crowd heard the remaining supports give way, cheering victoriously as the outer walls suddenly listed inward. The three they had trapped inside screamed only once as the beam collapsed. The crackling of the structure became the only sound. With the bloodlust of the gathering sated, they began to leave, one by one, until only a few remained to make sure that their job was indeed complete.

Zeke thought that the memory would have perished with the saloon, but all that was left were feelings—exquisite, unending pain, cavernous hate, and thick, tarry, soul-staining vengeance. The thoughts were so vile that they shook him back to reality.

Levi released his hold on the fur trapper, both men gasping for breath as if they'd run a competition.

"I..." Zeke panted as he attempted to catch his breath. "I had no idea. You poor boy. I'm so sorry."

Levi grimaced in hate, growling through gritted teeth: "It's far too late for apologies and condolences. You and this town are cursed. I've seen to it. If I can't have your souls, then I'll take the souls of your descendants. The guardian of the forest has granted me the ability to trap them within the same logs of your cabin."

A sudden realization dawned on Zeke's face. "That's why my house didn't fall in the quake!"

The smile that crossed Levi's lips sent a chill dancing down the trapper's spine.

Levi nodded slowly as the light came on in Zeke's mind. "I have one more memory to show you."

Again, laying his hand on the trapper's forehead, he recalled the construction of his cabin.

"'Tis all wrong, sir."

The voice behind Zeke gave him a start as he surveyed the forest for suitable trees to use. He spun on his heels to see a young man, barely out of his teens, if that. He was dressed as plainly as the Amish men had been, a wide-brimmed hat preventing the sun from reaching his eyes. Tufts of raven hair peeked from under the chapeau. Despite his appearance, his green eyes bore wisdom beyond his years.

"What's that, young man?" Ezekiel couldn't disguise his ire when he spoke, the visitor's timing catching him off guard.

"Your house should be facing the South." The newcomer, wearing a snake oil salesman's grin, stuck his hand out. "My name is Levi. Good to meet you."

Zeke shook it, introducing himself almost absently. "How do you know this?"

"Oh," he began, "I've helped raise my share of properties. I may look young, but I have plenty of experience." Levi stepped forward, looking past Ezekiel to the foundation they had laid. "I can fix it easily enough." He looked around the landscape. "Winter is coming soon. We'll have to work hard and fast."

"You don't talk like the Mennonites." Zeke scanned him up and down. He was undoubtedly a sturdily built lad, if not a bit skinny. "I'll take all the help I can get, but I can't pay ya too much."

"I am of an older religion." Levi strolled over to the foundation for a closer inspection, keeping his face away from the sun almost instinctively. "Where I come from, we help our neighbors. I'll get my payment in other ways. As for the Amish, their superstitions don't hold water with us."

Gooseflesh prickled Zeke's arms. "I don't recall mentioning why they wouldn't help me."

Levi waved it off dismissively. "It doesn't matter. I know what they say about this land." A low rumbling echoed over the rolling hills like distant thunder. It almost felt as though the earth itself was moving. Levi looked to the source and smiled widely, his grin appearing almost too toothy for his mouth. "Ah. Here they come now."

Zeke watched in the direction his visitor was gazing. Several bulky-looking men surrounded a tall, muscular steed that pulled a flat cart toward them. "Tarnation," Ezekiel uttered in awe at the crew heading in their direction. He was dumbstruck as the men approached at an oddly fast pace. "Where'd ya dig them up?"

Levi's smile never wavered. "Tell me"—his voice was soothing and silky, almost hypnotic— "are you willing to make the necessary sacrifices?"

Zeke slowly snapped from the trance in which the approaching crew held him, Levi's words barely registering. "Hmmm? What sacrifices?"

The young man turned toward the men as they pulled their cart to a stop. The stallion, a brutishly gargantuan thing, snorted impatiently. "You know. Sweat. Tears." He spun away from Ezekiel as his eyes glowed. "Blood. All of that. It takes hard work and long days to build a good home. Are you willing to do what it takes?"

One of the men Zeke had previously hired looked at the group as they pulled to a stop, horror etched on his face. He began to mutter things in Spanish, falling to the ground and pedaling backward as if trying to get away. "Ay, Dios mío!" He crossed himself, scampering to his feet. He pointed at Zeke with an accusing finger, speaking rapidly in his native tongue before retreating to town without collecting his gear.

"We don't need him," Levi said, seemingly somewhat amused by the display. Again, he put forward his hand. "Do we have a deal, then?" He saw a flicker of doubt in Ezekiel's eyes. He smirked knowingly. "I can take my crew and leave if you prefer, but you should change the direction of your house." He slowly lowered his arm.

Clasping his hands behind his back, he whistled as he strolled to join them. The whole crew began to look as if they were about to depart.

Desperation overtook Zeke while the few who remained of his original crew looked on. He rushed to Levi and took his hand, shaking it vigorously. "Okay! Okay! You have yourself a deal."

The strange visitor gave another signal, prompting the newly arrived crew to park themselves and produce tents and stakes. "Well then," Levi hissed triumphantly, "Let's begin."

Levi and his crew began rending the foundation up and remaking it the way he described it. Much to his surprise, Ezekiel had very little to do, and the redone foundation looked far better than before. On top of all of that, he could envision the view from what would be the sunny southern side. Before the final stones were placed in the corners and where the front door would be erected, Zeke thought he saw a sigil on the undersides.

"What's that for?"

Levi grinned. "It's traditional in my religion. It's for protection. As long as those stones remain whole, your house will always be safe."

The more Ezekiel saw that young man's smile, the less he liked it. *Why does this whole thing feel like a lie?*

As if reading his mind, Levi spoke: "It's harmless. Besides, it's what you wanted. You asked us to help. You have to allow us to put a bit of ourselves into it, don't you?" The day was almost over, the sun waning over the horizon for its final goodbye. The sky had turned an ominous shade of red without clouds to make it beautiful.

"Red sky at night, a sailor's delight. See? It's a good sign."

Ezekiel looked at the odd young man in confusion. "We aren't sailors."

That toothy grin flashed again. "Aren't we?" Levi seemed to take in the scene, relishing it, tasting it. He clapped his hands together, and his crew ceased work, awaiting his orders. "That will be enough for today. Tomorrow, we'll start putting up walls."

As he and his accompaniment retired to their tent, one of the other workers, built like a farmhand and a good foot taller than his host, approached the landowner. "I don't like them," he whispered, leaning down to make eye contact. "Not a one. I'll work for you one more day because I need the money. Beyond that, I'll leave you to it." He peered over his shoulder to see Levi watching intently. "There's gonna be death in this house. Mark my words. Be rid of them while you can."

Zeke watched the muscular man walk away. *There was fear in that man's eyes. What in tarnation got him so riled?* His gaze shifted from the employee to Levi and back, neither man removing their glower from the other as the worker passed.

Ezekiel didn't rest well that night, his dreams terrorized by an unseen force. When he awoke, he couldn't recall what his mind had played out in the darkest hours. Groggy and cold, he bundled himself before stepping out through the flaps of his tent. Levi and his lot were already hard at it. They sawed trees as quickly as any lumberjack, trimming them and placing them onto the cart. The gigantic horse pulled the logs from the forest to the house effortlessly. The original men, under the guidance of their foreman, notched the trees perfectly. Only the large man from the night before remained unseen.

"Where's Ezra?" Zeke felt a shiver overcome him, almost as if he'd suddenly fallen ill.

"I sent him to work in the forest. That's where I needed him." Levi barely turned his eyes toward Ezekiel. "You look like hell warmed over. Take the day off and get some rest. We'll get your house built."

"Hardly seems right." Zeke turned his head and sneezed. "I can—"

"I insist."

"Look out!" a voice thundered from the forest.

A scream echoed through the hills. A tree cracked and fell, sending a cold chill down Zeke's spine.

"How unfortunate." Levi leered in the direction of the commotion without any hint of remorse. He seemed more put off by the delay than by a desire to see what had transpired. He gave Zeke a sideways glance and sighed. "Let's go see what happened."

The landowner rushed to the forest, his foreman strolling along as if without a care. His mouth hung agape when he saw the large cedar on the ground, Ezra's head buried beneath it. The hardwood tree trunk looked snapped rather than cut, appearing exploded at its base. The victim's legs twitched for several minutes before finally becoming still. The crewmen stared as if expecting such an outcome. They stared as if it weren't an accident.

Levi shook his head, seemingly more from inconvenience than from grief. He swung his gaze to Ezekiel, seeing the shock, and rolled his eyes. Finally, he glowered at his workers. "Well? Don't just mope about. Get it off of him."

Ezekiel found a sudden need to regurgitate as the felled tree lifted. Even his dreams hadn't horrified him more.

Levi wrapped an arm around Ezekiel, spinning him away from the scene. "You go rest. I'll handle everything."

"I don't even know if he had a family."

"He didn't. I checked into everyone here myself." The foreman guided his employer back to his tent, comforting him along the way. "I tell you what—get some rest, and we'll give him a proper burial and funeral right here on your land. Does that sound okay?"

Ezekiel nodded solemnly. "It only seems right." All of his energy was gone as he crawled over to his bed. Sleepiness hit him like a locomotive as he lay his head down. "Poor soul."

Levi watched as the landowner fell into a deep slumber. Smirking, he walked back to the accident. No one had dared move an inch. He smiled an impossibly toothy grin as he looked at the blood-spattered tree, his gaze lingering on the corpse for a long moment. "No sense in it going to waste. You know what to do, boys."

The workers closed in on the corpse, practically climbing over each other for space. Flesh tore, and hungry mouths smacked. Soon, the crew hovered over an empty puddle of blood and bones where the body had once been, a ring of crimson around their lips.

Levi strolled over to the stain on the tree. Reaching a single finger out, he scooped up some of the viscera on the bark and savored it. Then, placing his entire hand on the spot, all of the limbs on the tree were razed smooth, the bark shorn, notches carved, and the length cut into three sections, with the bloody piece the shortest.

"I think this will make a fine mantle." As Levi held his hand in place, ornate etchings dug themselves into the wood, the imagery as disturbing as it was beautiful. In the middle was the likeness of Ezra, his face frozen in a tormented scream. "Don't forget to bury what's left of him, now. Boss's orders." He rotated to the two remaining workers who weren't part of his crew. "We need a few more souls for the construction. Any volunteers?"

The men had been frozen in place for hours, unable to speak, either by terror or by otherworldly means. Only their eyes were under their control. Ezekiel had been too distracted to notice. The unmoving men, rugged and weathered by the storm of frontier life, began to weep for their lives as the menacing foreman approached, his minions close behind.

When Zeke awoke, he stepped outside in the noon light, his body refreshed by the rest. He wasn't sure if it was a trick of the morning, but it looked almost as if his house was finished. "I must be dreaming." He rubbed his eyes in disbelief, never recalling hearing saws or hammers. The sounds of labor never stirred him from his sleep. "How long was I out?"

Ezekiel started as Levi seemed to appear from nowhere. "You were out for a while. We let you rest."

"But how?"

"My crew works fast when properly motivated." The foreman ignored Ezekiel's sputtering, casually striding to the door of the cabin and cracking it wide open. He gestured to the inside with an actor's flourish. "Welcome home."

The connection between them broke, leaving both men breathless once more.

"What have you done, Levi?"

"I did precisely what I told you. That structure will hunt them all down, and you will watch as it devours their souls, powerless to help. Once my vengeance is complete, it will take mine." Levi began to laugh. "Yours was damned the moment you left my mother."

"I'm not your father." Now it was Zeke's turn for righteous indignation. "You weren't my responsibility."

"I never said you were. The happiness you gave my mother washed away when you followed your dream for money, of all things. You left her when she needed you the most and when she loved you the most."

Sorrow burrowed into the trapper's heart. "I wanted to make a better life for her. I promised I would return."

"Twenty years, you old fool!" Levi screamed at the mountain man. "You left for twenty years. You had no intention of returning, leaving her and me to be ridiculed and outcast by the people of New Madrid for my whole life. It was only when your body became too old to ply your trade that you *decided* to settle down. By then, my mother had been gone for seven years." Again, the young man chuckled. "Oh, what the hell. I'm feeling generous. How about one last memory?"

Suddenly, Zeke was back at the card game in Little Prairie. The player across from him, a man with a ten-gallon hat and a sandy blonde handlebar mustache, glowered at the other players, his cash almost completely wiped out. To his left sat a younger man with a flock of raven hair peeking out from under a lid with a rim so vast it obscured his face in the shadows throughout the entire game, and he muttered obscenities as if trying them out. He snorted his disgust before pushing a parchment into the middle of the round table to sweeten the poker pot.

"That's it. That's all I have."

"Cash only," declared the dealer. He began to shove the paper back to the player, but Zeke stopped him, fishing it out from under his grasp.

"What in tarnation is this?" The trapper unfolded it with a slight crackle. "A land deed? Near Mew Madrid?"

The young stranger leaned back in his chair, his face still obscured. "As I said, it's all I have. If you can beat me, it's yours."

Zeke thought about it for a bit, glancing down at his pile of cash, thinking to himself.

It won't make me rich, but it might be enough to make a house. Having a plot of land to put it on would only make it happen sooner. Then I could call on Maddie and marry her.

"Let it sit." Zeke moved all of the money in front of him to the center of the pile. "I'm all in. I call."

"You'll have to pay out of your winnings what you owe to the house." The dealer studied both men, awaiting their answers.

The younger man nodded in agreement.

"I said I was all in. Spill your hand." Zeke couldn't hide the jitters this game was giving him. He fanned his cards one last time. Ace of clubs. King of clubs. Ten of clubs. Jack of clubs. The queen made a royal flush.

Nervously, he took the cards and ordered them. He'd never had such a lucky streak in his life as today. It was as if it were ordained.

"Full house." The dealer smirked knowingly. Other than Zeke, he'd been the only of the four who had taken any of the hands, and he was confident in this one. He laid down the other three aces from the deck, followed by two eights.

The tremble in the trapper's hand became noticeable. "Your turn. I called."

The youth leaned forward, first discarding a two. Taking his time, the stranger in the broad hat slowly revealed his hand, savoring what he thought might be a win. Seven of hearts. Seven of spades. Seven of diamonds. Finally, he completed the collection with the seven of clubs, a hand that shot the confidence from the dealer's face with a satisfying grunt.

The fourth man chuckled and nodded. "Good on you, kid. Good on you."

Zeke's hand shook, his heart thrumming as the attention turned to him. There was only one hand that could beat a four-of-a-kind, and he was holding it. Slowly, in wide-eyed disbelief, he laid his royal flush on the table, still fanned as they were when he'd been holding them.

Onlookers collectively gasped in disbelief. The dealer hung his head. Even with a foolproof hand, he'd been beaten, not once, but twice over. The man with the handlebar mustache just shook his head incredulously and slowly stood, collecting what little of his money he still owned. He began to speak, looked at the three hands on the table, turned, and left for the bar without another word.

Zeke was still so shocked that he never saw the smile on the younger man's face. "Good game. Damned good game." He stretched, almost relieved that the game was finished. "I'm tapped."

"Better luck next time," Zeke uttered robotically, extending his hand and getting to his feet. The youth took the trapper's hand in his fire-scarred mitt and shook it. "I can't believe I done it."

"Hard to beat a royal flush." Tipping his hat, the young man strolled solemnly to the door. "Don't forget me, now."

"I don't think that will be possi—" Zeke turned, and the kid had already disappeared, the double doors of the dusty entrance swinging back and forth like the flapping of wooden wings. The doors swung wildly, the fluttering becoming more and more frantic until it reached a fever pitch.

Zeke and Levi snapped from the final vision as a turkey flew out of the bush, startling them both from their trance. Zeke sneered at the youth and his snake oil salesman's smirk as they caught their breath.

"It was you!" the trapper growled. "It was you this whole time."

A slight chuckle escaped Levi. "Yessir." His joviality continued, infuriating the mountain man. "And you bought it. Hook. Line. And sinker." He inhaled deeply, finally regaining his composure. "You can thank my real father for that. He taught me everything he knew that day in the woods before the townsfolk of New Madrid killed him and my mother."

Zeke thought a bit. Then it dawned on him. "The priest? I thought they were supposed to be holy men."

"He was until he was cast from the church for talking about other deities. Then he made his own religion. He learned of the old ways and even older deities."

"That's sacrilege!" Zeke fumed. "I ain't the best Christian, but—"

"Sacrilege?" Levi's ire ignited. "No." He slithered unnaturally to the trapper like a snake considering its prey. In seconds, they were nose-to-nose, Levi's green eyes boring into his victim's soul. "It's freedom. It's power. And it's many, many years older than that book you worship. Even the Indians were afraid of this God. That's why the land you got was considered cursed. They knew who resided there. They called him the forest guardian and let his holy place be. Oh, but not the ever so arrogant white man." He laughed with malicious glee. "Not you. Now you're the one who's trapped, trapper."

Zeke laughed incredulously. "How the hell am I trapped?"

"Your cabin. It's made from that forest with your blessing. Now the guardian will hunt you down and take your soul." Levi chuckled. "With Ezra's sacrifice and the mantle inside your house, the guardian will make sure you, the townsfolk of New Madrid, and their kin pay for their misdeeds."

"It's a house." The mountain man's confidence puffed in his chest. "I can burn it down. I can move."

The awful smile expanded on the young man's face. "You can try." He sat up, then stood over the mountain man, his gaze never wavering, his smile never faltering. Reaching behind his back, he produced a dagger with a charred handle. "Now there's just one thing left. One final sacrifice and the pact will be complete. Your soul will be the first. Then I will have my revenge on New Madrid." Levi slowly raised both hands over his head, chanting in a tongue Zeke had never heard in his life. As his prayer reached a crescendo, his hands clasped together on the weapon as if he meant to bring it down on the trapper.

A shot rang out, and Levi froze in place, an odd mix of horror and satisfaction on his face. A pool of crimson blossomed on the front of his shirt as his knees gave, sending the young man crashing to the ground in a heap. He slowly turned to look his nemesis in the eyes as the life drained from them. "It. Is. Done." His laugh echoed, even as his life force left him, carried by the wind through the valley.

A blinding flash caused Zeke to scuttle backward from the dead man until he bumped into the Amish man, Hezekiah, holding a smoking shotgun. Both men gaped in awe as Levi's body became engulfed in flame. The column of smoke churned upward, then bent opposite the air stream and pointed toward Zeke's cabin. Only a few moments passed until the young man's body was nothing but a pile of ash dancing in the breeze.

"What the hell did you shoot him with?"

"An unnatural death to an unnatural creature." Hezekiah spat three times.

Somehow, Zeke could tell that the zealot was just as perplexed.

He offered a hand to help the trapper up. "I told thee thy land was cursed."

The ground shook once more, pitching both men off kilter. Sand blew up in geysers all around them, filling the air with dirt and the putrid stench of sulfur. The temblor didn't last as long, but when the dust settled, Zeke's cabin was right there! The door swung wide, that awful laugh of Levi's emanating from deep within. What was left of the young man flew away in the wind, the laughter along with it.

"That's impossible!" Zeke stepped away from the structure in disbelief.

Hezekiah started backward, terror in his eyes. "The devil's dwelling hunts for souls!"

The laugh vomiting from the cabin deepened as a shadowy, demonic figure swept toward the entrance. All that could be seen were a pair of glowing red eyes within the blackness. Tendrils of smoke snaked through the air from the figure as it approached the portal, reaching outward to the men, beckoning them to come within range.

The Amish man shakily reloaded his gun and let fire, the blast passing through the specter, leaving a hole that quickly healed itself. He began to pray in German as the hellish creature chortled even heartier. A tentacle flashed outward, wrapped itself around the legs of the religious man, and dragged him into the structure. He disappeared into the darkness of the cabin. A blood-curdling scream poured from within, cut short when a crimson spray fanned into view. The entire time, the vision in the doorway never relented its stare or position.

"Thou shall not kill." Levi's voice trilled, an added baritone layering within its message. "Now for you, trapper. Greed took you from those who loved you.

Cowardice prevented your return. Hell awaits the torture of your damned soul."

Zeke scrambled to his feet, turning tail and running from the house, his house, as fast as he could. He sprinted toward New Madrid, hoping to find safety among its population.

"No matter where you go," the voice within the walls of his cabin boomed, echoing throughout the land, "you will be hunted until your soul becomes mine!" That horrific, multi-layered laughter rang through the air, burrowing into Zeke's heart and mind, driving his panic into a frenzy. His eyes glanced at the charred remains of Maddie's saloon as he fled. He thought he saw two more shadowy beings boring their red glares through him as he passed. He shot a quick peek behind him, making sure that the cabin had stayed put.

The ground below him bucked just as Spitfire had, tossing him into the dirt once more. The air filled with dust and sulfurous sand. Lightning blossomed from the ground in front of him, creating another barrier to town. Every time he attempted to stand, the earth shimmied under his feet, mocking him, taunting him.

As the tremor ended and the air cleared once more, the cabin stood before him, barricading the path to town.

Zeke's mind couldn't grasp what he was seeing. A shrill shriek escaped him as he skittered back in wide-eyed horror. The door swung agape, but the shadow was nowhere in sight. The laugh, however, lingered from deep within the bowels of the building.

A wagon filled with equally frightened folk fleeing the city passed by, their huge eyes fixed on the house that appeared from nowhere. Women screamed, and children wailed in fear as they cleared the structure. Zeke tried to get them to stop, to take them with him, clambering to get into the bed of their wagon. A teen boy kicked at him as he grasped the handle of a lard can to gain hold, squealing his dread at a frightful pitch.

The trapper fell off the back with the can, some of its contents spilling onto his clothes. Without a second thought, he yanked the lid away and chucked the container into the cabin. He produced a match, struck it alight, and tossed it onto the spilled contents of the canister. The fire began to blaze, jumping eagerly from the puddles of oil and greedily licking up the timber walls. Soon, the entire structure was engulfed in a conflagration.

The delighted demonic laughter persisted, reaching a crescendo that caused the earth to shake once more. Water spouted from cracks in the ground leading to the cabin, dousing the fire effortlessly. The gap widened into an earthen maw, engulfing the retreating wagon and all of its passengers before snapping shut, cutting their screams short.

"You'll never be rid of your curse, Ezekiel Bane. New Madrid and all who reside there are doomed. Their bloodlines will end. Suffering will be their birthright. Only when the cabin is sated will it be over."

A shadowy rope outstretched from the doorway. It knocked Zeke to the ground, causing him to hit his head on an outcropping of upheaved stone. Blood pooled around him as another smoky limb wound itself around his leg. The world drained from his sight as he lost consciousness.

Zeke awoke with a start in the cold, wintry grasp of the Colorado mountains, his makeshift tent flapping in the brisk breeze. Age had gotten to him since that fateful day. For twenty years, he wandered the land, barely surviving off his skills as a fur trapper. He never stayed anywhere for very long. Nowadays, exhaustion overwhelmed him. His body ached from the constant retreat. No matter how much distance he put between his next stop and his last, both native and settler alike could never understand why the strange man refused to sleep in the cozy, inviting cabin nearby, the one none of them could recall ever seeing before.

THE CLAWFOOT TUB

The girls were raucous, hooting and hollering, baying at the full moon, most of them already two sheets to the wind from the bar they had just left. The late spring air was filled with the smell of apple blossoms as they began their transformation from flower to fruit, spraying the light breeze with nature's confetti as they opened the door to the cabin.

"Woo!" A tall, leggy brunette in a sequined altar top and a black pleather miniskirt led the charge into their nightly quarters. "And here we are!" Atop her head, a tiara declared her the *BRIDE*, as did the golden sash draped over her shoulder.

"I can't wait to get out of these damned shoes." A blonde with a mussed, angled bob swept to her right side popped through next, practically running over the woman behind the bride. True to her word, she doffed the spiked heels within three steps of the entrance. She plopped down into the rustic, log-framed couch, misjudging its depth with an almost comical pumping of her legs.

A final woman, just barely into her twenties, ambled through, her face pallid and expression miserable. "Um, where are we exactly? I didn't see another place for miles."

"Relax, Annie." The bride removed her shoes as well as the sash and tiara.

She hardened her gaze at the brunette. "You know I hate it when you call me that, Marcy." Her protest elicited a giggle from her sister. Looking around the rustic interior, a small smile crossed her face. "I'm just not sure this is the right place."

"Oh, will you relax?" The blonde finally peeled herself off the couch well enough to talk in more than just grunts of effort. "You got us here, and the key thingy worked, right?" She strolled over to the raven-haired brooder, throwing an arm over her shoulders. "Without you, we wouldn't have had such a fun night."

"But why a cabin?" Annie motioned around her quizzically. "We could have stayed at a hotel or something, like the other girls."

"That was their choice." The sandy blonde removed the sash that identified her as *THE MAID OF HONOR*.

"Jessie and Mary wanted to do a different kind of partying." Marcy pantomimed smoking a joint and

44

snorting cocaine. "I'm up for a lot of things, but getting arrested is not one of them."

"Those bitches had better not OD."

Annie shook her head at the bob-haired woman's remark. "Karen sure is a fitting name for you."

"Besides, I have something special in store, and they're going to totally miss out." Karen pulled her phone from a purse barely large enough for the device with more effort than was necessary. "Finally. Now. Just one phone call to make." She pressed *send* and waited for the answer, putting distance between herself and the others with mischievous intent. "Yeah. This is Karen Butler. I'm ready for that pizza delivery now." She paused briefly, listening to a smoke-addled rasp on the other end. She plucked up a welcome letter from the basket of goodies left behind by the turning service, skimming over its details to double-check the address. "Yep. That's the place."

Marcy slowly strolled about the living room, casting her gaze here and there, taking in the woodwork and country charm. "I really like this place." She swept a finger over a metal rooster cut-out hung on a supporting beam next to the kitchen. A metal sliver gave her exploring finger a prick. She drew back her hand in surprise, a small bubble of crimson beading over a small puncture in her finger. "Ow!" Instinctively, she stuck the digit in her mouth.

Both of the women looked at her, suddenly concerned. "What happened?" Annie rushed to her sister's side.

"That cock pricked me!"

Karen held her hand over her phone to muffle the conversation, calling back over her shoulder, "That's what they do. Then we have to raise them." She studied her friends, waiting until she felt things were in hand before returning to the gadget in her hand. "Yes. Extra pepperoni. We like lots of meat."

In spite of herself, Annie giggled at the order as she examined Mary's injury. "You're as subtle as a train wreck, Karen."

"Don't be jealous."

"I think I have a band-aid in my bag. Let's go to the bathroom and get you taken care of." She led her sibling by the hand, snatching up a large black bag covered with metal spikes en route. She fumbled through the contents, finally locating—

Her sister let out an ear-piercing squeal, making her heart leap into calisthenics.

"The hell?" Karen ended the call, her brow furrowed.

Marcy jumped up and down with glee, giddy with excitement. "The bathroom has a clawfoot tub."

Stationed about a foot away from the exterior wall was an old-fashioned iron soaker tub, oval and porcelain-coated. It stood on four-inch-thick legs designed to resemble a lion's paws gripping round balls. Jutting from the interior side of the lavatory, copper pipes terminating in two levers on each side of a spigot that looked like the head of a male lion. On the exterior wall was a rather small window, filled in with opaque glass blocks instead of a regular pane of glass.

She could barely contain herself. Letting out another peal of joy and completely forgetting about her slight injury, she scrambled over to the fixture, hands over the rim, marveling at the find as if it were filled with diamonds. She squeaked again, absently, as drops of blood fell from her finger into the tub and snaked their way down the drain. Her smile looked like it could crack her face in half.

"Oh, I have to take this out for a test drive."

Marcy scanned every inch of the furniture, finishing with the drain. Something seemed to move in there. Leaning in, the water in the pipe swirled and slushed, reflecting an almost hypnotic rainbow within. As she became more entranced by the spectacle, the pipes belched a low gurgle. Thick, black liquid rose up, startling her backward and onto her butt. She could've sworn that the tub moved for a second. Finally, it rattled to a stop with a weighty thud.

"You okay?"

Having forgotten about Annie, she let out another yelp of surprise. It morphed into a titter of laughter as she got to her knees and then stood. Brushing herself off, she winced as the cut on her finger hit one of the sequins just right, reminding her why they had been there to begin with.

Annie turned the half-peeled bandage to where it would cover the abrasion, adhering one side to the digit, then the other. "We'll get some of that liquid skin stuff tomorrow. That will help it heal, and it'll be less obvious than a band-aid during the wedding. Good thing it's your right hand. Won't be as obvious."

Marcy drew in a gasp. "I forgot! Oh my god. Ben is gonna kill me."

Annie's face soured cynically. "Over a little cut? I doubt it."

"Jeez."

The interruption caused both women to scream. Karen began belly laughing so hard that she wilted against the door frame and slid to the floor.

Marcy stomped over, feigning a boot to her friend's legs before stepping over them. "Bitch. You scared me."

That only deepened the fit. Soon, tears were streaming down Karen's face as she convulsed in guffaws at her friends' expense. "Is…" She tried to regain her composure, and Annie slipped by as she stood. "I'm sorry. Is your whole family this dramatic?" She could barely cage her chuckles, the weeping laughter causing her mascara to run.

Annie smirked. "You wanna see something really funny? Check out your makeup."

The joviality briefly died as Karen peered into the rose-tinted antique mirror hanging just above the pedestal sink. The looking glass swayed with the commotion. She tore free a square of toilet paper and dabbed at the run-off. "I can fix it." She dismissed the problem with a wave of her hand, tossing the used tissue into the garbage.

She hadn't seen the tendril growing out from under the bathtub, snaking its way toward her.

A knock came to the front door.

As she stepped out into the living room, the thing reaching for her from under the tub returned to the shadows without its prey. The sound of it scraping across the floor gave the women a collective chill.

"Marcy, that's probably the pizza guy. Get it, will you?" Karen tilted a wink at Annie, leaning onto the back of a brown leather recliner, no shortage of attention aimed at the entrance.

"Uh-huh," Marcy smirked. "I've seen that look on your face. It always means trouble."

Karen only waved at her innocently, shooing her to get on with answering the door.

As Marcy peered past her friend, she saw something move.

The harder Marcy stared beyond her, the more concerned Karen became with her surroundings. Slowly, she turned her gaze to the bathroom. Her face went pale when she saw it: a little brown field mouse scurrying across the tiles in a panicked fit of survival. Now it was Karen's turn to scream. When the rodent sprinted into a hole in the wall, she exhaled with relief.

"Is everything okay in there?" The voice on the other side of the door was deep, manly, and very concerned.

Karen continued to catch her breath as the door swung wide. A handsome man with shoulder-length blond hair stepped through, carrying a square cardboard box and a huge radio straight out of the '80s. Though his shirt declaring his devotion to Ricky's Rocket Pizza Delivery was tight enough to accentuate a proudly sculpted body, his pants doubled down, nearly revealing his religion with their lack of breathing room.

Karen cooed her approval, instantly forgetting their minuscule intruder, sauntering over for a view of the more rugged one. Annie rolled her eyes at the lust-inspired blond but still found it within her to watch the events unfold. He set the box down on a kitchen counter and hit the *play* button. Hot Chocolate's "You Sexy Thing" thrummed out of the speakers, and he began gyrating to the beat of the music.

"Seriously?" scoffed Annie. "That song is older than he is. Hell, that boombox is probably a family heirloom."

Karen slid over to the naysayer, positioning herself behind so they were back-to-back, and rhythmically bumped her backside against her. "Just. Have. Fun. Your sister is."

Indeed, Marcy was having the time of her life. As the muscled man began to dance and remove articles of clothing, Annie watched her sister's action teeter on the edge of suggestive before falling desperately into the lewd. It was both shocking and hilarious.

"See? The only thing keeping them from doing the horizontal mambo is a little good sense and a few articles of clothing."

"And the clothes are disappearing," remarked Annie, her mouth agape as the man thrust his hands forward, ripping his pants free with a single fluid motion.

His banana hammock proudly swayed to the tempo as he crouched to the ground seductively. He crawled like a predator toward the betrothed woman as she squirmed in bacchanal delight. He was just beginning to make his way up between her legs when the music cut off.

"A little too handsy, Magic Mike." Annie scowled at the entertainer.

The other women jeered as the pizza guy smiled and raised slowly. He could have been put on display at an art institute for all to adore. But for now, his audience, at least two-thirds of them, admired him hungrily, like a display of prime cuts behind a glass case.

"You must be the little sister." He gathered his clothes, still obviously showing off the wares as much as possible.

Annie blushed as he drew nearer. She loathed cockiness, yet his green eyes had her transfixed as he approached. "How did you know?"

He broke the spell as he reached behind her for the radio, pulling in close enough that she could smell his pheromones. "I have a protective sis, too. You know," he hissed seductively, "I could show you some of my benefits packages that come with the show."

Annie chortled. "Yeah. There's not much left to the imagination after that little display." She turned her eyes downward to emphasize her statement.

"I do love a challenge." He spun on his heel, one arm full of clothes, his boombox in the other. "Where's the bathroom?"

Karen jerked a thumb in the direction he wanted, waiting for the door to shut before stomping over to Annie with heated intent. She whispered through gritted teeth: "What are you doing? We could have seen the full Monty if we paid him enough."

"I have a feeling that, if I hadn't stepped in, that sleaze would do us all, give us each a different venereal disease, and murder us in our sleep for your hoop earrings."

"I can hear you," the voice from the bathroom sang, accompanied by a steady stream of water.

Annie mocked at the door between them, equally sing-song: "That makes us even."

Karen yanked her best friend's sister away from the door, still chattering in a hushed and firm tone: "You're ruining your sister's fun. First, you don't want to stay in the hotel because you might get bed bugs. Next, I have to get a last-minute reservation at this forgotten hellhole so you feel more comfortable. I'm way too fucking sober for this shit, Annie. Get a grip or go away and let us have fun."

"I just don't want Marcy to regret anything." Tears began welling up in Annie's eyes. "She's getting married tomorrow."

"Benny's a good horse, but that doesn't mean she can't ride a stallion right now."

"She's not a slut like you."

Karen slapped Annie loud enough to bring Marcy immediately to her feet.

Annie reared back, answering the slap with a balled fist, missing the target yet still managing to make Karen lose her balance.

Marcy raced over to get between the two. "Stop! Stop it, Annie. You too, Karen." She shot an authoritative glare at them.

"What the hell?" Karen raised her hand from the floor, a thick, transparent, gooey substance stretched from the wood to her hand. Her face contorted in disgust as she looked at what caused her to slip. It seemed to be coming from the bathroom.

"Do you think he's okay?"

Annie would usually use such an opportunity to chide her sister about her cluelessness, but even she looked confused. She rapped on the door.

No answer.

"Hey. You alright in there?"

Still no answer.

She knocked louder this time. "I'm coming in. I'd tell you to cover up, but I think we're way past that point." She twisted the knob. The latch clicked away from the strike plate, and the door opened an inch.

Her heart raced wildly. She heard the drain sucking as if the tub had been filled with water. The muck on the floor seemed to retreat further into the room as she creaked the door ajar an inch at a time.

Did he fall and hurt himself? Maybe he took a bath and fell asleep.

"Oh, for god's sake." Karen threw the door wide. "Stop being such a prude."

Nothing. The bathroom was empty.

"Did he sneak out?" Karen looked indignant at the slight. "I'm not leaving him a damn tip." A sudden realization hit her. She spun and retreated to her insignificant purse. "He has my credit card information. Shit. Shit. Shit." She rifled through her things, looking at the card she'd put his services on, contemplating calling the customer service number to cancel it.

"I don't think he left," Annie noted, pointing to the toilet, "not without his clothes and antique radio." The stripper's outfit was wadded up on the seat of the commode, the boombox resting on the tank lid. Still, there was no sign of him anywhere. Nor was there a linen closet in which he might've hidden.

"He probably climbed out the window," Karen continued, raging over her folly. Her husband would undoubtedly wonder why the card had been canceled, and she would have some serious explaining to do.

"That window? The one with the glass bricks cemented in place?"

Marcy approached the tub to make sure he hadn't fallen in. A pink substance, thick and translucent, very much like what Karen had slipped on, now exited the tub via the drain. Amidst the muck, the remains of a human face appeared: the stripper's face. It seemed to dissolve as it raced toward the pipe. Her eyes grew wide in horror, watching the face's deteriorating shape yawn a silent warning as it slipped into the pipes and out of sight. A scream stuck in Marcy's throat. She fell to her backside and pedaled away from the horror. As her back hit the jamb of the door, the wail building within found egress.

"What?" Annie rushed to comfort her sister, bewildered. "What is it, Marce? Tell me!"

All she could get in response was terror-filled caterwauling. Marcy pointed an accusing finger at the porcelain contraption, her eyes nearly catatonic with shock.

"Karen, get in here and help me! Marcy is having a meltdown or something." Annie lightly slapped her sister on the cheeks, trying to halt the screaming.

"Oh, it's probably cold feet or something." Karen peeped into the room, but as soon as she saw the abject terror on Marcy's face, she followed the finger to the tub. "What? Did she see the mouse?"

Annie's face was full of frightened concern. "I don't know. She's never acted like this before. I don't think this is wedding nerves."

The maid of honor walked over to the offending fixture and peered inside. It appeared slick on account of a lingering film of water, but there was nothing extraordinary. "I don't see anything." She shook her head in disbelief. Scanning the porcelain again—she half-expected a spider or something else creepy but innocuous—her gaze crossed the drain hole. In the trap, liquid shimmered a tantalizing rainbow. Her face slackened as the substance moved hypnotically, and she became engrossed by the rhythmic movements.

"Karen?" Annie stood, now a bit worried about the woman's sudden silence. She walked over, putting her hand on Karen's shoulder. "Hey. Did you hear me?"

The bobbed blonde shook herself from the trance and stood upright. "Sorry. I thought I saw something."

"Where?"

"In the hole." She bent back down to face the inside of the tub, pointing to the drain. "Right there."

The pipes belched, the liquid inside gurgling and bubbling. Suddenly, the viscous matter erupted upward, wrapping itself around Karen's head. She struggled to turn her face toward Annie, a stifled bubble of a scream forming in front of her rapidly dissolving features. Muscle, skin, and even bone began to liquefy. The scream bubble popped, but by then, it was barely a garbled groan.

Annie scrambled away. "Holy shit! What the actual fuck?" She clambered to her sister as they both yowled in horror, clutching each other.

Just as it finished melting away their friend's head, the mucus yanked, pulling the rest of her into the basin. Pipes clanged as more of that thick gunk vomited into the container, making quick work of its victim.

Annie shot to her feet, violently pulling her sibling up with her. "We're leaving." But no sooner did she get the traumatized bride-to-be to her feet than the bathroom door slammed shut on its own.

Marcy shouted in absolute agony. She hadn't only used her sister but the door jamb to help herself up. Now she looked at four bloody stumps where her fingers once were. Blood gushed from the partial digits in beat to an unheard inner tempo.

"Marcy!" Annie grasped her sister's hand, trying to quickly figure out a way to staunch the wound, crimson spattering her face and shirt. Soon, the bride's shouts tapered as she fainted from shock. "No. No no no no no no."

Annie lowered herself and her sis gently to the floor. She reached up and tried the door. It opened a crack before something shoved it closed with a might she couldn't overcome. Scouring the doorway and the immediate area for the cause, she saw it—a long, spaghetti-like vine had crept around them, following the floorboards until it reached the opening. That was what had snapped the door shut, and it seemed determined to keep it that way. The thing originated from under the bathtub.

Annie's eyes grew wide when the tub's feet popped to life, their claws clacking audibly on the cool porcelain tiles. They dared her to move closer so they could reach out and grasp her. Water began to pour from the faucet on its own, the stream first clear, then pink, as if mixing with a more sinister scarlet liquid. The torrent became darker, thicker, and redder, staining everything it spattered.

The mouse they had seen earlier began scurrying in panicked circles around the room. More vines blossomed from the underbelly of the fixture, blindly reaching, feeling. The critter deftly dodged the otherworldly appendages here and there, though it was just as trapped as the women were. As the rodent made another lap, one of the tub's talons snatched it up. The pest squeaked in fear as the claw maneuvered it to an unseen mouth. A sickening sound, a marriage of tearing sinew and crunching bone, emanated from under the tub.

Annie witnessed the spectacle, but her mind refused to acknowledge it, to accept it. One of the snake-like tendrils reached for her foot. She kicked at it in futility. It recoiled in the air like an agitated cobra. She wasn't sure if the thing hissed at her or if it was simply the sound it made as it moved across the tile.

"It's like a mimic." Her mind made the odd connection aloud. "How is that possible? They don't exist."

Her sister, draped over her lap and looking very pale, groaned weakly, snapping Annie's attention from the surreal beast. She felt her sister's neck; the pulse was weak and fading. Her own heart sank in defeat. She began rocking back and forth, cradling the woman she had grown up with. Memories flooded her mind, releasing the waterworks in a cascade. She scarcely saw the vine wrap itself around Marcy's leg and begin casually tugging her away.

"No." Annie fiercely held on to Marcy, her sibling's breaths short and weak. "No. You can't have her." Her strength grew, as did her efforts. With everything Annie had, she defied the endlessly hungry creature even as it mercilessly yanked. Spying a small pair of sharp-pointed scissors on the lip of the sink, her hand flew to them. Stabbing the tendril, accenting each word, she shouted, "You. Can't. Have. Her."

The appendage screeched in protest, releasing its grip and retreating. Heroic rage overtook Annie. She pummeled the impossible limbs with the tip of the weapon, trying to drive them from the door. Her sister hung from her clutches like a ragdoll as she pierced the tentacles with righteous fury. She stopped her assault for a second here and there, only long enough to shake her sister back into position, but the dead weight just wilted and drooped.

Claws clacked on the tile, the creature freeing itself from its station in the room. Drywall exploded, flooring upheaved, and water sprayed in fans as the beast slowly spun with a guttural snarl. The shower curtain, a swaying circle of fabric, followed the movement of the bathtub, reminding Annie of a pitcher plant. The rings rattled, the plastic sheeting sliding back and forth with each step forward. The spout turned to face the front, its lion's head roaring like an unearthly demon. All of the tendrils squirmed at its base now.

"I'm sorry, Marcy." Annie set her beloved sibling on the floor, pulling the door wide.

She then turned to collect her kin, but the thing already had her in its grasp. It pulled and digested ravenously, jostling the woman to life long enough for her to shriek in terror, reaching out in a plea for help before disappearing between the floor and the thing's underside. A purple, tongue-like thing mopped the floor, savoring each drop. It stomped over to the opening, collecting the last victim's missing digits.

Annie, wide-eyed in disbelief, jumped out of the room as quickly as she could. She scrambled to the front door, only looking over her shoulder once. The creature was unable to fit through the frame's limited space. She tried to get out but bounced off of the chest of a uniformed officer and fell to the ground.

"Whoa. What's going on here, miss?" He peered inside. The cabin was empty except for this very frightened black-haired woman. "I heard screaming as I was patrolling by. Everything okay?"

Annie couldn't speak. Relief enveloped her as she bawled and reached for the newcomer.

"Stay right there, ma'am." He turned for a split second, speaking into his two-way radio. "This is Jenkins requesting backup at 187 Mockingbird Drive. Send an EMT, too."

"Roger that. Help is en route."

The officer returned his attention to the inside of the structure, but the woman who had bumped into him was gone. He unholstered his sidearm, casting his gaze in all directions as he stepped cautiously inside. "Miss? You need to come out where I can see you."

His request was answered with an eerie silence.

He peeked behind the door and in every dark corner. Nothing moved. The familiar sound of a shower curtain being pulled shut rang from the lavatory. "This isn't a game, lady. Come out now. Don't make me come in there."

A scream pealed from the bathroom, causing him to drop his back to the wall just shy of the door. His heart raced. He gathered his courage, popping in front of the opening as the scream was reduced to a liquefied echo. A silhouette of the woman leaned against the opaque curtain, arms and hands splayed.

Was she melting?

"Last chance. I'm coming in." Keeping his gun pointed at the shadow behind the plastic, he pulled it away. There was nothing there, only a thick, oddly colored water moving into the drain.

A bubble formed as the officer watched. It burst, releasing one final, bone-chilling shriek into the air as the liquid fell into the pipes.

THE ROSE-TINTED MIRROR

"Oh, Howard! I can't believe you found it." The older woman, still striking for her seventy-five years, gasped with a schoolgirl's enthusiasm as she opened the front door to the cabin. Her eyes sparkled with glee beneath her age-dulled blonde hair as she gawped at the structure's interior. Her memories of their first honeymoon flooded back to her like a tidal wave. "It's almost exactly as I remember it."

"Wasn't easy to track down. Seems like the thing has moved," Howard huffed from behind her, dragging their suitcase on its one good wheel, struggling to get it over the threshold. Colorful language spilled from his lips as the slight bump began to prove itself a worthy adversary. "Maybe we should have hinted to the kids that we needed new luggage." One more mighty yank got the case over the finish line and into the vacation cabin, dropping him onto his aged backside in the process.

Tessa's hand flew to her mouth in a panic. "Howard, are you okay?" She rushed to her husband's side as fast as she could, wrapping her arms around his to help him to his feet.

"I'm fine, Tessa," he grumbled crankily as he stood, his posterior throbbing from the sudden impact. It took him a bit to regain his upright posture. His bruised pride and wild temper urged him to deliver a good boot to the luggage, an action that would have likely done more damage to him than the hard-sided suitcase.

When his blood pressure finally settled and his rear stopped aching, he took a good look around the old place. He ran a gnarled, liver-spotted hand through his gray hair. Years of scrawling on paperwork hadn't been kind to his joints, but the payoff for their golden years had made it worthwhile.

Tessa embraced her husband of fifty years, gently kissing him in the same way she had all their lives. She was never much for French kissing, but her affection never lacked passion.

When Howard was younger, that was the sort of thing that helped make a family. To that day, it still made his heart flutter.

Tessa was right. Beyond the marginally updated décor, the cabin was exactly as he recalled it. The woodwork within the cabin looked as if every inch had been meticulously polished just for their visit, everything perfectly clean and orderly. The whole place gleamed as if brand new. The wood-burning stove was still right between the bedroom and the kitchen. In the living room, the mantle was still there, though there was something different about it.

Howard's gray eyes puzzled about the carving, approaching it slowly to make sure he hadn't been seeing things. "Huh."

Disappointed by the sudden break of their embrace, Tessa decided to inspect the kitchen. She ran her hands over the butcher block countertops in the cooking area. Admiring the updated cabinetry, she began to say something but paused when she looked up and noticed Howard's bewilderment. "What is it, honey?"

Howard pursed his lips together, shaking his head. "Oh, nothing. I could've sworn this thing had a different face on it when we were younger. Looked like one of my uncle's. Same nose and everything." He traced the soft curves of the new figure. "Now it's a woman."

"They probably had to replace it when they relocated the cabin or something."

Considering this for a moment, Howard relented with a sigh. "You're probably right."

"Of course I am," Tessa joked. "You should know that after fifty years." She wandered out of the kitchen and into the bedroom before heading back to investigate the bathroom. "The clawfoot tub isn't here anymore, either."

Howard peeled his gaze from the mantle, turning slowly around to keep from aggravating his hip. As he did so, his heart rate spiked. He found himself staring into someone else's eyes. Shuffling backward, Howard nearly tumbled over the coffee table before regaining his balance. He laughed nervously, concluding that the face gazing upon him was his own reflection in an ornately carved mirror hanging over the couch. "I'll be damned." He arched his brows in recognition. "Tessa, get in here."

The odd urgency in his voice brought Tessa in at a run. "What is it, Howard?" Stopping short, she spied the object of his excitement. "Oh, my goodness. It's still here. The rose-tinted mirror." Tears and a peal of joy accompanied her claps and bounces as she saw what her husband gazed upon. She joined Howard in the center of the room, leaning lovingly on his shoulder and peering with wonder at their reflection. A broad smile crept across her face. "Do you think it still does it?" she whispered.

Howard beamed at his wife. "Only one way to find out."

Anticipation tingling on their skin, their breath caught in their throats as they both straightened to get a better view. They stared at their reflections with unblinking eyes, waiting for something, anything to happen. Soon, the smiles melted into dissatisfaction.

"This is just silly," Tessa uttered, shaking her head. Her shoulders slouched as she chewed her lip. "Besides, what if it did work? What if it showed us the future again? It's not as though we have that much time left at our age. I don't know if I want to see when either of us dies."

Howard remained transfixed by the looking glass. Attempting to clear his mind, he locked eyes with the man gazing back. *How did we get it to work?* "Uh-huh." Finally, he gave up with a sigh. "We were young then, barely in our mid-twenties." He turned away to gather their luggage and schlep it to the bedroom. "We probably imagined it."

Tessa attempted to keep her eyes from the mirror, training them on something—anything— else, but the shine of the pinkish glass called to her, tugging at her heart. "Everything we saw back then came true." She paused, disappointment weighing heavy in her soul that the relic had failed to respond. Her voice fell to a whisper: "All of it."

"We've lived a good life together." Howard's voice was distant and distracted as he strained to put the suitcase on the bed. "Mirror or no mirror." He dabbed at beads of sweat rolling off his forehead with a handkerchief and headed back to his wife. "Half a century in this together, and it was our doing, not some antique." He wrapped his arms around her from behind. "Now we're the antiques, and I still love you."

They turned as a couple, peering into the looking glass once more. The frame around the oval-shaped mirror was painted gold and featured intricate carvings of grapevines. A fleur de lis graced the top, the crowning detail in the ornate backdrop. It had looked old, even when they first encountered it back in 1975. Now, it seemed positively ancient; some of the foil behind the glass had begun to bubble and flake in places near the edges, giving it a grittier feel.

Howard smirked at his wife in the reflection. "Maybe we're not using the right words."

Tessa cast a cynical look at her mate. "Mirror, mirror on the wall…"

They watched as the surface appeared to ripple like a still lake disturbed by a pebble.

"It's happening!" Tessa gasped.

They locked their eyes on the glass, watching as the surface swam and clouded. Their reflections disappeared completely for a moment, lost in the ether. When the image returned, the couple gazed upon their younger selves, the ones who shared their first honeymoon in this very cabin five decades ago. Their faces were wrinkle-free, their eyes hopeful and energetic, and their youthful hair shades of blonde and brown.

"Oh, Howard—" Tessa purred in a gasping breath.

"Howie?" Mascara melted and ran down the young bride's cheeks as her tear-filled eyes looked to something beyond her new husband.

"Tess, I hope you can..."—Howie's voice trailed off as he studied his inattentive new bride—"...forgive me," he finished absently, turning his head to follow Tess's wonder at the antique rose-tinted mirror. "What's happening?" Their stress-induced tiff on the way there forgotten, she wriggled from Howard's grasp, hypnotized by the quivering surface of her reflection.

The images swam and swirled, finally clarifying after a brief, disorienting spell. The pair staring back at them were faded and aged, easily half a century older than the newlyweds were now. "Holy cow. I do look like my dad." Howie, just as entranced as Tess, glanced over at his wife. There was a look of sheer terror in her eyes as she patted her face frantically to make sure the wrinkles weren't actually there. Moved by sheer instinct, Howie caught her as she swooned, nearly fainting with the shock of it all. His eyes barely leaving the mirror, he sat his beloved down on the couch and rubbed her shoulders to keep her from passing out. "Tess? You going to be okay?"

Tess nodded, though her pallid complexion suggested otherwise.

Howie quickly fetched her a glass of tap water, helping to steady her trembling hands as she raised the glass to her lips. Within seconds, her sloppy slurping sounds had drained the container of its contents. "Who... What... What was that? Who was that old couple?"

Howie scratched his head. "No idea. They kinda looked like you and me. Maybe we had one too many."

"That's it!" Tess shouted, bouncing up and clapping her hands, a wild sparkle of glee lighting up her face and warming her ashen complexion. "This mirror"—she caressed the ornamental framework—"shows us... Well, it shows us *us* when we're older. Don't you see?" She squealed and clasped her hands in front of her face. "And darling, it shows us together after all of that time."

Howie shook off the notion, not ready to believe his wife's explanation despite what he thought he had seen. "I don't remember having that much fun in the sixties. I think our minds were playing tricks on us."

Silence enveloped the room as they returned their gazes to the mirror, which only reflected their youthful vigor back at them.

"See? We imagined it," Howie said, a twinge of unease running through his mind. He sounded like he was trying to convince himself.

In response, the mirror rippled slightly around the edges.

Howie's skin crawled as he weaved past Tess and lifted the luggage. "I'm going to go put the suitcases on the bed," he grumbled. "Maybe this second honeymoon was a bad idea."

The mirror responded to their unwavering glowers with a hypnotizing shimmy.

"I think I'm going to bed," Howie said. "That drive took it out of me."

"Oh, you old party pooper," Tessa needled her husband, watching him limp down the hall and into the bedroom. "I'll be in shortly." She wasn't sure whether he'd even heard her.

"Don't look at that thing too long," came a muffled warning from the other room. "You know what happened last time."

"I want to see what it will show me." Tessa smoothed the wrinkles on her face and twiddled the loose skin under her chin absently.

A young Tess examined her taut neckline in the mirror. "Who knows what this thing will show me?"

Dread washed over Howie, seeing how infatuated his wife was with the looking glass. Not wishing to start another fight, he shrugged and muttered, "Suit yourself."

Tess was enamored with the soft pink mirror and found herself waiting for a vision to be unveiled. *What if he decides he doesn't want to stay with me?* She hung her head as the thoughts surfaced, separating the anxiety of being a new wife from elation about the wedding like vinegar and oil. *Will he leave me? Do I really want to know?*

Soon, her patience was rewarded, the surface glimmering and undulating like a pond into which a pebble had been dropped. The hallucinations came rapid fire as if someone were changing the channels on the television, only giving her glimpses into the ether. She saw so many firsts: birthday parties, Christmases, sleepovers, their son's football games, and their daughter's dance recitals. Vacations on beaches were paired with sledding and snowmen as two children flashed through the years before her. There were flashes of her and Howie pushing a toddler on a board swing hanging from the bowed limb of a sturdy tree in front of a duplex. This scene was soon replaced by a candy-striped aluminum swing set, a slightly older boy of five being pushed by his dad on one seat while, in the other, a two-year-old girl giggled happily in her mother's lap. She watched her firstborn get married to his wife and then the birth of her grandchildren. Tess watched as her daughter tossed her college graduation cap into the air before her gown transformed into a physician's white coat. A sincere smile bloomed on her face as she watched the whole thing transpire.

The sudden touch of a hand on her shoulder made Tess jump. She had been so absorbed in the images that she hadn't noticed the hand enter the reflection in the mirror.

"Wow." Howie, allowing his curiosity to get the better of him, had come up behind her as the kids' lives unfolded. "That was…"

"Amazing," Tess finished, leaning her head on his hand, grateful that he had shared the experience with her after all.

"You know," Howie kissed her neck in just the right spot, "You and I didn't look much older than we are now when that first one was born. We'd better get started if we want it to come true."

Tessa watched the mirror within the mirror in shock as their children's lives unfurled in front of her for a second time. Only this time, she didn't see the same events she saw before. Same kids, same lives, different moments. Hidden moments, less celebrated: a twelve-year-old Barry experiencing summer camp, a growing desire for male companionship taking hold, and a high school teacher giving "extra credit" for work not done on paper. She witnessed him shoving a man out the back door of the house as Candace pulled into the driveway with their kids in the back seat of the station wagon. She saw her son in the hospital, as the mother of his children lay on her death bed, her body ravaged by cancer, an unheard confession spilling out as her son wept.

Ellen's life wasn't saintly, either. She had discovered the usefulness of certain drugs in her college studies, keeping herself awake with Adderall and Modafinil, sometimes with frightening consequences. Tessa saw her daughter go into hallucinogenic fits of paranoia when she tried to wean herself off them, barely passing the exams she studied for due to sleep deprivation. Ellen lost job after job in hospitals and rest homes for raiding the drug pantries or writing herself scripts until she finally had her license to practice revoked. Then, she got a job working in a factory, earning far less, still addicted, and still lying to her parents about being a doctor.

"Dear Mother of God." Howard had his gnarled hand on Tess' shoulder, though she barely noticed. He had been watching the whole time. She leaned into his grasp as the tears flowed. His breath hitched as the lump in his throat grew. "That was—"

"Awful," she interrupted. "Why didn't they tell us? Where did we go wrong?"

"I-I," the elderly man stammered, "I don't know. Maybe we put too much pressure on them." Turning away from the mirror, weeping and holding one another, Howard led his wife from the glass. "Let's agree not to look into it again."

Tessa nodded.

Howard blinked, attempting to erase the visions from his memory. His distraught wife leaned on him as he led her across the room, but the images replayed, fresh in his mind. Rage began a slow boil within him as he thought of his children and their deceptions. The longer he pondered their secrets, the deeper his ire grew. "How could they do this to us? How could they not trust us to love them?"

Tessa whispered between sobs: "Let them tell us when they feel it's right, darling." She paused, her voice becoming distant. "We all have secrets."

The last statement was barely audible, but there was something in the way Tessa had uttered "secrets" that caused Howard to gaze upon her with suspicion. "Let's go to bed, my dear. Tomorrow, I'll put a blanket over that thing so that we don't have to see what it shows us." His mind was a whirlwind.

What secrets? he wondered. *What are hers? I certainly don't want her to know mine.*

They fell asleep that night in each other's arms, as they had for the past fifty years.

Awakening the following day in a lover's embrace, the young couple were serenaded by the robins perched in a tree just outside their open window. Sunshine smiled in on them as they stretched.

"Good morning, wife." Howie beamed at Tess.

Her flirtatious smile widened as she answered: "Good morning, husband." She giggled lightly, sighing as she placed her ringed hand over his and stared. "That will take some getting used to."

Howie brushed his hand through Tess's long blonde hair as she threw her leg over his hip. "If the mirror's right, you'll have a very long time." Gently cupping her chin, he pulled her closer for a loving kiss.

"What should we do today?" She purred at his light caress, his hands exploring her.

"Oh, I have an idea." He pulled her closer, causing his wife to squeal with delight before she shoved him away teasingly, more than his interest growing.

"Behave yourself." Swinging her legs in the other direction, she kissed him again, her bright green eyes glinting.

"Never." He moaned his disappointment like a schoolboy being forced out of bed, tossing the covers away from their naked bodies in mock protest. "Fine!" Standing almost fast enough to make his head swim, he rushed to the bathroom. Tess caught him in front of the mirror, hugging him at the waist. He breathed deeply, cherishing her embrace. Opening his eyes, he glossed over the reflection of his trim, muscular frame as well as hers. "Do you think we'll still be this in love when we become that older version of ourselves?

"We'll have each other. That's what will count." Tess knew the words sounded heavier than she meant.

"You know what I mean." Howie shifted behind her, holding her tight as they admired themselves in their youth. "Don't you want to stay this young and beautiful?" He kissed her neck again. "And gorgeous." Smooch. "And voluptuous." Peck.

"You need to stop." An idea hit her. "We could always ask the mirror." Her eyes bore deeply into her reflection. "Mirror, will my husband always be a horny—"

"Stop!" Howie broke from her with a playful tap on her backside. "The last thing I want to see is my dad and your mom bumping uglies."

Tess swatted at his shoulder as he walked away to tend to nature's call. "Time and gravity are no one's friends." Her smile faded, her deep thoughts taking root while she studied her reflection. The surface of the glass shimmied in response to her unbreaking stare, distorting her near-perfect body with ripples and clouds beyond the veil.

Tessa sighed as she gazed longingly at her younger self, which appeared superimposed over her more experienced figure in the mirror. "Time and gravity are no one's friends," she said, recalling her words from years ago with startling clarity. She wound her hands over her chest, feeling where one of her breasts used to be. Pulling her half-stuffed bra into place, she thought of the ghost of her younger husband drifting behind, perfectly echoing past and present, like a double-exposed film of then and now, and she couldn't stifle the chortle that escaped.

"What's so funny?" Howard closed his robe, turning to her. Seeing Tessa watching the mirror, his rage from the night before blossomed again. "Stop looking at that thing. You know no good will come of it. You're becoming obsessed."

She brushed her fading blonde hair back, blushing. "I couldn't help it. I had to see." Her voice became small, looking down at the scars where her breast had once been. "I wanted to see myself as a woman again."

Now, it was Howard's turn to exhale deeply. Searching for the right words as he approached, he draped his arm around her. "That thing only brought us heartache last night. It'll only remind us of things we shouldn't worry about." His hand gently touched her scar. "You're still the woman I love. All of you."

Then the looking glass swirled again, the picture seeming to focus on Tessa in middle age. Not the pretty, ravishing beauty of her youth, but indeed not a wilted rose either. A man slid in behind her, his silhouette familiar but blurred at first. As the image sharpened, the dark complexion of Howard's best friend bore his eyes at the reflection, a whimsical, daring glower that drilled a hole in Howard's heart as the man wrapped his arms around his wife.

"Steve?" Howard released Tessa, his arms drooping to his sides.

After hearing the name, Tessa's eyes grew large, and her mouth fell open. She swung her gaze back to the mirror to see what was playing out on its rosy surface.

Howard's face contorted with disbelief, a slack-jawed look betraying his shattering heart, as his friend touched Tessa in a way he'd thought he only had. A wildfire of emotions tore through his soul. "How? When?" He fought against the urges he felt in his hands. He'd never raised a finger to harm Tessa. With an intense stare darting from her ashamed look to the reflection playing back at him, he felt his arms begin to quiver with unadulterated rage. Before his top half could act on impulse, his knees gave, and he slumped to the floor, his hands flying to his head. "I can't believe you would... And with Steven!"

Tessa stammered, trying to find an explanation or attempt to deny the truth of the mirror. "T-that was a mistake from a long time ago, Howard." She fought back the impulse to send something solid through the plate of glass. "It was only the one time. I was weak. It was a mistake. I still love you and haven't done it since." She knelt in front of him, trying to pry his hands from his tearful eyes. "We can work through this. I have faith in us." She stood, frowning into the looking glass. Her heart leaped to her throat as the mirror's surface began to warp and quiver again, replaying images they had seen on their first honeymoon.

Howie sat on the couch in the cabin living room, instinctively opening his wallet and glancing at the shrinking cash within. "We'd better take it easy today. Tight budget and all."

"Stop being a tightwad for a week. We're on our honeymoon."

As if in response, the mirror shuddered to life once more.

"Oh, look! It's doing it again."

Howie rushed to his wife's side. He and Tess watched as the fog cleared, showing Howie in an office, staring across a mahogany desk at a somewhat intimidating-looking bespectacled man with a crimson beard. "Isn't that Mr. McElroy?"

The two men rose from their seats and shook hands, huge smiles decorating their faces. The suit-wearing redhead then toured him around the high-rise facility. "It looks like you got the job."

Flashes of checks after growing checks flitted through the years; his loyalty paid for in benefits seen and unseen.

The doors to the place where the fire-haired man had shaken Howard's hand eventually shuttered. Then Howie opened his own firm in a much more modest space.

Tess could see piles of unpaid bills stack up and then disappear. The worry on her husband's face transformed into the confidence he had built over the years. She could see him snap his logbook shut as a very smartly dressed client entered with the greeting of the old world and older money. "Who is that man?"

Howard shrugged in response. "I have no idea. I've never seen him before."

In the forecast of the looking glass, their house went from a single-bedroom rental to a multi-floor Mediterranean with a vast, open floorplan. Their cars exchanged themselves from a dusty, green, barely functioning Maverick to one so foreign, sleek, and shiny black that Tess couldn't make out the manufacturer.

Each time their lives improved, that man showed up with his non-American-style hello. And every single time, without fail, the future looked just a bit brighter.

Howard coughed, sitting on the edge of the bed, well out of view of the mirror, still reeling from the visions of his wife and best friend that the infernal thing had wrought. Tessa left his side at his request, leaving him to his thoughts as he caught his breath. He'd had to slip nitroglycerin under his tongue to keep from having another heart attack. He stood, testing his ability to remain upright.

"Who's the man that keeps coming into your office, Howard?" Tessa asked herself as much as the mirror.

"Why's it showing that?" She studied the glass, trying to read the lips in the silent conversation. Both the man and Howard seemed to be tangled in a heated discussion inside his modest office. Judging from her husband's age, she'd guessed this little trip down memory lane was a recent replay. The well-dressed man pointed an accusing finger at the accountant as he took a stack of ledgers from him with authority.

"He's the reason I'm retiring." Gasping and wheezing, Howard joined his wife, unsure if his heart could take much more. His head slumped, and the color flushed from his face as appearance after appearance of the man in question hit him like a ton of bricks.

"You can't just close shop like that," Tessa said, her words heavy yet pointed. "What about all of your clients?"

"He's the only client I've ever had." He grabbed his wife by her shoulders firmly. "He took good care of us, but he's a dangerous man."

Tessa began to feel ill. She shook her head in confusion. "What happened? What did you do?"

"I quit." Howard began to feel weak again. Guiding her over to the bed and sitting her down, he locked eyes with his beloved. "I cooked his books for so long that he never noticed when I skimmed a bit here and there. Now, he's out for blood. We aren't just reliving our honeymoon; we're hiding from Don Santini."

Suddenly, things were starting to make sense, the way Howard had been acting before the trip, the sudden desire to buy an RV and get on the road. All of it. It had been a ploy to escape fate.

"Who are you?" Tessa glowered at her husband with an accusing stare. Her breathing became rapid as she clutched at her neckline, her face awash with disbelief. Tears began flowing. With trembling lips, she blurted, "You're a criminal. That's who you are."

A jolt of pain tore through Howard's chest. He gripped his shirt, wadding it in his fist as if the tightness in his ribcage could be readily grasped and torn away. "And you're a cheating whore," he snorted through shortened breaths and gritted teeth.

Tessa stomped over to her husband, slapping him hard enough to rock his head back. A red handprint blossomed on Howard's face. "My God, you're awful." She pointed a finger at him, beginning to turn to leave.

Howard's eyes grew wide with fury, the erratic thudding in his chest momentarily forgotten. He bolted to his feet, his hands shot out. Spinning his wife, he wrapped his fingers around Tessa's throat.

The pair twirled as they struggled in the bedroom. Tessa's face changed shades from porcelain white to a deep purple. Her arms flew to her husband's shoulders while they spun in their macabre dance.

Al Green's "Let's Stay Together" played over the radio in the living room. Howie held Tess close as they twirled, her arms draped over his shoulders, careful not to trip over the shag area rug. Only when the newlyweds had looked up from each other's gaze did they notice that the mirror had once again shifted perspectives.

"Oh look, Howie," Tess cooed, and although their reflection was still a good distance from them, they could make out the barest of details. "They're dancing, too."

They watched in awe as the elderly couple in the mirror mimicked their movements perfectly.

Howie chortled. "Looks like they chose the bedroom for their setting. Maybe we should follow their example."

Tess blushed, giving her husband a light, playful swat on the face. "My God, you're awful."

Howie's heart thumped in his chest. *I love this woman.*

Tess halted their slow rocking, now watching their pink-hued selves with locked interest. Their elder images continued their dance over to the bed, clumsily falling over each other in a heap on the mattress. The view obscured their faces. All that could be seen was Howard collapsing atop Tessa, both apparently spent.

Tess gasped softly. "They're falling asleep in each other's arms."

The glass showed Tessa with her arm over Howard and his over her, facing each other. That was the final vision the mirror offered the newlyweds during their honeymoon, fading away as Tess and Howie closed the distance.

The life faded from Tessa's eyes as Howard collapsed on top of her, his breaths even shorter than before, the pang in his heart reaching an alarming crescendo. His arms ached. His head throbbed.

Vision quickly darkening, he pulled her to her side toward him, cupped her chin, and positioned her face to meet his eyes. With great effort from his failing strength, he tugged her arm, draping it over his side. It became too difficult to breathe. With a solitary tear falling down his handprinted cheek, he leaned in to give the love of his life a kiss.

I loved this woman.

Slowly, Howard closed his eyes, his heart thumping one final time.

The life, that happy, fairytale existence they had foreseen in the mirror on their first honeymoon, had been a lie. Their love for each other, however, was a truth even the rose-tinted mirror couldn't ignore.

THE FOREST GUARDIAN

"Grandfather! Tell us a story!"

The children of the village all rang in chorus, echoing the sentiment of the young native boy. At first, the weathered older man appeared pestered. Still, his resolve melted into satisfaction, then into happiness. The quickly gathering youth of the tribe eagerly wanted to hear him speak around the crackling campfire.

The elder woman next to him, mistaking his prolonged silence for weariness, attempted to send the children away. He raised a leathery, unsteady hand, ending her efforts and the mournful protests of the collected youth. She studied him, their eyes sharing a silent conversation.

Slowly, he nodded to his wife, and she relented, directing the children to form a semicircle around him, keeping them a safe distance away from the fire.

With the bustle of the feast barely behind them, the rest of the West River Folk quieted, some to listen to the timeless tale about to unfold. Painfully, the elder stood with the aid of his walking stick, decorated with eagle feathers, as he scanned the valley for a subject that might interest his audience. His gaze met the forest canopy off in the near distance, a single tree lording above the rest.

He began with a rhythmic chant as he raised the stick above him with slow and deliberate timing, his patchy summer clothing shifting in the slight breeze. A drummer joined in, accentuating the beats of his instrument to match those of the chant. Immediately enthralled, the children's eyes locked onto the gray-haired man with awe and respect as the flickering fire lent him a supernatural glow.

The pace of the chant quickened, his face stretching with the seriousness of the tale, reaching a crescendo as he held his arms high above him and stared at the star-strewn night sky. The elder hit one final note, joined by several hoots of praise, and then went silent for several seconds.

"What's he doing?" one of the French explorers whispered to their young translator.

"Jacques, be respectful," admonished his companion quietly in their native language. "This is a wonderful opportunity." The other man produced a scroll of paper, a quill, and some ink, scribbling rapidly on his parchment as he drank in the scene.

The young tribesman, who had invited them to join the feast as guests and trade goods and medicine, kept his gaze on the elder, leaning in to explain. His broken French at times confused the translations, but he and the explorers had come to understand one another through trial and error. "Chief Atowatua begins all of his stories with a prayer to the Great One to show appreciation."

Savages, thought Jacques to himself, a curl of disgust slightly raising one end of his handlebar mustache. His partner, Remi Passaud, could see the growing disdain in the eyes of his company and nudged him with an elbow. Jacques nearly sneered at him as he nodded in the direction of the tale-teller. Finally, the sage began his tale, and the young scribe the explorers had met kept up as best he could. And the story unfolded.

"We are all children of Mother Earth, guests, as we pass from one spiritual plane to the next. Like all children, we need to be taught from time to time. Sometimes, those lessons are as easy as a tale around a fire. Other times, we must learn through suffering, joy, sorrow, and sickness.

This story is the tale of the Great Tree and the guardian who protects it. The Great Tree lies at the center of our forest, its roots digging deep into the ground and connecting to others like it. It is the home of the Forest Guardian. He protects all of the trees to prevent man from taking more than he gives.

Once, when I was young and foolish, I believed myself above the laws of nature, the laws of Mother Earth. When I ventured into the forest to take wood for a fire, I chose not to accept the freely given wood rotting on the ground but to take it from the living trees. Such was my arrogance.

Reckless with my hatchet, I took one sapling, then another for my pile, ignoring the trees' cries for their lost children. As I gathered the fuel and piled it, the earth shook under me, toppling my pile before I could flick it ablaze with my flint. Determined, I set back into the woods to gather twigs to catch the sparks.

I took twigs from trees instead of branches discarded to the ground from wind and disease. I gathered fresh leaves in place of the dried ones rustling and crunching beneath my feet, stripping limbs bare. Again, the earth below me jolted angrily, knocking me into the dust.

'Take no more.'

The voice came from all around me, shaking the very earth. Still, in my defiance, I gathered my spilled collection. I knelt, then stood proudly. 'I take what I want. I am a man! I listen not to orders from man or beast.'

The ground vibrated and thundered once more. 'Men dare not tread here, boy! Take no more.'

The voice boomed so loud that I had to drop my load to cover my ears. The forest blurred with motion. My ears hummed and rang from the warning, bringing me back down to my knees. Behind me, I heard the creaking of a large tree. There was a loud snap! A gust of wind rushed by me. It felt as if the air could have sliced me in half had I not been kneeling already. A tree trunk as thick as my leg exploded at its base from the rush of air, first listing, then fainting to the earth, dead.

'Arrogant child!'

Now, the growling voice was more evident. It no longer made the ground tremble but felt as if it were breathing down upon me. A shadow overtook me, blocking out the sun, a threatening tower. Slowly, I turned to face the spirit I had angered. My eyes grew wide as I gazed upon its carved wooden face. Yellow eyes bore into my soul. Vines bristled wildly upon its head and visage in the place of hair. It was the size of five men. There was a hole in the ground that once accommodated its roots, the tree once there looming over me.

'You will leave without your fire, without food in your belly. Your kind is not welcome here.'

Each breath it took smelled of the dirt from which it had come, reeking of time and wisdom and danger. It blew its air upon me as I cowered beneath its gaze, trembling. Sensing that I meant no more harm, it huffed on me one final time, slowly turning back to the hole in the ground from which it had uprooted. With the earth shimmying from the impact of its steps, it spun and looked at me, giving me one last warning as it changed back into the tree it once was.

'Take no more. This forest is my home. Whosoever touches it shall be cursed, and their soul will be mine.'

So, I took no more, and I left the forest empty-handed, with a newfound reverence for Mother Earth and Her guardians."

While the elder finished his tale, Jacques and Remi watched with expressions as amazed as the children surrounding the man. Soft murmurs of approval rang from the kids at the ends, their dark eyes as wide as saucers from the yarn.

"Superstitious nonsense," Jacques snorted quietly.

Again, Remi reminded his traveling companion of his manners. "This was a wonderful experience. Do you see how alike we are to them? We all listened to stories as children." He stood and stretched, rolling his scroll tight before tying it shut. "We should go back to our camp. The day is over, and I have much to write about in the morning."

Their business concluded before the feast. The men thanked their hosts, said their goodbyes, and headed toward their tents near the forest. They chatted in their native French along the way. Their young translator had remained with his people.

"My God, that was most amazing!" Remi babbled on. "So much to write about. So much to tell."

"Quit your gushing," huffed Jacques. "They're savages. Brutes worshipping false deities and nothing more. Do you believe it was a coincidence that the elder told such a tale before us?" He studied his partner for a reaction. Losing his patience, he nearly shouted at the man beside him. "They mean to prevent us from making our settlement right here."

"I thought it was quaint," Remi retorted, no hint of ire in his voice. "The story merely hinted at not taking more than you need. Do we not have fables like that back home?"

"Superstition and folklore will not prevent the French from taming this wild land." Jacques knelt to duck into his dwelling for the night. "Or its people, if need be. Tomorrow, we begin our work. Bonne nuit."

Remi gave a routine yet distracted wave, his nerves still thrumming from the excitement of the day. He sat on a log by the fire as the workers slept soundly in their shelters all around him. He scribbled his thoughts by the campfire until the sun kissed the horizon good morning. Catching himself nodding off in mid-stroke, he set his quill aside, capped his well, and sleepily rolled his finished work before heading off to his tent.

His dreams were haunted by a nightmarish wooden giant with glowing yellow eyes brutalizing the workers and terrorizing their livestock. He kicked and groaned in his slumber late into the morning.

It seemed as though only minutes of sleep had passed when a commotion startled Remi awake. Men screamed in terror, shouting profanities and absurdities alike. The cries filled the wind with confusion as he heard the familiar snapping of felling trees. Peeking outside, disheveled dark mane and all, he saw a tree collapse in the forest. The impact shook the ground, perhaps more than it should have. The restless, bleary-eyed man, still catching his bearings, watched as workers fled the tree line, unfathomable terror in their eyes.

"Take no more!"

Groggily, he exited his tent and faced the source. Footsteps, large and thunderous, vibrated the ground below. One of the workers was thrown backward from the woods, smashing against a rock outcropping with a wet, crimson splatter. Remi's mind immediately snapped wide awake in disbelief. As the body slid down the stone, more tortured yowls emanated from the thick of the forest, one of them sounding familiar.

More men scrambled from within, one snagged by a set of vines and dragged back inside just as he made the clearing. Another scream ended abruptly, a small fountain of red peaking above the canopy. Now, it was Remi, and not the ground, who shook in fear of what he had just witnessed. Something launched from the wilderness at him, causing him to shut his eyes, raise his arms, and fold in on himself in reflex. A wet thud landed next to him, a pair of recognizable, bloody trousers with Jacques' lower half still in them. The bare left foot twitched while the booted right appendage danced to its own tune.

Remi's jaw dropped, and a horrified screech knotted in his throat. Another of the workers fleeing the forest scrambled in his direction. The explorer heard a loud grunt as something of immense size launched itself into the air toward them, blacking out the sun in its flight. Remi retreated in an attempt to get out of the object's path. The hired help wasn't as lucky; his life snuffed under the foot of a giant man-like creature of wood as if he were a mere ant. Remi's bladder released itself as fright overtook him.

He covered his eyes to prevent the madness of what he saw from locking itself into his reality. "Show mercy!" he whined, stealing a peek at the being.

The monstrous protector leered down at the stranger to its land, regarding him with menacing, glowing yellow eyes, the sound of wood cracking and creaking with its every move while it decided the visitor's fate. A low growl bubbled from within, its mouth widening in a sneer of disdain as it reached out for the cowering, trembling man.

"Stop!"

A voice cried out to the thing grasping for the explorer, briefly halting its desire to eradicate him. Remi and the giant both turned their attention to the approaching natives. Chief Atowatua led an army of warriors, some of them with their bows trained upon the being. The elder looked at them and gestured for them to lower their weapons, his walking stick in hand. Slowly, he lifted the staff into the air, accompanied by shouts and chants. The entity followed the piece of wood as if hypnotized. As the mystical sage continued his calls, the beast straightened, seeming to relax at the prayer. At last, the chief ceased, signaling his tribesmen to stay back as he approached the guardian.

"Great Atwuskniges, his kind is foolish and arrogant, as I once was." He closed to a respectful distance, never losing eye contact with the creature, his staff still held in front of him.

The wooden man regarded the token held out to him, memory seeping into its gaze. "I remember you." Its face contorted and slackened as if deciding what to do with the interloper. "What do you offer in return?"

The chief took a deep, slow breath, looking lovingly at his people. His wife forced her way to the front, her aged eyes glazed over with fright and sadness. When the chief nodded to his other half, she appeared to understand what was about to happen.

"I have spent my life telling your story," the elder explained. "When we met, you offered me a part of you in exchange for my spirit when I was ready. I have lived a long and happy life. Spare this man to tell your story to his people as you once did me."

The wooden giant considered the offer before him. "Are you ready to give your soul to me?"

Without hesitation, the Native agreed. "I am."

The creature twisted its awful gaze upon the explorer. "Will you accept this offer? Will you warn your kind to avoid my forest?"

The Frenchman nodded enthusiastically, still fearing for his existence.

The being directed the chieftain to relinquish his wooden staff to the white man with an outstretched hand.

"Take this and remember our bond. Tell of the consequences of trespassing. Take not from my great tree, my home. Any man who does will surely be cursed for me to hunt their souls. When you are ready, I will collect your soul to help me serve Mother Earth."

As the colonizer silently agreed, the creature set his eyes upon the Natives. With uncanny quickness, he pointed an open hand toward their chief. The man breathed his last as a human. His feet became the roots of a great trunk, leathery, aged skin morphing into bark. Outstretched arms grew and contorted, his fingers thinning and sprouting leaves. Only a vague resemblance of a face remained at the base of a yawning fork of the newly formed tree.

The elder woman howled in anguish to see her mate so transformed. With a pained stride, she slowly approached the tree, her unbearable grief and great cries filling the air as the creature coldly spun, wordlessly returning to the wood from which it came. Thunder shook the ground with each of its steps, matched only by the mournful wails of the West River People as they gathered around the large, lone oak.

The explorer quietly regarded the staff in his hand. He felt its power, electric and clear. He would keep his promise, not for the sake of the being, nor his own, but for the great man who had sacrificed himself so that he might live.

"That's why this house is built from wood far away." A gray-haired man rocked his young grandchildren as he spun the yarn. "One day, I'll be a memory, a part of this forest." He gazed lovingly at the seven-year-old boy and then his younger granddaughter. "You must never take from the forest behind this house, for a great chief protects it, as it will be by me someday.

A teenage boy sneered from the table, shaking his head at his aged patriarch in disbelief as he skinned a rabbit for dinner. "Grandfather, why do you fill their heads with such fables?"

"Take no more."

The thunderous voice shook the cabin violently, causing the younger children to cry out in fear. They leaped from their grandfather's lap and hid under the table, quaking from fright. Wide-eyed, the sage man looked at his oldest grandson. "Where did you hunt that rabbit?"

With his heartbeat becoming rapid, the boy turned to his elder. "I got it from the forest."

The Frenchman stood from his chair. Painfully, he retrieved the gnarled wooden staff mounted above the mantle, sorrow welling in his eyes. "Come," he directed the young hunter, "it's time to pass this to you."

CRICKET SONG

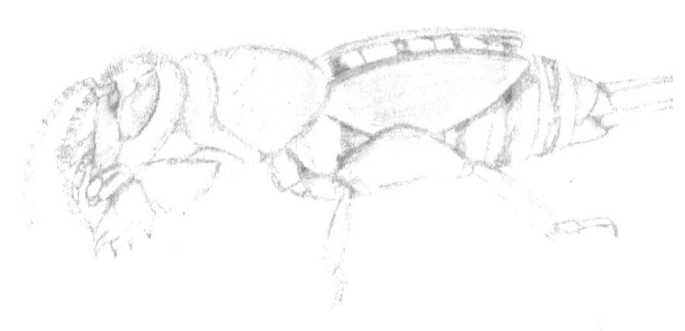

"This will be perfect!" Isabelle Merced stepped out of her cream-colored 1953 Oldsmobile, the metal hinges squeaking a slight protest. "I can do my dissertation here. Maybe I'll even discover a new species." She shut the door and absently traced its sharp angles back toward the trunk, looking up at the leafy summer canopy and around the brushy forest floor with an ear-to-ear grin on her face. Inhaling deeply, she savored the dusty smell of the Ozark Mountain air. Leaves rattled in a slight breeze, making the Midwest morning warmth tolerable, though the promise of a humid day lay ahead.

Just as she popped the trunk, a ticking began behind her.

Tzeeeeeet. Tzeeeeeet. Tzeeeeeet.

Isabelle expertly stalked the high-pitched thrumming hidden within a thick raspberry bush. A brilliant green grasshopper with a pointed head cautiously crawled amidst the thorned branches.

She offered a finger in its path. Reluctantly, it accepted the new perch. Isabelle slowly stood and brought it into the open. "Nebraska conehead." Her smile returned as it unfolded its wings and flitted off into the safety of the brush once more.

Struggling with the sparse selection of scientific equipment she had borrowed from the laboratory where she worked, Isabelle unloaded the luggage from the trunk. The smile faded to a scowl as her gaze came upon the cabin. "Less than ideal conditions," she snorted. "It'll do in a pinch, I suppose."

She had driven for two days from Massachusetts to be here. Her master thesis on the Northern Mole Cricket would take a month or more of hands-on research if she were to be taken seriously by the etymology field. Most women shied away from anything with more than four legs, but insects and arachnids had always given Isabelle a sense of wonder, even as a little girl.

The scientist plopped her equipment into a neatly organized section just right of the door. A musty smell assaulted her, making her nose crinkle. "Windows first," she thought aloud.

Isabelle started with the panes on either side of the door, opening them wide, the light breeze from outside barely shifting the curtains. Next was the small but adequate kitchen and the half window above the sink. Upon finishing her rounds, the bedroom windows finally allowed a beautiful cross-breeze to waft through the building, billowing the sheer curtains pleasantly.

The grin returned to her face, and she habitually peered around the central area, locating outlets and light switches.

"Today is about getting set up and familiar," she reminded herself. "Tomorrow, I'll do my first real expedition."

Isabelle stretched as she lay in bed the following morning, the rising sun peeking in through a corner of the bedroom window. It had taken her several hours to fall asleep that night. She had stayed awake, trying to identify the different calls of the local bug population. She had fallen into a deep slumber while making notes in her book of some of the suspects trilling outdoors, a trail of ink arching from a partial word on the last page.

This morning, she was well-rested, but she knew most of her work would likely happen at dusk and when the moon shone down.

I'll have to force myself to stay up a bit longer each night.

She set up a makeshift lab on the dining room table. It didn't have much space to offer, but it would be fine for specimen jars and making notes. The lighting was better in the dining room for her microscope—the sun's natural rays peeking beams of light through the leaves. The propane stove had a percolator filling the air with the bitter smell of strong coffee.

The night prior, Isabelle had tested the camping lantern she had borrowed from a friend. The soft glow would be ideal for her strolls. It would also be far less likely to frighten away any proper specimens while they called for their mates. Several skeins of brightly colored yarn awaited, marking her paths to prevent her from getting lost at night.

Noon had struck before her stomach gurgled for sustenance. She looked down at her midsection, annoyed by the intrusion into her thoughts. Strolling over to the fridge and popping open the door, she leered into the empty space, realizing she had forgotten one major thing: food.

During her rampant, insatiable quest for knowledge, it wasn't unusual for Isabelle to forget to eat. In her excitement for the trip, even with the long drive, it simply hadn't dawned on her. During the trek, she ate at roadside diners, with her mind lost in thoughts about her studies and the possibility of discovery. Now, here, a good drive into isolation, it hit home.

Slamming the appliance shut, she threw her head back with an exasperated sigh. "A whole day wasted," she grumbled, thinking of the nearest town that might have a grocer. "Stupid. Idiotic." Her self-deprecating murmurs continued as she stomped back out the door and to her car for the long haul.

After the hastily made shopping trip, Isabelle's stomach was finally satisfied, and her refrigerator had supplies. Fresh fruit filled a wicker basket on the dining table for easy grabbing before entering the field. Some of the berry bushes she would encounter might also have ripe treats for her to enjoy.

Afternoon blossomed into evening, the Midwest heat and humidity bringing with it a sticky sweat. Had there been a breeze to cool her off, Isabelle still would have paid no mind to her drenched clothes as she rifled through her field bag for what she needed. Specimen bottles clanked together with each motion, seemingly impatient for use.

Her eyes combing the forest floor, she slowly made her way through the thick underbrush, savoring the various trills of her quarries. Most of the insects would halt their music at her approach, fearful of the possibility of a predator. She quickly located and identified several species of tree and ground crickets, as well as katydids and locusts. The nearer the sun came to the horizon, the more active the chorus became until she finally had to set the lantern alight to see where she was going.

As the near-full moon gleamed among the starlight, peeking through the dense trees, she heard a sharp, whistling vibrato that her keen ears couldn't recognize.

Brooooot. Brooooot. Brooooot.

It was the most beautiful thing she had experienced, nearly mesmerizing in its cadence. The sound invaded her mind, overtaking her and making her oblivious to everything else around her.

"Could this be it?" she wondered. "Could this be the new species I discover?" Her eyes dilated, and her heart raced with adrenaline as she scanned all around to find the source.

Another chirp, this one of a slightly higher pitch, joined in from behind her. Then another. And another, each a different octave of the same melody. The fluttering of unseen wings joined the choir, moving the origin of the noises before she could successfully pin them down. They called all around her, enveloping her in a nocturnal musical cocoon. A huge smile radiated on her bookish face as she drank it in. It hypnotized her, causing her to feel light-headed. Slowly swooning to the ground, she allowed the song to wash over her like a moonlit sea tide amid the Ozark Forest. The choir engulfed her, the hypnotic highs and lows lulling her to an unintended slumber.

Isabelle awoke, dazed and confused, as songbirds broke the morning silence. Dried, decaying leaves were tangled in her long brown hair and clung to her dress. She sat up, looking around.

What happened?

She stretched serenely, entirely at ease, oblivious to her disheveled appearance. The memory of the natural concerto unfolded in her mind.

She bolted to her feet, a newfound thrill pounding in her heart. Rifling through her bag, she found the brightly colored yarn, tying one end to a tree branch as high as she could reach. Locating the direction she had come from, she gathered her things and headed back to her cabin with studious enthusiasm.

"I must return tonight to see if I can locate one of them."

The smile never wavered from her lips as she hummed to replicate the song trapped in her mind. It took three of the skeins of yarn before finally relocating her base and securing the opposite end near the door of her makeshift lab. While unloading the sample jars she had collected throughout the night, she snagged an apple from the basket and devoured it. Flopping a notebook open, she busily penned her experience as best she could recall before her unintended nap, noting the tempo and pitch of the pattern of chirps. Unable to contain her excitement, she snapped the journal shut and stuffed it into her bag before heading out of the cabin to chase her marked trail. Nightfall would be hours away, but she had to study the surroundings to see what made last night so unforgettable. The rasp of the creatures, whatever they might be, echoed in her mind as she lovingly traced the yarn deep into the wilderness.

Finally reaching the clearing where her marked trail ended, she began to view the immediate landscape, taking in as much of the minutia as scientifically possible.

What sort of vegetation is here? What variety of minerals? Where are they hiding?

Isabelle first stood in place and observed, hoping to catch a glimpse of movement, any indication of last night's unseen creatures. The dense carpet of dewy, decaying leaves brought forth no signs of motion. Something didn't feel the same. The energy she experienced last night wasn't there. The forest felt empty.

Then she noticed it: her surroundings weren't just empty; they were silent. No birds sang praises to the morning sun. No other insects made their presence known. If the wind hadn't kicked up a few of the leaves, the quiet would be discomforting.

Then, a small, raspy chirp echoed over the breeze.

Creeeeeeeeeeeeeeeeeeeeeeeeeeeeeeeeeeeeeeeeeeeeee

Her head swiveled toward the source so fast that her neck popped painfully. Stars shot behind her eyes as her hand flew to the injured area. Soon, the agony subsided as she tilted her head to relieve the soreness. Another continuous, gravelly chirp hit her ears. It sounded deep and hollow as if coming from…

A cave?

Her gaze locked on a small black opening in the ground. The crevice was so well camouflaged that she'd missed it in her earlier observations. The opening merely appeared like a large flat slab of limestone jutting from the ground. The cave's maw hinted nothing of its contents or depth, only a darkness so hungry that it swallowed the light. Stepping softly, she returned to her discarded pile of equipment, lit the lantern, and brought it back to the crack in the earth to peer inside. The closer she got with the light source, the more frantic the noise within became. Lowering herself to the ground, along with the lamp, she tilted it in an attempt at a better look. A pair of red eyes regarded her from the blackness, and a sharp chirp emitted from inside, startling her backward and listing the lantern over on the drying leaves, setting them ablaze.

Isabelle quickly stomped out the fire, smothering it with loose dirt. As she quelled the flames, the rattling in the cave grew more menacing. This time, it wasn't welcoming; it was a warning. One song became two; two became five. The mouth of the dark cavern filled with pairs of glowing, demonic eyes. They glowered at her from the safety of the underground. Soon, the air filled with a different melody. The sound followed her no matter which way she spun her body. It spiked inside her ears, rattling Isabelle to her core as she wilted to her knees. Her hands flew to her ears in a futile attempt to silence the commotion as it climbed to a crescendo. It pulsed in her skull, throbbing like a migraine in time to the beat of her heart.

Through pained and tearful eyes, she saw that the entrance to the cave wasn't the only port to the underbelly of the forest. Several openings surrounded her. She was in a natural amphitheater, the reverberations bounding off each other perfectly. Isabelle screamed at the sound, hoping to frighten the insects into retreat, blood trickling from her ears and nose. She wiped at it, looking at the crimson on her fingers in wide-eyed disbelief.

I'll die if I stay here.

She clawed back toward where the yarn could lead her away, the sound eating at her psyche little by little. Just as she reached the pathway, the chittering ceased as quickly as it had begun, diminishing in layers until all that remained was quiet. She turned her body, leaning against a tree, her lungs heaving for life-giving air as if she'd been holding her breath. Her heartbeat slowed, and her breathing returned to normal as she tilted her head against the trunk, peered at the sky, and let out another blood-curdling scream.

The tree she'd thought she'd been leaning against was a man. Skittering backward like a crab in retreat, she yowled again at the perplexed person. She shot a frantic gaze around her, worried that she may have recoiled back into the nest where the crickets lurked.

The man held out his hand, causing Isabelle to wince away as if he meant her harm. "Come on. Let me help you."

She grasped his arm. As he assisted her upright, her eyes explored him. He was tall and muscular, wandering through the woods with nothing covering his bare chest. A large, clunky canvas backpack plopped lightly to his opposite elbow as the stranger gently pulled Isabelle to her feet.

"May I?" He motioned, indicating his meaning: he would help dust her off if she would allow it.

Still unsure, she approved with a slight nod. The newcomer's touch was light and unthreatening as he brushed the leaves and dirt from her clothes. Once finished, he straightened, his body glistening with sweat, which she supposed resulted from his hike. As her gaze poured over him, the silence became awkward. He smirked and cleared his throat, causing Isabelle to feel the blood rush to her face.

She turned away quickly, her face becoming redder with each passing second of silence. "Sorry."

He wrestled with something from his gear as she watched through her peripheral vision. She saw a flash of white go over his head and down his perfect torso while she pretended not to pay attention.

"Better?"

Isabelle turned around slowly, taking in the magnificent man in front of her. He was square-jawed and rugged, with a dark brown ponytail and the most striking brown eyes she'd ever seen. The t-shirt he'd slipped on hugged every part of his torso.

Isabelle's studies and work had kept her more interested in things with six legs than two. However, if her dreams had ever had a personification to them, he was standing in front of her now. Her heart fluttered nervously, words still stuck in her throat.

He smiled widely, revealing a perfect set of white teeth, and tilted his head in curiosity. "Are you sure you're okay?"

A churring began again, seemingly accompanying his every syllable. This time, it was more akin to what she experienced in the first round: calming, soothing, captivating, and just a bit more baritone in its cadence.

Did his shirt flitter?

The song burst through the air once more, lowering her guard. She was sure that she saw sudden movement come from behind him. Closing her eyes, she shook her head to dispel the tricks her brain was playing on her, stumbling as the world swam around her.

He rushed forward with unreal speed, catching her as her legs gave out. Scooping her up into his arms, he held her close as he stood. He seemed to marvel at the transformation from the bookish scientist that drew him in to the lovely creature he now cradled. Her tightly wound bun of hair had fallen around her shoulders; her strict and upright posture had given way to a guarded and shy countenance.

He carried her, following the yarn-marked trail, barely releasing his gaze from the captivating woman in his arms. With each stride, the cricket song rang through the woods, just as alluring and enticing as the first time.

Instinctively, her arms carefully wrapped around his shoulders as her aqua-blue eyes met his. His back rippled with each step, rocking and soothing her, his voice humming along with the sound of the insects as if it were his favorite tune. She felt as though they were dancing to the sound of the cricket song throughout the forest.

She lulled and relaxed, savoring the surreal moment, the midday sun adding a touch of warmth that made it perfect. His boots hit the wood planks of her cabin's stoop. Her heart sank, knowing that this would be the end of her encounter with the handsome stranger. Yet, he didn't set her down. She leaned her head into him, inhaling his masculine scent.

He struggled somewhat to unlatch the door, causing Isabelle to giggle. He shifted to carry her through the threshold like a bride on her honeymoon night. Past the makeshift lab on the dining room table, he ushered her through the living room.

The man gently placed Isabelle atop her mattress. An emptiness washed over her as his arms uncoiled from her body. She could no longer hide the wanting in her soul as he released her.

He grinned coyly. "I should go. You need your rest." He turned to leave.

Isabelle stopped him, grasping his hand in hers, and he peered softly down to her. She whispered, "Stay."

Sadness overcame his face once he understood the tension between them. "I can't. If I do, it will only cause you pain."

"Please stay with me," she pleaded, her face reddening once more.

There was a finality in his forlorn expression. "Are you sure?" As she nodded, it melted away, replaced by a hunger. "This can't be undone." He searched her face, again finding approval. Hovering over her, he bent down, offering her the gift of her first lover's kiss. Soon, he embraced her as she wished, and they made love deep into the night.

Night gave way to morning. Isabelle's hand searched her bed and felt the man beside her twitch repeatedly. She slowly sat up, turning to him. His back was turned to her as something moved under his shirt. Curious, she lifted the clothes to peek at the source. A pair of iridescent black wings fluttered, a slight chirping noise emanating from the friction of the movement. Gaping in horror, she tugged on his shoulder gently. His body flopped flat on his back, the fog of death clouding his once radiant eyes.

She felt for a pulse in a panic, but none met her touch. Tears rolled down her cheeks, the shock of the discovery morphing into the grief of loss.

I can't. If I do, it will only cause you pain.

Laying her head on his chest, she was shocked at the hollow sound within and the cold, hardened texture of his skin.

She reached up to caress his face, only then noticing his outer shell, now cracked it was, how it flaked away like the bark of a hickory tree. With shaking hands, she delicately peeled off a chunk of the façade. Peering underneath, she sat bolt upright, her hands flying to her mouth, a scream lodged in her throat.

I'm imagining this. It can't be real!

The thing below the surface wasn't human. As Isabelle peeled away more of his face's shell, large red eyes, now cloudy and lifeless, stared back at her. What she'd believed to be a strong jawline were palps tucked into the proper position. A small seam split his chin where the joints met. The knotted ponytail proved to be the creature's antennae tied behind him and camouflaged by the other hairs on his head.

Finally, a yowl of terror escaped her lips, echoing throughout the valley, frightening a flock of songbirds conversing in a nearby birch tree into flight. She shoved the husk away from her in an attempt to place some distance between her and the body. The soft lines of what she had believed to be toned muscles had darkened into harsh lines of flesh-colored armored plates, caving to a hollow pile of chiton under her abrupt and violent reaction. Another dread-filled yell pervaded the cabin as she fell off the bed, backpedaling in disbelief as the night's illusion and her lover shattered before her

Isabelle scrambled to her feet, skittering into the cabin's main room, knocking papers and vials to the floor with a mixture of flutters and shatters.

What the hell is going on?

Her heart raced as she stumbled around through a fog of panic. She peered back at the bedroom, falling to her knees once again next to the fireplace. Placing her hand on the mantle as she caught her breath, she felt the wood shift beneath her touch. The carvings vibrated beneath her palm, coming to life. The screaming family at the center of the mantle morphed, as they moved to one side. Isabelle watched in horror as the wooden face of the man who had made love to her last night appeared before her eyes.

Her hand flew to her mouth in another silent scream.

While her mind scrambled to grasp what she was seeing, a sharp pain shot through her abdomen, pulling her back from the shock. Slowly getting to her knees, flares of agony sparked within her stomach. Isabelle held herself as her body cramped and ached. At last, she stood, hunched over, unable to fully straighten while something writhed inside her.

A new insectile song began to warble through the forest, seeking her, growing louder with each second.

Yeeeeeeeeweeek. Yeeeeeeeeweeek.

Isabelle's brain vibrated from the sound.

Slowly, the chirps morphed, becoming words she could understand, a phrase repeated in a female voice: "You seek answers. Come to me."

Pain stabbed at her anatomy. Isabelle's eyes widened as she glanced at her midsection. Her torso stretched and expanded, things writhing just below the surface of her skin.

Pregnant? Am I pregnant?

"Yes," the voice answered, even though Isabelle hadn't directed the query at it. "Quickly. Come to me. I can offer comfort and knowledge."

Despite her expanding belly and fearfulness, the scientist felt compelled to obey the mysterious disembodied command.

Isabelle treaded naked through the woods, her stomach ballooning outward and heavy, each step weary and burdened as she traced the yarned path back to the clearing.

"Welcome," the voice's metallic ring in Isabelle's head soothed as she approached the entrance to the caverns she'd recently discovered. "You are in no danger."

A previously undiscovered insect species, some as large as rats, scuttled about, feeding on nearby rotting vegetation and a possum that had died in the night.

Or had they killed it with their song?

Wings rubbed together, crowding her cranium with conversation. The creatures' forearms were brutish and cupped, digits turned inward, obviously meant for the sole purpose of burrowing. Their heads closely resembled a conglomeration of humanoid and bug-like skulls in various stages of development. The things gathered by her feet inspected the intruder with their antennae. She snatched up a smaller one for closer inspection. It wriggled in her grasp. Dual stingers protruded behind its thorax, offering a warning against predators and rivals.

"Mama," cooed the critter.

Isabelle's body seemed to rebel against her, contorting and stretching. Sunlight began to become painful. Mindlessly, she stuffed the animal into her mouth and chewed. It crunched and squished as she masticated and swallowed, her mind never contemplating what she had just consumed. Something else was overtaking her. Fear had given way to an insatiable hunger so fierce that it grew to anger. The other insects at her feet kept a distance but seemed to know that their guest wouldn't harm them further.

She knelt at the tiny crack in the ground, looking at the blackness beyond with newfound hate. "I can't fit in there!"

As if on command, the bugs clawed at the opening. Dirt and rubble fell at their misshapen hands, rapidly relocated in a ring around the ravine by their instinctual skills, growing the entrance within seconds.

Isabelle crawled into the opening once it became large enough for her, her belly now dragging behind her like a plump bridal train. Her legs struggled to straddle the protrusion and shove her forward at first. Isabelle adapted to the pain of her rapidly changing body, her limbs strengthening. The trek became more manageable once the cave opened further, and she could stand. Her eyes adjusted to the absence of light with shocking ease, the pain from the direct sunlight gone. The damp coolness of the cavern, something that would have customarily offended her senses and filled her with dread, felt more welcoming with each blindly guided footfall.

"This way." That once commanding voice now sounded weak and weary. "Please hurry. There's not much time."

An alcove yawned in front of her. Rocky stalactites and stalagmites seeped, reaching for each other through the passage of time like the pointed fingers of Michelangelo's "Adam and God" on the ceiling of the Sistine Chapel. Water dripped all around her as she surveyed the structure. A solitary beam of sun sliced through the black like a spotlight.

"Come closer."

Now, the command was no longer in Isabelle's mind but out loud, reverberating off of the cavern walls. Something shifted beyond the beam of light, the entirety of it unseen, yet the size of a human.

"Hello?"

Deeper into the cave, her eyes adjusted to the dimness of the surroundings. Isabelle's stomach now stretched behind her a couple of feet, still increasing in size as she advanced on the mysterious thing beckoning her. She could hear labored, raspy breathing as she closed in. Tiny legs skittered in the shadows, joined by a more extensive set that matched the motion of her host.

The shape moved once more, remaining in the shadows as much as possible. Light from a crack in the earth above flashed upon a pair of large compound eyes halting to regard their guest. They blinked slowly, meekly, as a dying patient in an elderly ward might.

"I see my king chose his queen." The disembodied voice seemed relieved. "I can finally rest." It gasped and coughed, turning away. "Our kind will be able to continue."

More of the rodent-sized crickets shuffled around her feet toward the light of the entrance. "Who are you?"

"I lost my name decades ago," the creature gasped, restless in the darkness.

Isabelle approached further, curiosity far outweighing the pain of her body's transformation. "What are you?"

The creature laughed, an insectoid thrumming accompanying it, followed closely by another coughing fit. "We are an ancient race, hidden both amongst and away from humans for millennia. As our kind progresses, we must evolve."

"I don't understand." Isabelle felt her voice crack. "Why is this happening to me? How?"

A clawed limb swept into the light, directing attention toward the crawling things retreating from the underground. "As we... As they mature, their bodies begin to resemble humans more closely. Only a select few, usually males, will make it to full adulthood. Fewer still find a mate and begin a new colony." The still-shadowed speaker rasped and chittered. "I finally brought forth a king to carry on this hive, to take it forward to the next step."

At last, the creature paused and leaned into the light, revealing her nearly skinless skull, the bug-like eyes protruding from their dark sockets. "You will take my place. You are our next step."

No lips formed the words coming from the thing before Isabelle. Her face contorted in a silent screech, hands covering her mouth to stifle the terror. In seconds, the shock wore off, morphing into scientific curiosity when the life form in the cave took no retreating shift. She shuffled closer, her gigantic, ant-like thorax twitching behind her, holding out a hand to caress the pained matriarch. A sympathetic tear flowed down her face as the creature leaned into her touch.

"It has been so long since I felt a human's caress." Weakly, it raised its head from her guest's hand. "My time is done."

Isabelle stepped into the beam as the creature's weight began to lean toward the ground. The light allowed her to finally see the entirety of the manifestation that had called to her. It had been human at some point, having evolved into this entity, the mother of who knew how many creatures.

Slowly, the queen began to lie down, her exhausted body experiencing its final moments. "Please stay with me so that I won't slip into the darkness alone."

Isabelle began to hear a new song from the darkness. While their mother lay dying, the insects issued mournful sounds, like something played at a wake. The sources of the sad music surrounded the matriarch. There were hundreds of them, all in various stages of evolution, naked, humanoid, some parts still very much insectile. A fully formed man stood bereft of clothes beside the fallen creature. His resemblance to the human Isabelle recently loved was uncanny, causing more tears to flow.

The etymologist, now resigned to her fate, wept as she held her slipping predecessor, comforting the creature as it left this plane.

The pain of childbirth was challenging to get used to for Isabelle, but it eventually got easier. Others tended to her needs as dutiful workers to their queen. She held one of her beautiful living creations in her arms, made possible by her love. Though they still had the bodies of misshapen crickets at the beginning of their lives, their cooing now came from the well-formed lips of a human child. She rocked it as it slept in the safety of her caress, sucking one of the pointed digits of its shovel-like hands.

Deeper in the cave, songs of praise comforted her. To her, it was a chorus, relaxing and inviting. For now, the rest of the world only heard cricket songs.

THE NORTH SIDE
OF THE TREES

"Okay. Let's wrap up here." The voice was muffled and tinny through the odd-looking orange protective suit's helmet. The man's face shield fogged with each breath as he stuffed a sample of the smoldering rock into a lead-lined container and snapped the lid shut. "The thing's too heavy. We'll have to get a team out here to collect it."

"I'm not done with the readings yet," answered another man in a similar getup as he swept the area with a Geiger counter that angrily clicked away. "Radiation is off the charts."

Thunder rumbled in the sky.

"You hear that?" The man in charge stood up painfully. "It's about to rain. We need to leave."

"Why? We're protected."

"We are, but our equipment isn't. The truck isn't." He placed his sample and all of his tools in the back of a black truck with no markings. "In these parts, so close to that coal-fueled power plant, that's likely to be acid rain. Look at those pines over there." He gestured to a grove of wilted and dying Douglas firs around the crater.

"Good point. Wait. Are you sure that's not because of a pine borer or something?" The other man hefted his device into the back.

"If it were just the pine trees, I'd say yes. Look again."

The other man squinted through his breath-fogged face shield. It wasn't just the firs but the aspens, the brush, everything. They all had the appearance of dying. "Someone should do something about those power plants."

"Never happen. Not as long as people like cheap electricity."

They mounted the vehicle and shut the doors before removing their helmets. Both bespectacled men looked rather scholarly. The leader had a huge bald spot crowning his head; the other, a slightly younger man, had thick brown hair. The truck kicked up gravel and dirt, leaving slight tire marks as the scientists drove away from the site of the meteorite crash. As the rain began to fall, the smoking celestial visitor cracked from the temperature change. The crater it had gouged into the earth on its arrival aimed toward a run-off. That creek led to a lake, a body of water made completely useless from the pollution. The fish in it were long gone. Reptiles and amphibians had avoided the area for some time. In fact, most of the wildlife had either died out or moved into kinder pastures. Nevertheless, Mother Nature had ways of adapting to things like this. Next to the space rock, a purple, glowing moss began to sprout.

"Me and Bobby McGee" blasted through the static-filled airwaves, barely audible out of the AM radio. Janis Joplin faded in and out as they climbed to a higher altitude in their Chrysler New Yorker. The sunshine-yellow beast sputtered in protest at the change in oxygen levels.

"Should we be concerned about that death rattle?" The blonde in the middle of the back seat popped her gum as she spoke.

"Nah." The driver patted the dash lovingly. The sun reflected on his cranium just as it did the hood of the car. "This baby is a tank. She'll get us there. She just doesn't like heights very much."

"I can tweak it a bit when we stop, Jim." One of the men in the back seat offered, leaning in to look at the driver. "I may not be a mechanic, but I've rebuilt a carburetor or two. It just needs a richer mix. It's a pretty simple adjustment."

"That'd be just fine, Gary," answered the woman in the navigator's seat with a sultry voice. Her long, light-brown hair draped over her left shoulder so the fresh mountain air could hit her neck.

"I..." he stammered, his face flushing with embarrassment. "I just feel like I should help somehow. I wasn't able to contribute as much to this trip as the rest of you."

The other man in the back, behind the driver, reached to put an arm on his shoulder. "It's fine, man." He smiled and leaned back into the seat, enjoying the view and pulling the woman next to him in tight. "We've got you covered. Besides, I've heard all about your cooking over the years but have never tasted it. You can be our little kitchen bitch."

Gary rolled his eyes and pulled back into his corner of the car, the feigned smile on his face wilting away as he turned to watch the scenery. "Thanks, Tuck."

"Tucker Baker!" Jane smacked him on the arm playfully.

"What?" Tucker feigned innocence. "He said he wanted to contribute. I've heard he was a good cook. I figured it might give him a chance to show off and afford the girls a break from doing it. Lord knows you don't want to eat my cooking."

Everyone in the car chuckled except for Gary. He was deep in thought, the jab forgotten. "Guess I'd have to see what we have. I tend to improvise a lot in the kitchen."

"That's the spirit!" Jim beamed. "We'll go to the store after we get settled in. It's a bit of a drive, so you'll have plenty of time to plan a menu."

Gary brightened, his demeanor completely switching from morose to exuberant. A good deal of the conversation for the rest of the trip became about what people liked to eat.

A long gravel driveway snaked the sunshine-yellow car midway up the north side of a mountain before leveling off to where the cabin stood. It looked small from the outside but still probably large enough for the five of them to be comfortable. The front of the cabin displayed huge picture windows facing due north to overlook the neighboring peak and the tree-filled valley below. The sun hovered just to the west. Male mourning doves sounded a series of *coo-OO-oos*, and interested females answered, their distinctive vocalizations providing the soundtrack to mating season. Hawks shrieked overhead, the sounds echoing for miles, as they sought to prey upon those smaller, more musical birds.

The heady scents of pine, lilac, and sweetspire wafted all around them. Wildflowers sprang up randomly in the clearing, swaying in the cool breeze, providing a most inviting landscape around the cabin. Charlene got out of the car, popping her seat forward to let Gary out while Tucker and Jane exited through Jim's side. They all stretched, happy to finally be free of the vehicle. Gary inserted his key and turned it, opening the deep trunk.

"It's a bit chilly," Charlene noted, adding, "but it's absolutely breathtaking."

"You can say that again." Tucker inhaled deeply before sneezing.

"We're about seven thousand feet up. You'll get used to it after a while, but everyone should be sure to drink lots of water. The air is very dry here. You might get nosebleeds, too." Gary yanked the last of the suitcases out and shut the trunk. Looking at the rustic structure, he smiled brightly. "Come on. Let's go in."

"You're just saying that to cover the fact that you want to punch us in the snout," Tucker joked.

Gary clapped him on the back as he passed by. "Just you, Tuck. Just you."

Tucker stood there, speechless, as his shoulder-length brown hair moved with the wind. Finally, he peered over to Jane, who was looking at the log structure with nothing resembling the reverence everyone else had. His brow furrowed as he drew her close to him. "You okay, babe?"

She leaned into him, her sun-bleached blonde head on his chest, arms folded defensively, her face remaining a contortion of uncertainty. "I guess so. I just have a bad feeling about all of this."

"Your women's intuition going haywire? What could go wrong out here?" He squeezed her reassuringly. "Come on. Let's go claim a room before Gary takes the big bed."

Gary left nothing to chance after he saw that the house only had two rooms and a loft above the living room. Climbing up and down to the loft would be scary, the old ladder creaking and groaning under his weight. The space was tight. He could barely sit up to read a book. Still, he didn't allow it to dampen his spirits. He wasn't at home. He wasn't at work. He was on an adventure with friends.

"You about ready to head to the store?"

Gary peered over the railing to see Jim smiling up at him. "Yeah. Just about got things the way I want them. Be down in a minute." He set his gas lantern next to his sleeping bag, rolling up the open end to prevent any little critters from making themselves at home. Carefully kneeling back to prevent from braining himself on the rafters, he decided he was satisfied with the layout and swung his body to line up with the ladder.

"Careful now." Jim watched his friend descend the rungs."

By the time Gary heard the crack, it was too late. Halfway down, one of the rungs broke when he put his weight on it. Gravity grabbed the hapless man, sending him sprawling onto his back against the hardwood floor. Air evacuated his lungs upon impact. Stars danced in his eyes, his head ringing like a church bell. Charlene rushed over as Jim stood above him, a look of grave concern on his face. The room spun a bit as their garbled concerns fell momentarily on deaf ears. He thought he heard a door open and someone else joining the couple that watched over him.

Finally, his senses cleared, and he slowly pulled air back into himself.

"Are you okay, Gary?" Charlene leaned down to look at him. "Maybe you should see if there's a doctor while you're in town. You could have a concussion."

Gary's head swam as he leaned up slowly. "I think I'll be fine once you guys hold the house still."

"I think she's right," Jim agreed. "We'll see if there's a clinic and have you looked at, just to be safe."

The world returned to focus. Gary studied the offending rung as best he could, gradually standing on spaghetti legs. He took in deep breaths. The broken part was in the middle of the ladder, so his fall wasn't far. "I'll be fine. We need to get some hardware to fix this, though."

"Please go see a doctor," pleaded Jim's wife. "For me."

Gary sighed and smiled at his hostess. "Okay, Char. For you, I will." He looked over and saw that Tuck and Jane were in the room as well. Tucker was half-clothed, Jane not far behind. Neither had said much, possibly due to the shock of what happened. He glossed over them with a pang of jealousy. "Fresh mountain air getting to you already, Tuck?"

Jim took him by the shoulder and led him to the car. "Let's go. The nearest town is still an hour away. We may be gone for a while. Sometimes, these little mountain towns roll up the sidewalks early."

The men strolled out to the New Yorker. It rumbled to life, and they left with a list of chores. Jim practically chatted Gary's ear off, specifically to keep him from going to sleep on the ride out. It wouldn't have been an issue. Gary wasn't about to let a little tumble ruin this trip for anyone.

The little town was quaint and certainly one that thrived on tourists as much as locals, but as the day waned, so did their chances to complete everything. Much to Gary's chagrin, the first stop was a local physician. Luckily, the aged man's office was empty, so they were able to get in.

"Well," the doc said, setting down his otoscope, "I don't think there's a concussion, but you'll be sore in the morning. Take some aspirin for any pain and ice down any swelling, if there is any. Maybe reconsider using the loft space."

They left the doctor, having relieved Jim's worries. The sun was starting to go down.

"Maybe he's right. I can sleep on the couch. We'll fix the ladder later this week." Gary looked at his watch.

"We'd better get to the store. I need to have stuff for tonight's dinner and breakfast, at least."

They hastened to the local grocer and found they had more time for shopping than they had thought. Afterward, they loaded their bags into the trunk and got in. Jim turned the key. The Chrysler whined but refused to come to life. "Dammit. Our milk will go bad if she doesn't start."

"Did I see a tool kit in your trunk?"

Gary nodded at Jim.

"Pop the trunk and the hood. I'll take a look."

Jim released the latch and got out to open the trunk. Fetching the small toolbox, he joined his friend under the hood. He already had the top of the carburetor off and a peculiar look on his face.

"What's going on? What do you see?"

Without a word, Gary reached daintily inside the machine, pinching out a long string of oil-smoked purple substance. Both men examined it with dumbstruck wonder. "What the hell is that?"

Gary shook his head and shrugged. "I couldn't tell you, but I bet it's the cause of the problem." He walked the thing over to a nearby trash can, giving it one last curious twist and turn before depositing it. "Go ahead and give it another shot. I'll look at the air filter and fix the mix problem while we're here."

Jim returned to the cab and cranked the key. The engine popped to life, still sputtering for a few seconds before Gary made his adjustment. At last, the car began purring as if nothing happened. He heard a screw being tightened, and his mechanically inclined friend closed the hood, wiping his hands on his jeans.

Gary returned the tools to their place and closed the trunk. "Seems to be fine now. Air filter was a bit dirty. You're going to need new belts and hoses when you get home, though. It should last until then. They weren't too bad."

"Well, aren't you the grease monkey?" Jim quipped, clapping his friend triumphantly on the shoulder.

Gary smiled coyly, a sense of accomplishment on his face. "My dad insisted on teaching me a few things about cars. He didn't want me to get ripped off by a shop when it was something I could do myself. I change a mean tire, too." As the men began their long drive back to camp, his face soured. "I still can't figure out what that stuff was or how it got in there."

"That is odd," agreed Jim. "You got it working, and that's what matters." Several moments of silence fell before he spoke again. "I've talked to Charlene. Our offer still stands."

A flush of shame overcame Gary. "I can't impose."

"Nonsense. Since Janette left for college, we have a spare room. You need a roof over your head and food in your belly."

"I..." Gary turned away to hide his emotions. "I don't have any way of pulling my weight. I don't have a job."

"You can help me get some things done around the house, maybe fix my car for me." Jim smiled softly. "We've been friends forever, man. Let us do this for you. Char loves you almost as much as I do. Besides, with those talented hands, you could find odd jobs somewhere, I'm sure."

Gary fell silent for a long time. He brushed a tear from his cheek and looked at his buddy. Though his smile suggested defeat, his eyes filled with gratitude. "Okay. Just until I get back on my feet." He paused. "Don't mention it around Tuck. You know how he loves to be a smartass. I'll never hear the end of it."

"He gives you shit," reminded Jim, "but he cares for you in his way. He's just too damned macho to show it. You know that." Jim returned his eyes to the twisting road and chuckled. "I hope Tucker isn't rocking the cabin too much."

They both laughed and continued chatting the rest of the way home. By the time their tires crunched to a halt in the driveway, the mood was light and cheerful once again. Charlene was out on the porch swing, reading a romance novel with a contented grin on her beautiful face. The men began lugging the paper grocery sacks into the cabin.

Jim nodded toward the inside. "They still going at it?"

Charlene peeked up from her book. "Hmm? Oh. I don't think so. They went quiet a while ago. I just got so into this book that I tuned them out." She placed a bookmark between the pages, set it down, and stood with a slight stretch. "Here. Let me help."

Jim handed off one of the lighter bags as the three strolled inside. "You put them away." He leaned over and kissed his wife tenderly. "We'll get the rest."

As both men made another trip to the car, Gary spoke: "Tuck isn't the only one who's going to get some love. I know what those novels do to her." He elbowed Gary knowingly. "That's why I encourage her to read them."

"I'm so jealous of you and Char." Gary grabbed the gallon of milk with one hand and the sack of canned goods with the other. "Hell, I'm a bit jealous of Tucker, even if he doesn't stick with any one woman for long."

"You'll find someone." Jim closed the trunk and grinned. "We can set you up with one of Char's single friends if you like."

"We'll see. I'm more of a romantic like you, not a playboy like Tuck." Gary felt the weight in the can-filled bag shift and heard the paper start to tear. "Shit. Better get these inside. I have to start cooking soon."

"Make something hearty. We'll need it for our hike tomorrow."

"You asked for it."

"That was the best stew I've had in years, Gary," Jim raved, raising his scotch on the rocks in salute before taking a hefty gulp and sighing in satisfaction with a pat to his belly.

Charlene feigned shock at her husband before she smiled at their cook. "I could get used to this."

"Absolutely." Jane clinked her mimosa against Charlene's. "We didn't even have to clean up. This is truly a vacation."

"Man, with cooking skills like that"—Tuck drank heartily from his can of Coors—"why aren't you running a restaurant?"

Gary blushed in silent appreciation at the praise, nursing his can of beer. "I just never thought of it, I suppose." He pondered his friend's advice for the next few minutes, tuning out the others. Eventually, he heard his name called, breaking from his trance. His eyes shot around the room to see who was talking to him. "Huh?"

Jim smiled at the lost expression on Gary's face. "I said that I can't wait to see what you come up with for the morning. It'll have to be quick, though. Our hike will take a good part of the day." He stood, finished off his glass in a single swig, and stretched. "I suggest everyone get a good night's sleep and make sure you have plenty of film for your cameras. The trail we'll be on is beautiful, but it's rugged. We'll all need our energy." He looked at Tucker with a knowing grin. "That means you might need to save your hormones and let Jane rest, too."

Everyone laughed at the comment.

Tuck lifted his can once more. "No promises." He chugged his drink and crushed the container triumphantly. He drew his paramour closer to him on the couch. "How can I keep my hands off of such a beauty?" He gingerly capped the can pyramid in front of him with the bent container.

Jane giggled and squirmed to face him. "You're so bad." She placed her empty glass on the coffee table and kissed him deeply. "I know what will help you sleep."

"On that note," Charlene got to her feet, collected the empty glasses, and stepped into the kitchen. "I believe I'll retire."

"You're all so lucky." Gary's sentiment looked as if it caused a bit of discomfort for everyone else. It made him feel awful. "Just leave them, Char. I'll clean them up. It's my contribution, remember?"

"You gonna be okay on the couch?" Tuck, in a rare moment of concern for someone else, looked at his pal.

The lone man nodded solemnly. "Yeah. Gravity can't hurt me from that height."

Tuck put a hand on his shoulder. "That's not what I meant."

"I'll be fine. I'm going to clean up and get a bit of fresh air before going to bed. The stars are out, and I want to enjoy it for a bit."

The friends parted company for the night. Gary washed the few glasses, gathered the empty cans, put on his jacket, and took a deep breath as he stepped onto the wraparound porch. Constellations and planets twinkled at him from above as his exhalations hung in the air like a phantom before dissipating. A smile wilted from his face as loneliness crept in. He shook the feeling away before it took root. "My God, it's beautiful out here."

The sun rose on the cabin, peering in the east window directly onto the couch. Gary had already been up, frying eggs in the leftover bacon grease and buttering toast as it popped up. The aroma of the breakfast had already awakened Jim, Charlene, and Jane. Tucker was still snoring loudly from the second bedroom, causing them all to giggle at his thundering as they ate.

"I'll go wake the lumberjack," Jane announced, popping the last bit of her toast in her mouth.

"Better make it quick, or his food will get cold." Gary plopped the second egg onto one plate before populating his own.

Jane just smiled coyly before disappearing into the room and shutting the door. The snores morphed into moans, terminating in a yowl of sexual ecstasy. Gary chuckled as he ate, shaking his head. Jim and Charlene looked at each other in mock shock.

"Oh, to be young and full of vitality," Jim joked.

"You're the same age," Charlene scolded. "You hold your own just fine."

Jim kissed his wife. "As long as you're happy."

The door popped open, and Tucker emerged with an ear-to-ear grin. He saw the expressions on everyone's faces. "Helluva wake-up call. I'm starving." He spied his dish and unashamedly began devouring the meal.

Gary collected the egg-sopped dishes and cleaned them, setting them to dry on the rack. Charlene began drying without a word. "I've got that, Char."

"Nonsense. It'll get done faster this way."

Jane came out of the bedroom, dressed in jeans and a flannel shirt tied in a knot over an undershirt. She hesitated to make eye contact with anyone, but her smile told the tale.

With the dishes done and the crew dressed and ready, they all set out for their hike. The path started at their cabin and extended down the north face of the mountain. They chatted as their trail switched this way and that, opening up to a view of the fog-filled valley in front of them, the low-hanging clouds obscuring the trench. As the day wore on, the sun evaporated the mist, revealing a little river carving out its path below.

"Breathtaking." Jane snapped pictures absently, stepping forward without looking.

"Look out!" Tuck screamed as the rocks under her feet slid away. He attempted to reach out for her, but it was too late.

Jane hung from Gary's arm as he clung to a cliff-rooted tree with the other. Her face was drained white from shock.

"Careful." He slowly returned her to the trail.

Her blue eyes began to fill with fear.

"You're okay," he reassured her. "I've got you. Help me, Tuck."

Tuck gathered his wits, then his girlfriend. He soothed her as she trembled in his grasp. "You're fine. You're safe. It's okay."

The other pair had been a few steps too far ahead to do anything but watch in horror, rejoining the group after she'd been pulled to safety. Charlene kneeled in front of her, awash with concern. "Are you okay?"

Jane breathlessly nodded, her pounding heart finally slowing its tempo.

Gary rubbed the blonde's shoulder comfortingly as she calmed. "Let's take pictures away from the edge next time." His quip elicited a small giggle of relief from her. The reaction he wanted.

"You gonna be okay to continue?" Tucker seemed to express a pang of jealousy at his friend before his gaze fell on his date.

Jane agreed, her pulse finally slowing to normal. She stood, face red from shame. "I'm such a klutz."

"It's okay." Jim breathed a deep sigh. "Just watch for loose rocks on these thin trails. "There's a clearing ahead. We'll stop there and have a bit of jerky. Jane can rest a bit after that harrowing adventure."

"Yeah." Charlene adjusted her pack. "I think I could use the little girl's room right now."

A nervous laugh poured from Jane. "I think I already did."

Everyone except Tucker joined in on the joke. "You scared me. I thought I was going to lose you." He hugged her uncomfortably tight, pressing the air from her lungs.

Gary detected an unusual bit of sentiment in his friend's eyes. Was he falling for her? "She's safe now. Let's get to the clearing and take a break. This morning, I made some granola to go with our jerky."

They marched forward, Jane keeping as much distance as she could between her and the trail's edge. Finally, it snaked away from the mountainside and back toward the forest plateau Jim had told them about. An up-cropping rock formation gave them places to sit as they caught their breath. Gary passed around a paper lunch sack of the homemade cereal treat: raisins, cashews, oats, and broken bits of pretzels mixed with chocolate chips. Jim offered up the jerky he had bought specifically for the hike, and they all sipped from canteens and thermoses of cold water.

"Don't drink too much," Gary warned. "It needs to last until we reach the stream, at least."

"Ew." Jane's face scrunched in disgust. "Fish pee in that water. I'm not drinking it."

"We can sterilize it by boiling it. I have a pan to do it in." Gary patted his pack, and Jim nodded.

Charlene returned from the brush, her face a mixture of wonder and amusement. "You guys should see this." She waved them to follow her.

Gary and Jim stuffed the food away in their backpacks as the other slung theirs into position. They caught up quickly, noticing the trench dug through the tree line, the groove growing deeper as they went. Upturned black dirt accented the ditch. A purple substance lined the hole, overgrowing the edge and reaching into the canopy-darkened forest floor.

Tucker bent to examine the slimy, violet lichen. He reached out, its vining iridescence flashing hypnotically in the sunlight. "What is it?"

Gary stopped his friend's hand before it touched the odd plant. "Don't." He looked at the scenery, his brow furrowed. "Best not to touch it."

"I've never seen anything like it," Jim mused at the sight, his eyes resting on the empty, purple-covered crater at the end.

They stood in dumbstruck awe as they scanned the forest. "Whatever it is," Jane pointed out, "it's everywhere."

She was right. The substance covered the tree trunks surrounding the plowed earth. It reached up the trees toward the sky and carpeted the ground in smothering abundance. As they stood there and took in the sight, they listened. Soft clicks and pops came from everywhere.

"I think you can actually hear it growing." A cold shiver visibly crept down Charlene's spine.

"You okay, hun?" Jim walked over to his wife and wrapped an arm around her.

"Yeah. I just wanna leave. This place gives me the creeps." She spun, leading the way. "You ever seen anything like that?"

"Not even in one of my hiking books."

Gary stooped, watching an outgrowth of the nearly amoebic plant as it crawled and reached with alarming speed, worming over everything in its vicinity. It almost seemed to take a swipe at his boot before he backed away. "Did I imagine that?" As he glowered at the purple gloop spreading in front of him, his hackles stood at attention. He stepped away, the plant seeming to click angrily at the missed opportunity. "We should head back to the cabin. We should head into town and let someone know about this."

"It's just a plant," Tucker insisted gratingly.

"It's invasive," Gary added. "They may have to burn it off. There's no phone in the cabin."

"You've seen how fast it grows," Charlene pointed out.

"Let's get out of here." Jane barely peeled her eyes from the expanding lichen before practically sprinting back the way they came.

Tucker straggled behind for a bit before catching up. Just before leaving the clearing, a rabbit hobbled out of the bushes, hopping to one side as if drunk. It came toward them, rushing as fast as it could in its state. After seeing them, it veered back into the bushes, a purple vine trailing behind it like a second tail. The group's eyes widened collectively at the vision. They followed it with their stares. Before the small mammal could drop out of sight, it fell to the ground and breathed its last. The rabbit's skin came alive from underneath, tendrils squirming beneath the surface. In less than a minute, the hide burst open, blossoming in the purple substance. The animal's body dissolved into a bloom of shiny, blood-stained, iridescent fungus.

"Did..." Jim stammered. "Did you see that?" He went white.

"Let's get back to the cabin." Gary took the lead, a renewed sense of urgency in his voice. Jane practically attached herself to him in her haste to get off the plateau.

He held her back. "Easy. We still have to be careful with the ledges. You don't want a repeat, do you?"

Her eyes were filled with fright. She shook her head, holding back for Tucker to join her. She buried her face in his shoulder and wept softly. Tuck shushed and comforted her. Soon, she regained her composure and peered up at him. "I get to choose our next trip. No camping."

The joviality of the day had taken a screeching turn earlier from the incident at the ledge. This was an entirely different feeling. What they had witnessed caused a degree of alarm that none of them had ever experienced. A black cloud hung over their trip, silencing them into a deep concentration on their retreat.

By the time they returned to their cabin, the sun was beginning to retreat behind the mountain for the day.

"We should wait until morning." Jim gazed at the sunset with an odd mix of hate and worry. "My eyes aren't the best, and I barely know these roads well enough to drive them at night."

Gary glanced at his watch. "By the time we get there, it'll be close to seven o'clock anyway. No one will be open in that small town."

"Besides, who the hell would you tell?" Tucker plopped his pack down by the door of the cabin and doffed his boots in an unceremonious heap.

"Probably call the forest service or something." Gary set his own pack next to the ones in the corner, removing the paper sack with the few remaining kernels of granola. "Police won't care enough to deal with it." He reached inside, felt something, and let out a surprised yell: "Holy shit!" The bag dropped from his hands with a light thump.

Everyone gathered around as something within the sack wriggled against the sides.

"What is it?" Jane gasped, her horror born anew.

The group watched breathlessly in anticipation. They collectively inhaled as whatever was inside began to peek out with a flick of its tongue. A copper brown head poked out, tasting the air for safety before cautiously exiting the treat bag. The women screamed, chorused by Tucker, as they danced away in fright. Jim let out the breath he'd been holding.

Gary held a hand to his chest, relieved. "It's a night snake." He began to reach for it but drew back his hand rapidly as if it had struck at him.

"What's wrong?" Jim puzzled at his friend's reaction.

"Its eyes." He indicated a closer look at the reptile. "They're purple."

'Get it out of here!" Tucker scooped the critter up with a thumb and forefinger, holding it as if it were the vilest thing on Earth. Rushing to the door, he tossed the animal out, not caring where it landed or went off to. He stampeded to the sink, washing his hands vigorously with hot water and dish soap.

Charlene felt her gorge rise, making a beeline for the toilet. She heaved into the bowl as Jim and Jane approached, the other men close behind. "You okay, honey?"

She looked up, her eyes wet from her upheaval. "Too much excitement, I suppose."

Jim moved in, feeling his wife's forehead. "Maybe you got too much sun. You're burning up." He helped her up once she indicated that her stomach had settled. "Let's get you to bed."

"I'll make some chicken soup." Gary assisted his friend until Jim waved him off politely. "That will make everyone feel better, I think." He popped open the refrigerator door and stood there in shock. "My God!"

Tucker and Jane hurried to see what Gary was looking at. The inside of the fridge was overgrown with purple moss as if the contents had been left for years, not hours. Vines of the substance reacted to the new air, creeping out to touch the newfound freedom. It moved much slower from being exposed to the cold air than the stuff the group encountered on the mountain. Nothing within the seal of the appliance had been spared. The thawing chicken was a lump of Saran-wrapped purple tendrils. The veggies, including the onion and garlic, had been parasitized. Even the condiments and jar of pickles had given birth to the lichen.

"How?" Tucker practically screamed in a deep baritone. "How did it get into the fucking jar of pickles? How did it open the lid?"

Gary shut the door. "The better question is, how did it get here? We left it a good hour behind us. I didn't see any of it around."

Jim resurfaced from the main bedroom. "May have to go to town after all. Char's temp is out of control." He looked up and saw the others' faces. "I'm sure she just has a bug or something." He paused. "What's wrong with you all?"

Jane's voice hitched between soft sobs. "Everything in the fridge has that awful purple stuff on it."

Jim's eyes went as wide as saucers. "What?" He plodded to the refrigerator door and pulled on the lever. It opened with a wet, peeling smack. The shelves inside writhed in a violet landscape, sprigs of the moss reaching for the refreshed air. He quickly shut the portal, some of the branches wriggling, trapped in the seal, his air coming to him in fits. He leaned against the appliance as if holding back a bear.

"What will we do?" Jane continued her keening.

"Let's grab Char and—" Jim saw his wife standing in their bedroom doorway.

"I don't feel so good." Sweat ran down her in rivulets, her normally immaculate hair hanging from her head in sopping, brown strands. She reached for her husband with pleading purple eyes.

Jim's face contorted into grief. "No. Not my beautiful Charlene." He began to run to her, but Gary held him back. "Let me go! I have to get to my wife!"

Unseen things wriggled beneath her skin as Charlene clutched at her head in agony and wailed. "It hurts! It hurts so much! Make it stop, Jim!"

Gary struggled with his friend, and Tucker finally woke up from the nightmare long enough to help restrain the aggrieved man. "Stay back, Jim!"

Charlene glowered at her companions with empty, tortured eyes. She lurched forward in one final attempt to have her pleas answered, only to be met with retreating steps. She put forth a cry that would make a banshee's blood curdle in fear. As the others watched, she zig-zagged her way to the front door, staggering out. Jim broke free from their grasp, his face a flood of emotion as he pursued his beloved.

"I'm coming, Char!" He disappeared through the door, the others giving chase as the sun said its final farewell for the day.

Gary snagged a lantern by the door, lighting it on the run. Charlene stood on an outcropping ledge behind their cabin, looking out toward the valley below.

Jim stopped short, extending a hand to his love. "Char? Dear? Come away from there. It's dangerous. Let's take you to town and get you some help. C'mon."

Her skin seemed to take on a life of its own as she slowly turned to face her husband. Those horrific purple tendrils had replaced both eyes. The things flailed in the air from her ears, nose, and gaping mouth. She managed a deeply garbled sentiment: "Love you, Jim." Then her feet tangled in themselves, careening her over the edge and out of sight.

"Charlene! No!" Jim scrambled to the cliff's edge.

It was all Gary could do to keep his friend from jumping off after the unfortunate woman.

One by one, they all peered over the cliff. Though the darkness was now cut by the light of a waning gibbous moon, there was no sign of her body, only a purple mound shaped like their friend on the craggy rocks below. Jim wept, lying on the ground, staring at the outline of otherworldly moss that used to be his beloved.

"We're leaving." Tucker pulled Jane away from the edge. "Gary, grab Jim. We're leaving now."

"I'm not going," Jim stated softly. He stood, still looking at where his wife landed. "Not without my wife."

Gary put an arm around his friend. "Come on, Jim. You can't do anything for her now."

Jim shrugged his embrace off angrily. "Don't." He pointed a finger at them all in turn. "She loved you all. Now you want to leave her like she didn't exist."

"Jim, it's not like—"

"Charlene wanted to help you most of all." His disgust gave Jim's grief-stricken eyes a psychotic edge as he turned his ire on Gary. "She was willing to open our house to you!"

Tucker stomped up and clocked Jim squarely in the jaw, knocking him cold.

Gary barely caught him before his head hit the ground. "What the hell, Tuck! What was that for?"

"We need to get out of here. Now." Tucker helped Gary drag Jim to the car. "He has the only set of keys to that tank. It's our only ticket out of here."

Jane's scream broke his next sentence before it could surface. She clasped her hands to her face in petrified disbelief. The purple moss was on every inch of the car, growing on the tires, out of the tailpipe, bubbling up through the paint. It had even found its way through the vents to the inside, where it had rooted itself into the leather seats.

Gary felt Jim's weight lurch, pulling him sideways as Tucker fell to his knees, his skull cave agape. The clicking of the plant's rapid growth on the vehicle seemed to have a different tone as it digested the metal. He set his friend down on the ground, unable to hold the dead weight by himself.

They all jumped in unison as the tires popped one by one, rocking the car violently with each explosion. Gary took the lantern from Jane, lobbing it at their ride as it rotted away. The tank struck metal, broke open, and the vehicle was set aflame as the fuel splattered.

The unlikely lichen seemed to shriek in agony as fire lapped at it, a high-pitched, hissing squeal reserved for tea kettles or green firewood. The piercing sound caused them all to clap their hands over their ears and woke Jim up from his sleep.

They watched as the violet vines went up like seasoned tinder, each polyp in the organism setting the next ablaze. Only the outlying spots surrounding the area were spared the full wrath of the fire, though the ones that were too close to the bonfire withered away.

The moss on what was left of their transportation caught the connecting vines on the ground leading to the cabin. They went up like a fuse to dynamite, sparking and slicing the air with that shrill sound.

Jim bolted to his feet, wide-eyed, that same ungodly tone vomiting from deep within him. Flames belched from his mouth. His clothes caught. Jane screamed in horror, scampering away as their host stumbled toward her, threatening a fiery hug. He let loose one final yowl and sprinted off toward the forest. His dash, however surreal and unlikely, was cut short when he ran headlong into a large aspen, bursting like a Molotov cocktail against the trunk.

The forest floor crackled to elemental life as the flames from the impact spread to last year's layer of sloughed leaves and needles. The acid rain-wilted pines blazed like match sticks, growing the inferno exponentially within minutes. The cabin was flanked on all sides by the blaze. Soon, it succumbed to the conflagration as well.

Tucker pulled Jane with the urgency of a father leading a toddler to catch the next bus out of town. Sizzling vines swatted as they passed, Gary only a short distance behind the couple. Fire licked greedily at their retreating feet. Tuck artfully dodged a falling pine, yanking Jane along for the ride, but not unscathed. Her jeans caught on the cinders of the tree, burning her leg in seconds. Her love stopped to put her out before continuing the escape.

Gary and Tuck wrapped arms around her, carrying her off the ground and down the treacherous driveway in an attempt to outrun the wildfire engulfing their camp behind them. The wind picked up, favoring them by redirecting the fire toward the northern face of the mountain.

The inferno took most of the dying timber on the mountainside throughout the night, including the ill-fated clearing. A spring storm then rolled in from the sea, bathing the entire county in enough rain to douse the licking flames and glowing embers. Wet and exhausted, three strangers stumbled into a small town in the valley of Rogers Peak.

Wrecked and abandoned cars smoked in the streets. Lights flickered on and off. The whole town was deadly silent. The only thing making any noise was a familiar clicking sound.

Everywhere in sight, purple moss had taken over.

The northern plateau of Roger's Peak was once again bustling as scientists, covered head to toe in safety gear, took samples of the charred remains of plants and animals alike. Nothing was spared their scrutiny. The CB radio popped to life as a static-filled voice got one of the gatherer's attention.

"Hey Bob, you there? Over."

The man standing by the vehicle pulled his helmet off cautiously. "Yeah. I'm here. Whatcha got, Frank? Over."

"I think it's best that you come see. We found some live samples. And something else. Over"

The men exchanged locations as Frank boarded his vehicle and left. Once he arrived, he bounded out of the cab and stared in complete awe. In front of him was an unmarked cabin nestled in the middle of the swath of the forest fire. The melted remains of a sturdy car smoldered in the cold mountain air. Behind it was the cabin, as pristine and unmarked as the day it was built.

"Ever seen anything like it?" Frank asked. Then, a coughing fit doubled him over until he caught his breath.

Bob chuckled. "You need to lay off the Pall Malls, Frank. Those things'll kill ya."

Frank held up a hand as he stood and adjusted his helmet. He turned toward his cohort with a smile. "Maybe someday."

Bob furrowed his brow as he studied his friend. "Huh. I never noticed that you had purple eyes."

CURSE OF THE PIASA

"What the hell?"

Madeline's Audi dashboard screamed at her to brake as a golden blur ran across the road in front of her. She twitched, her reaction causing the car to fishtail slightly. Her heart thumped in her chest as she pulled off Illinois Highway 100 into a small roadside park. She parked, allowing her heartbeat to slow, her hands visibly shaking as she exited the car. Wide-eyed, she scanned the road to see where the creature had scampered off to but could find no trace of wildlife nearby.

"Is something wrong, Miss Perdue?" Harvey's voice echoed through the car speakers, somewhat distorted and inconsistent due to a weak connection. He sounded more aggravated at being interrupted than concerned for his boss's safety.

"No." Madeline inhaled deeply to calm her vibrating nerves. "Something ran across the road in front of me." She slowly turned, tracing the rocky cliff up to a crude painting on the stone.

A chill danced down her spine as she watched the monster looming over the highway, its golden-scaled wings spread wide. Fierce claws reached down for her, threatening to pull her toward the sharp-tusked mouth of the half-man, half-dragon. The dark, narrow eyes appeared to lock on her.

Did that thing move?

"Miss Perdue?"

Madeline shook herself from the trance, slowly returning to her car, never breaking her stare from the antlered menace on the mural until her door snapped. "This place is weird, Harvey." She let out another deep breath. "Did you find me a place to stay? This groundbreaking has to go off without a hitch, and I plan to oversee it."

"That's good because court costs from this one have eaten up profits from Fulton and Westlake retail locations."

Madeline scoffed, a disgusted look on her face. "Don't remind me. Cahokia sacred grounds, indeed. That restraining order delayed construction for a year." A small grin perched on the edges of her lips as Harvey confirmed he found a nice cabin outside of town with the amenities she wanted, including Wi-Fi, a soaker tub, and a television. "We still won. They're just mad that our ancestors stole their land."

"Let's leave that part out of the ceremony speech, shall we?" Harvey said before rattling off the address of the cabin.

"Of course," Madeline huffed. "I'm not stupid." She checked herself in the mirror. Red lips— immaculate. Hair—perfect. The designer sunglasses added a Manhattan touch that would express to anyone the style and class she was bringing to their town.

Plugging the address into her navigation system, she pulled back onto the highway, shaking her head as she glanced at a peeling billboard in her rearview mirror depicting a cartoonish version of the same creature she had left on the cliff behind her. Beneath the figure were the words *NOW ENTERING PIASA TERRITORY*. An uneasy feeling remained with her in the pit of her stomach, even after the billboard vanished beyond the bend in the road.

"Where are you now?"

"Just northwest of Alton on I-100 near McAdams Parkway."

"You're cutting out. Are you there?"

"I'm fine, Harvey," Madeline reassured. "Thank you for everything you do for me. I wouldn't be able to find my stockings without you."

A relieved chuckle escaped from the other end. "Too true. Try and get some rest."

The call ended, and she slumped in her seat, left with nothing to do except think about today's groundbreaking ceremony. From here, her week would become increasingly hectic, with plans to review with contractors and undoubtedly more trouble from the Cahokia Historical Society.

She recalled an elderly Native American man approaching her and her lawyer as they descended the courthouse steps in one last vain attempt to convince her to reconsider. "I'm Chief Ouatoga. You may have won the legal battle, but you have no idea of the forces you're toying with."

Her lawyer stepped between his client and the native. "Is that a veiled threat?"

Chief Ouatoga shook his head sadly. "If you continue, you will awaken a dangerous spirit."

Madeline sneered at the man, barely pausing to acknowledge him. "I don't have time for your superstitions, you old fool."

"That land has been under our protection longer than your ancestors have been here. The ground will shake from your arrogance and greed. You'll awaken the Piasa." Two more angry-faced tribesmen surrounded their elder, gently guiding him away from the unshaken woman. As they ushered him, he shouted one final warning: "Once it finds its prey, it never stops."

"Turn left ahead."

The monotone voice of her navigation system snapped Madeline from her memory. She glanced at the onscreen map. Three Highway, which would eventually lead to Route 67, would turn into Piasa Street.

Piasa Street? Seriously? These people are obsessed.

The GPS guided her to the construction area, only to find a group of Native American protestors on site. They shouted expletives, barely giving her enough room to pull onto the dirt pathway leading to the grandstand. A familiar disapproving glare caught her eyes as she stopped and rolled down her window. She rested her hand on the can of mace in her purse, ready to use it if needed.

"Chief Ouatoga. I should have known." Madeline gestured to him and the assembled group, seething. "You and your people are trespassing. Leave now, or I'll have you all arrested."

The Chief gazed at her with sad eyes. "Miss Perdue, please reconsider. I am begging you. You will put yourself in grave danger. You've seen the signs. The Great Spirit gave you a warning."

Madeline scoffed. "The only signs I've seen are the billboards bearing your little tourist trap graffiti. Now leave." She ignored the rest of his admonitions, rolling up the window as she drove past.

Pulling up to the parking area, she slammed the car into park, opened the door, and immediately stuck her new, one-inch, electric-blue heel ankle deep into a mud puddle. "Dammit. What else can go wrong?"

A hefty man in an ill-fitting suit rushed to her side. Despite the care the makeup artist had provided, it couldn't hide his wrinkled, haggard face or tired eyes. He favored her with a fake smile, undoubtedly saved for just such occasions, and assisted her the rest of the way out of her car.

"Mayor Huffman." Madeline produced her hand as she stood, ignoring her mishap.

"Careful, Miss Perdue," the mayor instructed, guiding her to more solid ground with her next step. The muck suctioned at her shoe, intent on keeping it. "I apologize for the conditions," he continued. "Can't control the weather, you know." He motioned for an assistant before seating her beside a cordoned patch of exposed earth in front of the stand. Golden shovels pierced the corners of the dirt, awaiting their time in the limelight.

"Can't you do anything about those protestors?" Her finger blindly flew toward the entrance as the mayor's helper removed her shoe and began carefully cleaning her slacks with a damp towel. Madeline impatiently waved him away.

"What protestors?"

Madeline glared at the mayor as if he were blind, twisting in the direction of the entrance. "Those—" She stopped. No one was there except for a couple of news vans pulling in. A chill danced down her spine again as she felt her face pale. *They cleared out fast.* Shaking it off, a triumphant smirk edged her mouth. "I must have scared them away."

"I assure you there have been no protestors here." The mayor seemed confident about his oversight.

Madeline listened as he rattled off the itinerary of the event, paying more thorough attention to her mud-soaked pants and shoes than his grating voice. After he had finished, the makeup artist began working on her.

Despite the rough start, the ceremony went off without a hitch. Orators delivered speeches flawlessly to a small, approving audience. Madeline answered questions without stammering.

The time came for the groundbreaking. It was nothing more than bluster, pomp, and circumstance to most. To Madeline, however, it felt more like a final spike of victory in a long battle. She took up the golden shovel and, with photographers snapping pictures and the audience cheering, planted its blade in the ground.

Reverie collapsed into panic as the ground heaved violently. The standing thrall pitched, many falling into their seats, some onto the rain-soaked ground. The mayor stumbled backward over the rope and landed face-first into the muck. Madeline barely managed to keep her heels under her, using the gold-plated tool as leverage. The podium tumbled, sending a screech of feedback from the still-live microphone. Car alarms blared in protest.

As the temblor faded away, the screaming subsided, and the mayor's assistant clumsily wiped at the politician's soiled clothes and skin. Another of the mayor's charges rushed over, whispering something in his ear. He nodded, holding up his hands to get the bystanders' attention.

"Nothing to worry about, folks!" he shouted as he wiped away more of the mud. The helpers righted the podium, and Mayor Huffman took up the squalling microphone. "I have just been informed that a fracking mishap caused the quake."

As the mayor gave his spin, the tribal elder's dire warnings bubbled up from Madeline's subconscious. Her fingers tensed around the shovel as sweat beaded on her forehead.

Was it really fracking that caused the earth to move or my actions?

It seemed ridiculous. The notion that she had anything to do with the tremor was totally illogical.

You're letting his superstitions get to you. Stop it.

"Just to be safe, we would like everyone to leave. Thank you for coming." The pundit turned his back to the crowd, grumbling orders through gritted teeth. The crowd dispersed hastily. Stationed in front of news vans, reporters offered their viewers conspiracy theories while the mayor refused to answer any further questions. Madeline headed for her car, closing the door on curious newscasters, grateful that the event had ended abruptly.

She didn't rattle easily but today had her nerves on edge. The short drive to her cabin, though quiet and uneventful, did nothing to soothe her anxiety. She hoped that a nice, long bath would do the trick, followed by a potent drink. Or three.

Gravel crunched under the tires as she pulled up to the log-style home. She stepped out, a bit more cautiously this time, and surveyed the quaint rental. Harvey had leased the "honeymoon" cabin.

Once inside, she was pleasantly surprised. In her mind, she thought the cabin would smell musty and dank, but it was pristine and freshly tiled. In fact, the woodwork and country décor were almost exactly what she would want in a rustic getaway.

Madeline squealed with delight—something she wouldn't have let herself do if there'd been anyone else around—when she saw a large basket of fruit on the dining room table. Beside it was a second basket, brimming with beauty products and spa goodies.

I need to give Harvey a raise.

She wheeled her suitcase to the main bedroom and plopped it on the bed. She sprawled out next to her luggage, letting out a long sigh of relief. The rest of the day was hers. "This is perfect." As she soaked in the rustic atmosphere, she relaxed, and sleep took her.

She awoke with a start, sitting bolt upright, the waning light barely illuminating the room. Regaining her bearings as she strolled into the living area, her stomach protested, unflinching at the meager offerings of the fruit basket, wanting something a bit more substantial. She located a laminated listing of nearby restaurants, settling on a pizza.

Carbs or not, I'm splurging and enjoying myself.

In the meantime, she had forty-five minutes to kill, just enough time for a nice soak in that inviting clawfoot tub. She grabbed a bath bomb from the spa basket, headed to the main suite, collected her robe, and undressed.

Something golden flashed past the window above the tub as she drew her bath.

Too big for a bird. Are there mountain lions around here? Don't be an idiot. Mountain lions don't fly.

She approached the dusty panes, peering in all directions, trying to catch another glimpse of whatever she'd seen. Nothing. Just woods surrounding the cabin obscuring the background. Playing it off as stress, she turned to step into the tub. Madeline's wet foot missed the bath mat, slipping out from under her, sending her tumbling to the ground in a heap, her head striking the tiled floor in the process. The bath bomb shot from her grasp, exploding on the tiles and blanketing the bathroom with debris. On her way down, she'd grabbed the curtain, the rings all snapping from the rod in sequence. The curtain fluttered down, laying over her like a death shroud.

"Son of a bitch!" Madeline held her hand to the back of her head, where a knot was already forming. As the stars and pain faded, the ridiculousness of the situation sank in, causing her to giggle. That made her wince, and she laughed even harder, imagining how foolish she must have looked.

The window shattered. Glass shards rained into the tub. A gigantic, golden-scaled paw reached inside, grazing her feet with its extended claws. The wounds leaked crimson. A thunderous snarl echoed through the room. Madeline had heard large predator cats roar in documentaries. Whatever this was, it was deeper and more guttural.

Madeline screamed, pedaling herself upright. The creature peered inside, its maw filling the window as it growled again, reaching around for purchase like a cat pawing at its prey. She shrieked and scrambled away from the tub, her bloody feet almost slipping out from under her again.

Someone pounded on the front door and shouted, causing the monster to retreat from the portal. She ran down the hall and then stopped, leaving bloody skid marks behind.

Oh god! What if that thing went around the front? Whoever's out there will get killed. So will I if I open the door.

"Ma'am?" More drumming on the door accompanied the male voice. "Is everything alright?"

Maybe it's gone. It would've attacked by now.

"Holy…" The young man nearly dropped the pizza as Madeline flung the door open with a crazed look. His teenage face turned bright red. "Ma'am, you need to put some clothes on." He averted his eyes to her feet and widened when he spotted the blood. "Are you okay, lady?"

Without thinking, Madeline grabbed the kid's shirt, yanking him past the threshold, causing him to yelp in surprise. "There's something out there. It's not safe." She spun to grab her robe. It was only a second. A garbled, choking yelp followed by a dull plop caused her to face the door again. The pizza box was on the ground, but the delivery boy was gone. Somewhere overhead, she heard him yell, the scream cut short by a squelching. Patters came from the rooftop above the door, stopping as rapidly as they had started. The creature let out a mighty roar, shaking the rest of the windows in the cabin.

Thinking fast, Madeline slammed the door shut. Standing clear of the entrance, she jolted forward again, clicking the deadbolt. Her hands tensed and shook. She backed away, bumping into the dinette table. Pulling out one of the hardwood chairs, she collapsed into it, brought her knees to her chest, and began to sob.

She recalled the chief's words: *You'll awaken the Piasa. Once it finds its prey, it never stops.*

Ouatoga's warning kept replaying in her mind. Her phone rang in her purse on the table, snapping her from her trance with a startled scream. Her trembling hands fumbled with the zipper, the phone nearly squirting from her sweat-drenched palms as she brought it to her ear.

"Harvey," Madeline's voice croaked. "Thank God. There's something out there. I think it killed the pizza boy."

"Say that again. You're breaking up."

Madeline broke down into tears. "I'm in danger here, Harvey. There's a monster. So much blood."

"Wait... What?" Harvey sounded like he didn't believe what he was hearing. "Blood? Are you hurt? I'm on my way. Get out of there."

"I can't," Madeline cried. "It'll get me."

"Call 9-1-... Madeline? Are you there?"

Before she could answer, the phone went silent. She glowered at the black screen in her hand in disbelief. Madeline reeled her arm back, tossing the device across the great, open room, shattering it against the wooden mantle. The face carved there seemed to scream for her to escape, the man's eyes as wide as hers.

Madeline retreated to the bedroom, wanting to put as much space between herself and the front door as possible, forgetting about the bathroom window. A chilly breeze eased through the broken panes; the curtains fluttered hypnotically in the corner of her eyes. A shiver raced down her spine. Shadows danced in the corners of the room to rhythms unheard. Tree branches creaked through the portal. An owl hooted outside, causing a small shriek to escape.

She looked at the window, wondering whether she should make her escape now that the creature had eaten. Cautiously, she approached the small opening. Broken glass littered the inside of the tub, the screen a gnarled net bordering the gaping hole. Madeline carefully stepped onto the tub, peering outside. The woods surrounding the cabin seemed to devour the light of the stars and moon, offering nothing but more dark ghosts. Trying not to alert the creature, she leaned out of the window, managing to get her body almost halfway out.

An unearthly roar pierced the night air. Madeline's blood ran cold as she scrambled to pull herself back inside. A shard of glass scratched her stomach. She winced in pain as it drew a line of scarlet across her midsection. A loud thump hit the roof above her. Claws raked against the heavy tin, like fork tines against an empty plate. Gooseflesh rippled across her body.

Another shrill growl echoed in the night. Madeline retreated from the bathroom, the new gash on her skin barely registering.

It smells my blood. I just know it.

Climbing onto the center of the bed, Madeline trembled and folded her legs against her body. Hours felt like years as she kept herself as small as possible in the center of the mattress while rocking back and forth. The heavy steps and clacking nails pacing the roof kept her petrified gaze skyward. Every time the monster emitted a frustrated growl, her entire body quaked.

A few hours passed. A knock at the door sent a yelp of surprise.

"Madeline… Um, Miss Perdue?"

Harvey. At last.

Madeline shot from the bed toward the door. To her horror, the thing on the roof had the same idea. Picking up her pace, she reached the front. Flinging the door wide, Harvey started to speak but screamed instead as she violently yanked him inside. He spilled to the floor, and she slammed the door shut. Outside, a deep roar pierced the air. Unsteady hands fumbled with the deadbolt and lock chain.

"What the hell?" Harvey stood, brushing his khaki shorts off and straightening his shirt. "What's going on, Madeline? And what was that noise?" He finished collecting himself and looked around. His eyes came upon the scarlet footprints on the floor, widening when they finished at Madeline's wounded feet. "Well, there goes the cleaning deposit." He faked a smile in an attempt to lighten the mood, but Madeline concentrated on the roof. "Come on. Let's get you cleaned up."

Harvey led Madeline to the bathroom. And that infernal window. Her struggles were meek at first, but when the portal came into view, she slammed on the brakes, shaking her head wildly from side to side. Her stomach knotted. Above them, nails clacked impatiently.

"What's wrong with you?" Harvey looked incredulously at his employer. Madeline began backing away slowly, her finger raising, directing his gaze toward the window. He squinted outside, seeing nothing but trees. "There's nothing—"

A man's face stared back at him. Its glowing red eyes glowered back hungrily. The creature opened its dagger-toothed, blood-drenched mouth, unleashing a roar that nearly knocked them both off of their feet, the mouth almost gaping wide enough to fill the small opening. The golden scales around its features dripped enough crimson from the fresh kill to serve as a lubricant as it attempted to fit itself through the opening. The antlers atop its head prevented a full ingress.

"What is that thing?" Harvey's voice quivered to match his knees, his eyes widening as far as they could while Madeline positioned him in front of her.

"P-Piasa," was all Madeline could muster.

Another otherworldly growl shredded the air inside the cabin as the thing struggled to pull itself free of the opening, one of its antlers wedged against the frame.

"Nope." Harvey grabbed Madeline without a second thought. "We're leaving. Now."

Madeline's heart played a drum solo on her ribcage as she stood and froze in fear.

Another screech.

Wood cracked as Harvey spun Madeline away from the bathroom. He peered over her shoulder. The frame was gnarled on one side, but the thing in the window was gone.

"Let's go!"

Feet stomped above them, sending wafts of dirt to the floor. The Piasa appeared to be predicting their retreat as it headed toward the front door. They both stopped in the center of the living room, listening, waiting, huddling together. Nails screeched against the tin roof, setting their nerves on edge.

A loud thump rattled the wooden slats of the modest front porch, vibrating the door. The frame shook as talons raked the barrier. The sound of splintering wood elicited fresh terror from both Harvey and Madeline, causing them to back further away from the entrance.

"I think it's trying to get through the door," yowled Harvey.

Madeline could feel him trembling even more than she was.

"What do we do?"

As they stood by the kitchen, Madeline glanced toward her purse on the dinette. *My mace. I should get my mace.* She stiffened up, her chest puffing. "Find the biggest, meanest-looking knife that you can, Harvey."

"What are you thinking?"

"We have to defend ourselves. That thing *will* get in here."

Another resounding thud shook the door, the panels of the wooden slab and the frame beginning to give in. Harvey's frozen feet released, allowing him to do what his boss suggested. Madeline shot over to the table, grabbing her bag. She fumbled with the contents, unable to find the can. She dumped the purse's contents on the floor, finally able to locate the canister.

A window-rattling snarl enveloped the cabin, turning her blood to ice. Harvey screeched, returning to her side, holding out the largest knife he could find in the rental with a trembling hand.

The Piasa burst through the front entrance in an explosion of wood. Shaking off the debris, it locked eyes on its targets, sounding a thunderous growl that quaked the walls, drowning out their terrified screams.

Its head lowered. With a constant, breathy grumbling aimed at the pair, the Piasa stalked toward them, its enormous eagle talons gouging the plank floor. The bearded, mannish face growled, the nose and forehead crinkling in rage. One of its antlers had broken off midway from when it escaped the bathroom window.

The long, snake-like tail slithered through the air toward them, a golden-scaled menace with the end like a fish. It unfurled its wings with another heart-stopping grumble, knocking over the standing lamp next to the couch, reducing the light to half when the bulb shattered.

Harvey stabbed at the tail as it shot forward, knocking it away with a metallic clash, though it remained unscathed by the weapon.

"Madeline, do something!" Harvey screeched. "I don't think this knife is going to hurt it."

She pulled Harvey out of the path of the tail as it swiped at him again. A glance outside allowed Madeline to see her Audi. "If we can get outside, we can get in the car and leave."

"How?" Panic overtook Harvey's voice. Tears of fright leaked down his face as he continued to slash at the prehensile tube that reached for them. The pair quickly put as much furniture and space between them and the beast as they could.

"I don't know," Madeline shouted back, her finger on the trigger of the can of mace. "I need an opening, but I don't know what this thing's range is."

"Well, try something!"

The Piasa reached out with one of its talons, shredding the leather armchair before tossing it away as if it were made of cardboard. Dust and foam shrapnel floated in the air, briefly obscuring the creature's vision.

Madeline ducked another swipe by the tail and took a step forward, depressing the button. A peppery stream erupted through the air at the Piasa, hitting it directly in the eyes until the canister was empty.

"Bingo!" shouted Madeline, a sadistic sneer of satisfaction on her face.

The cryptid howled in agony, its limbs and tail flogging at the air blindly. Its eyes scrunched shut while it pawed at them.

"Get ready," Madeline stooped down like a sprinter readying for the gun.

"Bitch, who are you telling?" Harvey kept his eyes on the long golden snake-like limb whipping around.

The Piasa thumped its head on the area rug, rubbing its eyes on the coarse shag. It whined as it wiped its injured face. The long, rope-like tail whipped through the air just as blindly.

"Now!"

Madeline grabbed Harvey, dragging him, expertly ducking the thrashing appendages. The creature let out an angry roar as it slashed at the air around them with its talons and extra-long tail.

It was only a few steps to the shredded front door. The Audi was in sight. They could feel the night breeze flowing through the open maw where there once was a slab of wood.

"Watch out!"

Harvey yanked Madeline back as a burst of air hit them from a different direction. With a single thrust of its mighty wings, the Piasa leaped in front of the door, crashing into furniture but blockading their escape. Had Harvey not pulled his boss backward, the thing would have landed on top of her, blind or not. Again, he pulled the screaming woman just in time, as the floorboards where she had fallen exploded into slivers by one of the talons.

The Piasa carefully pawed at its stinging eyes, squinting through the blast of pepper spray still assaulting its sight. It reached again, this time swiping with more dangerous accuracy. The chemical seemed to be wearing off.

Harvey gathered Madeline from the floor and led her down the hallway to the main bedroom. He slammed the door behind them, located a large dresser, and shoved it toward the thin wooden barrier separating them from certain doom.

A thunderous growl rattled the hallway. Nails ticked on the wood slats, etching deep gashes as they approached.

"Help me, Madeline!" Harvey struggled with the heavy furniture, scooting it in front of the doorway.

Madeline snapped from her trance and sprang over to help her assistant relocate the dresser. Once they got it where they hoped it would do some good, they both melted to the floor, panting.

"I'd like to take this time to put in for a raise." Harvey chuckled between breaths. The knife he'd armed himself with slipped to the floor.

"If we both get through this," Madeline huffed, "I'll double your salary."

The door began to shudder as the beast pawed at it from the other side, eliciting screams from both Harvey and Madeline. The growls deepened, and the barrier shook again. The flimsy obstacle began to splinter as the creature clawed and pulled. The door buckled, and the dresser budged as a talon broke through to the other side.

Madeline grabbed Harvey's knife and shot upright next to the doorway as a long, jagged tear appeared, pulled wider by the claw. Harvey stood to the other side, eyes just as wide as his boss's.

The Piasa gashed a wide enough opening to peer through the hole with the crimson eyes set in its somewhat manly face. It tore at the wood until it could fit its blunt snout through, snuffing at the air.

A flash of comedy snapped through Harvey's fear-weary brain, seeing Madeline holding the knife to her chest as the thing leered through the hole. *Here's Johnny.* He wound back a hand and slapped it in the face, connecting with its flat nose. "Back, bitch!"

What he hadn't planned on was Madeline swinging the weapon at the same time. She stabbed at the gash in the door, the knife burying itself through Harvey's hand and into one of the Piasa's eyes.

The menace in the hallway and her assistant both let out a chorus of yowls, his hand pinned to the creature. It withdrew, pulling Harvey's limb with it. Fingers bent unnaturally with an audible snap as his arm began to disappear through the opening.

Madeline's hands flew to her mouth, tears flowing at her miscalculation. They heard the knife clatter to the floor in the hall. Harvey quickly yanked his limb back into the bedroom, screaming in agony at his mangled digits and gushing hand.

A meaty talon reached through the opening, grasping at the air. Madeline clutched the screeching Harvey, yanking him toward the center of the room. The Piasa retracted its paw and glowered through the opening once more with its good eye.

A slight sneer of satisfaction crossed Madeline's face when she saw the other eye was bloody, gashed, and swollen closed.

With a final swipe at the air, the creature bellowed its frustration and disappeared from the opening.

Madeline returned her attention to Harvey. His complexion had begun to pale from shock and blood loss. She led him to the bed, gently sitting him on the edge. He tottered, slumping onto the mattress on his side with a weak groan. She reached over him and grabbed the other pillow. Removing its case, she fashioned a crude tourniquet and caressed him as he turned onto his back.

"I'm so sorry, Harvey." Madeline turned her back to the bed and slumped to the floor, weeping, her face in her hands. "I shouldn't have gotten you into this." She didn't recall the barely open window above the bed. Nor did she see that the screen had been pulled free.

A long, golden, snake-like appendage slithered through the opening, searching blindly. It felt its way through the air until it came to the warm, moist breath emanating from the bed. Slowly, it wrapped itself around the source like a constrictor.

Harvey awoke wide-eyed, gasping, clawing at his neck. He had just enough time to let out a small shriek before the thing ensnaring his throat choked the scream away. His face began to change colors as he kicked at the mattress.

Madeline sprang to her feet at the commotion, unsure of what was going on. Harvey held out his hands in a gurgling plea, his complexion quickly turning purple. Madeline backed away, her legs threatening to give underneath her in her retreat. Her backside bumped against the dresser propped behind the door.

Harvey began to fade into unconsciousness, the squeeze on his windpipe unrelenting as it pinned him against the window frame. Wood splintered, and glass crackled. Harvey locked eyes with his boss one last time.

"No. You can't have him!" Something within Madeline took over as she burst from the door, grabbing the thing that tried to pull Harvey outside. She planted her bleeding foot against the wall and tugged on the serpent-like limb. Working with her other hand, she struggled to pry the tail from his throat. Then she noticed the softer, furry underside of the extremity and bit down hard, tearing a chunk of flesh from the tail. The Piasa let out an agonized roar that echoed through the night as its prey slipped from its grip.

Harvey thudded to the ground, unmoving and pale blue. Madeline quickly pulled his dead weight far from the reach of the window. She tapped his cheeks lightly but got no response.

"Come on, Harvey," she pled, salty tears blinding her before falling onto his shirt. "Come on. Don't leave me."

She hyperventilated, her mind racing. Bending down, Madeline blew into his mouth, her own heart drumming in her chest as she massaged his. She repeated the steps, an almost comical lesson in CPR that she barely recalled from movies.

Harvey finally coughed and sputtered, the color flooding back to his face as he gagged. Relief washed over Madeline. She hugged him so tightly that she practically choked the air from him again. Finally, her grip loosened while she sobbed on his shoulder.

Still gasping for air, Harvey patted her lightly. "Thank you for saving me." He pushed her away from him and looked her in the eyes. "For a moment, I thought you were going to let me die."

"You're..." Madeline began between sniffles. "You're the closest thing I have to a friend. I couldn't let it take you."

She helped Harvey to his feet. Working together, they slowly slid the dresser from the opening, each of them cringing as it squalled across the floor. Peeking into the hallway, Madeline could feel the breeze from the front door. It smelled like freedom. And it reeked of danger.

Slowly, the pair crept down the hall, jumping at every slight movement on their sight.

Madeline spied the Audi next to the cabin. *I'd have to go outside to get there. Outside. With that... thing.* "I can't."

"It's okay, Madeline," Harvey tried to soothe her. "We need to get out of here. The car's right over—"

As Harvey pointed at the parked car, a flash of gold took him by the arm, pulling him into the open so quickly that Madeline thought she'd hallucinated it.

"Harvey. No!"

Retreating from the entrance, her heart felt as if it were trying to escape its cage. Clacking came from the roof. She jumped and squealed, spinning to that sound. Her gaze ping-ponged from the front of the cabin to the tub. As she regressed, the rooftop steps echoed her movements. Hands came to her mouth, muffling her cries of terror, as she continued backing away from both.

"This isn't real. This can't be happening."

Forgetting about the chair behind her, she tumbled tail over teakettle to the hardwood floor. Claws etched the surface of the tin roof. The creature was trying to shred it open. Another loud, shrill utterance pierced the night air. The pawing on the ceiling became frantic, impatient, and hungry.

Madeline slowly stood, pain in her left ankle and elbow shooting lightning to her brain.

No good. Sprained? Dislocated? Possibly broken.

Her weight shifted to the right as she steadied herself and searched for a new escape route. She grabbed a chair, the seat rocked, nearly reacquainting her with the floor. She limped past the bathroom entrance as quickly as possible without so much as a glance. The thing on the roof seemed to track her retreat.

The back door!

Her ankle gave a reminder with each hobble as she lumbered toward the rear of the cabin.

"Stop following me!" Tears flowed down her cheeks. She picked up a vase off a hall table and lobbed it at the ceiling. It arched close to one of the beams and fell by the front door, shattering into oblivion in a spray of glass. The thing atop the cabin shuffled to the sound. Her mind suddenly calmed.

It's hunting by sound.

Frantic and desperate, she looked for more things to throw. She began tossing anything she could get her hands on. Her throws demonstrated a lack of athleticism, but they still did the trick, luring the monster away from the back door. Spinning the deadbolt carefully, the rear door creaked open. Her heart thudded as the noisy hinges refused to allow her a silent escape. A wooden screen door stood sandwiched in the frame, its torn screen unlikely to keep mosquitoes out, much less some kind of demon.

Something reached through the broken screen and grasped her wrist. A scream froze in her throat. Chief Ouatoga slowly appeared with an index finger held against his lips. He pointed to the roof and repeated the gesture over his mouth before letting her go. Madeline nodded that she understood.

Slowly, he opened the screen door and assisted her outside, barely taking his eyes from the rooftop. A pair of middle-aged Cahokia women carried her between them down the rotten wooden steps to prevent sound. Madeline followed their silent directions implicitly.

Several Native American men positioned themselves in the woods around their chief, each bearing bows and arrows. A greenish-black liquid dripped from the tips of their projectiles. The women aided their charge away from the cabin, their moccasin feet barely rustling last fall's leaves.

Once they reached a safer distance, they sat Madeline on the ground and began to look over her wounds as she watched the scene unfold.

The roof and the creature were in sight from where she sat. The beast spun its gaze, and Harvey's carcass dangled from the corners of its blood-soaked mouth.

The thing that had hunted her clacked its nails and screeched, trying to get its prey to make a sound. It was the size of a horse, with the face and beard of a human, antlers of a stag, and saber teeth jutting from its bottom jaw. That long whip of a tail flitted back and forth in agitation. The crimson, feathery, spiked devil's wings flapped impatiently. Its feet ended in those damnable talons she'd heard scrape the roof.

Her fright morphed into anger. One of the women took Madeline's ankle in her hands and twisted with a pop, bringing her emotions into check in a flash of white. They splinted her leg and fashioned a sling for her elbow.

As Chief Ouatoga began to chant.

Madeline was entranced by the scene. "He's got that thing's attention!"

The other braves hid themselves in the trees.

"Piasa," corrected one of the Cahokia women. "It was once defeated long ago. Your construction awoke it."

The chief raised his arms high, backing to where the chimera could see him, continuing his native prayer. The beast was enraptured, stalking slowly to the edge of the house with a famished growl.

Madeline felt a pang of fear for the elder as he baited the monstrosity. *What if it attacked? Would he be able to get out of the way?*

The Cahokia's modern garb all faded into traditional garments. It was as if she were watching a daydream.

The creature positioned itself like a cat preparing to pounce, wiggling its hips left and right, red eyes fixed on its target. The leader voiced a renewed torrent of chanting to entice the demon into action. The other men took careful aim with their bows. He let out one final series of whoops before the being flapped its wings and leapt. Arrows whooshed. One final cry echoed into the woods.

The Piasa crashed to the ground with a thud. The Cahokia encircled the animal, more weapons at the ready. The monster rolled onto its belly, snapping one of the arrows away. It made an attempt to stand, but the coating on the arrowheads started to take effect. Taking one stumbling step forward, it howled its pain. It made a half-hearted swipe at one of the men, who answered with a shot under its wing.

As the creature fell, Madeline stood and hobbled painfully toward the beast. She almost felt pity for the dying thing as it lay there, agony etched into its fading gaze. Then she gave it a swift kick in spite of her splinted leg, nearly toppling herself on top of it. "That was for Harvey." The triumph on her face quickly melted away as she looked around. "Where's Ouatoga?"

A few of the men had gathered around a body, their faces painted with sorrow. Madeline's good hand covered her mouth as a tear leaked down her cheek. Chief Ouatoga had been gashed by the creature's claws, rending him open. She wilted to her knees beside the heroic chieftain.

"What's going on here?" A rotund, middle-aged man ran up to a kneeling, injured woman, brandishing a shotgun. He looked around. "The neighbors heard screaming." His gaze spun to the cabin. "What the hell happened to my house?" Then his eyes rested on what was left of Harvey. As a crowd from neighboring rentals began to gather, he turned a wide-eyed stare to a woman in a gown. "Call 9-1-1, Gladys! Someone's been murdered and a woman's hurt."

"Help him! Please!"

"Help who?" The owner shifted his sight from her to the corpse by the cabin. "I'm pretty sure that guy's dead."

Madeline scanned her surroundings. The Cahokia were still there. "No! Chief Ouatoga. Get an ambulance." She picked up the chieftain's hand and held it to her weeping face. "I'll make this right. I promise."

"Lady…" The man motioned around him, confused by the lone woman. "There's nobody there."

Plans were changed, much to the chagrin of the politicians and workers alike. Madeline, regarded as ruthless and straightforward less than a month ago, decided to move the store's location to the site of an abandoned building only a few blocks away. She worked with the Cahokia Historical Society to place a memorial park on land she donated back to them.

She paid for Harvey's funeral, too. The papers had called it a wild animal attack. They didn't know how right they were.

No one believed her story. She didn't care. People scratched their heads at the change of heart in the iron-willed Madeline. They thought she might have been driven crazy by the stress of success.

A few months later, her Audi was found half-submerged on a Mississippi riverbank. The roof had been peeled open like a sardine can. No trace of Madeline Perdue was ever found.

WHEN THE WIND CHIMES STOP

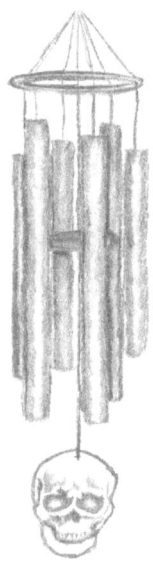

Saturday, October 3, 2015

This is ridiculous. I'm a city boy. I belong in this time-forgotten cabin about as much as teats belong on a boar. It was my therapist's idea. So was keeping this journal. Dr. Framhausen told me to get out of the city and decompress. It would help my stress levels.

He said, "Patrick, go someplace you wouldn't normally go."

Well, we compromised. Camping was one option. But I had never pitched a tent in my life. So, we settled on a stay in a cabin. I could get the "country feel" without embarrassing myself or dying of malaria or whatever bug bites give you.

I have to admit, the scenery on the drive to the country was nice. The trees on the winding road had just started to turn. This trip might mean that I'm missing out on my pumpkin spice-flavored everything, but I need to cut my caffeine intake anyway.

This cabin is decent, albeit with a tad too much woodwork for my taste, but I suppose that only adds to the rustic charm.

The wind chimes outside are almost zen-like in their pitch, the tones calming and melodic. I believe I'll enjoy my decaf coffee—yuck!—out here in the mornings.

Why is it that when someone like me snaps and has a bad day, the first thing they do is take away one of their vices? It's ludicrous. What am I? Twelve? The root of the problem is people, not coffee. I've had arguments with guys named Joe, never a cup of Joe.

Sorry for the tangent. Framhausen suggested I write things down as they come to mind. It's not like I'm writing a book, after all.

I got settled into the place, put away my groceries, and decided to relax. There's no television here, which is just as well. I'd be lucky to get three channels even with using a tower and a roll of aluminum foil. All that would be on would be the news and sports, both things on the list of things to avoid raising my blood pressure.

I wish I could quit my job and coworkers instead. I thought being an investment banker would be a piece of cake, easy money. I've always been good at making pennies grow. Why not help others with it? That's not the issue.

The problem is the people. The backstabbing, the competitive bullshit, the manipulation of paperwork and regulation involved—all caused by people. It's not as simple as I thought. Maybe it's because I'm still considered the "new guy." I've been there for over a year, and I still feel like an intern at Tango & Crouppen. Sounds like a "buddy cop" zombie movie. I actually don't have any friends there.

My head is starting to hurt. I think I'll take a nap and come back to this later.

I slept longer than I thought. Must have needed it. It's dark out. The crickets are chirping. I even heard an owl hoot. It's still warm enough that the occasional bullfrog will croak. Plus, there are the wind chimes. The tinny ring as the clacker strikes is almost hypnotic. The air hasn't quite gotten the autumn smell yet, but I can hear the crisp leaves rustle in the slight breeze.

Okay, I have to admit, Dr. Framhausen may have been right. This time away is relaxing. I think I heard a loon or something. Never heard one before, so I don't know what one sounds like. There's supposed to be a lake nearby. I think that's where a loon would live.

Sunday, October 4th

Woke up this morning, and, despite the bed being brick-hard, I feel refreshed. Renting this place for a week might not be so bad after all. Coffee on the porch was all I imagined it could be. I watched squirrels bury acorns for the winter as deer wandered by without a sideways glance. Listening to the growing carpet of leaves crunch in their steps, the chimes continued their wind-blustered lullaby, causing me to want another cat nap. What is it about this place that makes me want to do nothing but sleep? I could live here. The commute would kill me, but it might be worth it.

This therapy is really working. I don't even get anxious when I think about turning on the news. Television is nonexistent, and the radio is full of static, but it tells me all I need to hear. I listened for a few minutes until I felt my temperature and pulse rise. Then I turned it off, just as my shrink instructed. I don't even listen to what passes for music nowadays. Grunge is a joke; too tame to be metal, too edgy to qualify as pop music. Shame about that Nirvana guy, though.

I think I'll pack a small picnic lunch and see if I can find the lake. It's too cold to swim, I'm sure, but a stroll around the water's edge might be a good way to burn some time. I can only play so much solitaire before going stir-crazy. Besides, I want to see what a loon looks like. I wonder if they eat bread.

Found the water. It was amazing. There was a deck I could dangle my feet from. The lake was cold but not frigid yet. I got too much sun. My face, arms, and legs are on fire. Good thing I left my shirt on.

It was more of a trek to and from the cabin to the lake than I thought, or maybe it just felt like it. The lackadaisical lifestyle here, compared to the city, has me feeling lazy. I don't want to do much of anything and enjoy every second. In fact, that hammock on the porch is calling to me.

I ate my dinner al fresco. I have to say that it was lovely. There was one odd thing, though: a woodpecker drumming a tree for its dinner. I figured they'd be louder. It seemed muffled. The wood was probably rotten or soft. I can hear the squirrels scampering just fine. The chimes do seem a bit out of tune tonight, though. They must have really gotten knocked around. The notes sound sharper, more piercing, somehow. Might be my imagination. Or I could have slept wrong.

The sky is clear. I hope there are a lot of stars out tonight. It's been too overcast for me to see them since I've been here.

Monday, October 5th

It amazes me how quiet some animals can be. I can still hear the various rodents scampering on the ground and in the trees, but I never heard the deer as they approached this time. I let out a startled scream as they passed in front of me, causing them to bolt in response. If I hadn't seen them, I'd have never known they were even there.

I may be in for some storms tonight. I can see menacing-looking clouds on the horizon. Lightning flashes, but it must not be hitting the ground. I never hear the rumble of thunder to accompany it. Maybe it's going away. Still, gusts of wind harvest the remaining dried leaves from hibernating branches. There's something wrong with the chimes. Their melodic rings have become tinny and flat.

I think I've been misled. Rain on a tin roof was rumored to be relaxing. To me, it sounds muffled, like an impatient person drumming their fingers on a pillow. I was looking forward to experiencing it firsthand. Disappointing. Oh well. At least it will help me sleep.

Tuesday, October 6th

My coffee pot must be broken. Typically, I can hear it gurgle as it finishes making that godforsaken fake nectar. I want some real caffeine, not this unleaded, sorry excuse for a hot beverage. If not for the fact that I could smell it, I'd have never known that the pot was done. I was afraid if I took the carafe out too soon, I'd burn myself or at least have a mess to clean up.

How do people live out here? There's nothing to do but sleep. I mean, I know that relaxing was the name of the game, the reason I came out here, but I seem to nod off every other minute. Also, I went trudging through so much muck and mud before giving up on another trip to the water.

I must be sleeping badly. I don't feel rested anymore. Now, I can't even hear the squirrels pad around the forest floor. The birds still sing songs of greeting in the mornings, but the crickets have fallen silent at night.

I may need to get my hearing checked when I get home. I put a kettle on for some tea. After several minutes of not hearing the whistle, I stupidly placed my hands on it to check the temperature. I got lucky with a few blisters, but it could have been much worse. The steam escaping from its spout should have been an indicator.

I can't sleep. All I can hear right now is a constant, rhythmic whoosh. It won't stop. I get out of bed and nearly fall over. My balance is off. I stepped outside for some fresh air and heard the wind chimes. They were even more distorted, almost mocking and malicious. I wanted to grab them and yank them from their hook. Still, the sound seemed to bring my equilibrium back to zero.

It's a cold night, but I'm sleeping with the window open wide. I need to hear the chimes, even as ragged as their tones have become. They lull me to sleep.

Wednesday, October 7th

I think I made myself sick by sleeping with the window open. My nose is somehow simultaneously clogged and runny. There's also a pressure and ringing in my ears. The only thing that makes me feel better is the chimes, even though their ringing has become demonic. It makes my hackles stand, my flesh to goose. Even through all of that, the toning makes the constant, monotonous humming in my head stop.

At least I got a few hours of rest last night. Once I opened up the cabin to let the chiming in, I could sleep.

It's supposed to be frosty tonight. I don't have enough blankets to be able to keep the window ajar.

That damned whooshing is back with a vengeance. It's maddening. I can't find where it's coming from. I've also begun to hear creaks and groans when I move. I tried to keep a window agape to let the now unearthly music of the chimes in, but it wasn't long before I could see my own breath in the cabin. I can hear them through the walls of the structure, but that other sound—the infernal, incessant whooshing—drowns them out with the glass down.

Thursday, October 8th

I found a fan in the spare room that someone left behind. I have a plan. If I can't have a window cracked to let the sound of the chimes in, then I'll bring them indoors. I'll hang them from the spanner that divides the structure into two and put the fan on them at full blast. It's foolproof! Anything. Anything to rid me of that pumping sound that I can't shake.

Fuck! I tried to remove the chimes from their spot, and the clacker broke off. I need string, yarn, fishing wire, anything to make this work again. Anything to get the melody back on track.

I got the ringer back in place, but it's not the same. They don't sound right. There's a sinister pang to them— out of tune, echoing and grating as if they're pissed that I touched them and damaged them. Can inanimate objects have feelings?

I moved them by the fireplace. The fan is pushing gusts at them, yet they refuse to move. The hammer has gone on strike from its job. I even attempted to strike them myself with a spoon. Nothing. All I hear is that whooshing noise.

Why won't they toll? Why won't they help me?

Friday, October 9th

No sleep. Been up for two days.
Wick whoosh
Wick whoosh
All day. Every hour. Every minute. Every second. That is all I hear. I dare not move. When I do, the groaning echoes in my mind.

Windy outside. Supposed to be a nice, sunny day. Don't care. The chimes have stopped. They hate me. Don't care. Every part of me is tired.
Wick whoosh
Wick whoosh
So tired.

I know what that damned sound is. I figured it out! That wicking and whooshing. It's my heartbeat. My joints creak and groan like a rusty door hinge with each movement. I can fix this. Yeah. A knife! That will do it. That will end that horrible sound once and for all.

LOCKED

"Uh oh."

"Uh oh?" His face, framed in shoulder-length brown hair, withered from the jovial and excited appearance he had after they got out of the car to a serious look as he watched his friend frantically pat himself down, looking for something. "What is 'uh oh?' What do you mean by 'uh oh'?"

"I think I forgot the set of keys for the cabin." Doing one final round of turning his pockets out as if the absent item might magically appear, a sudden look of despair blossomed on David's face. "I... I don't have them."

Jessie snorted an incredulous giggle as though expecting a punchline or a big reveal, and they'd both have a great laugh over s'mores and a roaring fire in the fireplace. "Okay. You've had your fun. Come on. Get it open so we can start this whole camping extravaganza."

Ignoring his friend's normal sarcastic nature, David brushed his fingers through his short, spiky, black hair. "I don't have them, Jess."

"Are you serious?" Jessie watched David throw his hands up wordlessly. "Do you have a hidden key or something? Does anyone have a spare set?"

David began to get frantic. "I could call a locksmith, I guess."

"At eight p.m. on a Sunday, with the nearest town over three hours away, in the middle of Vermont, in winter, with a nor'easter heading our way within an hour? Jesus, you're brilliant, Dave." Jessie began to rub his arms a bit as the cold air began to bite into his flesh. "Why didn't I think of that?"

"Not helping." David looked around the cabin, willing the door to unlock itself so that this would all be over. "I'm perfectly aware of how badly I screwed up."

The longer-haired man scoffed in disbelief again. "No, I don't think you do. You're about to, though, because if you don't get us inside soon, I'm gonna take a huge steaming dump inside your car."

Finally, David snapped back, "Go take a shit in the woods with the other brainless animals and let me think in peace. Christ, you're a drama queen for a straight guy." He watched as Jessie stomped back to the small pickup truck, reached inside for a fistful of leftover fast-food napkins, and resumed making his way to where his friend of twenty-plus years couldn't see him do his deed in the thin carpet of light powder on the ground. "You should probably bury it when you're done."

"The only thing I'm about to bury is you if that door isn't open by the time I'm done. Dumbass." He laughed in spite of the situation. The further he got from the house, the heartier his guffaws became until it seemed he was struggling to concentrate on the task at hand.

David wasn't in a laughing mood. The heat from his anger and embarrassment had been keeping him warm until now, but even that quickly faded to the point that he retrieved his coat and slung it over his portly frame. His breath hung in the air like a ghost. A light popped on in his head. Hesitantly, he walked over to each window framing the door and attempted to pry it open. But his father had always secured everything almost neurotically when they left from their visits. It was a habit he took up without realizing it until now.

"You find a way in yet?

The unexpected reappearance of his friend gave his heart a jump-start, sending his buddy into a fit of laughter as the color drained from his face. David let his traffic finger fly at his buddy. "Why are we friends again?"

"I hate you, and I wish you would die." Jessie could barely contain himself, his shoulders shaking from the joviality. "I wish I knew. Right now, we need to find a way inside. The snow's starting to come down."

David finally noticed. His friend was right. They were big flakes, too. This storm was going to be a bad one. Another realization popped into his head, shooting the lightening mood. "Great."

"Now what?"

"I just remembered." David's heart sank even deeper than before. "No keys means no electricity. No electricity means no lights or heat or water."

Jessie raised an eyebrow with a smirk on his face. "You need electricity for water?"

David leered at his friend. "Do you want to take cold showers? The water heater's electric. Plus, the water pump is electric. And how are we going to cook to eat?"

In an attempt to calm his friend down, Jessie smiled and shrugged. "We can boil water, and I know how to cook some killer meals by campfire. I'm a chef, remember?"

"You're not listening. Without the pump, we won't have water at all unless you want to brave this storm to schlep it from the lake a mile away."

"We can melt snow for water if we have to. Now who's the drama queen?" Jessie put a hand on David's shoulder. "Just get us inside. We'll figure it out from there."

David's mind went into a whirlwind of thought. "The back bedroom! Maybe if we break that one out, you can crawl in there and get us in. We can board it up from the inside to keep the wind out after."

"Why do I have to do the climbing?"

David patted his jutting gut. "Do I look like the athletic type?"

Jessie shrugged in agreement. "Point taken. Let's go. This storm is picking up."

The snowfall quickened its pace. Snowflakes increased in size and frequency with each jaw-chattering minute as the temperature continued to plummet. The men rounded the corner to the back of the house, their footsteps deepening in the growing drifts.

"Dammit!" David clamped his arms around himself as the wind cut through him. "I forgot about the cages my dad had installed on the windows to keep people from breaking in." He gripped a set of bars encompassing the panes of glass, a padlock securing each in place, preventing them from being opened.

"What sort of paranoid nutjob was your dad, anyways?" Jessie shook his head, still laughing. "Maybe we'd better just call this trip a wash. As much as I love winter, even I don't want to get caught out in this storm."

"What can I say? He did love his security." David pondered their predicament. "Okay. Let's go back to the truck to get warmed up a bit. If it starts getting worse, we'll head to the nearest town. I don't think we'll make it home before this gets impossible to drive in."

Both men shambled through the growing snowfall back toward the front of the cabin.

Jessie began braying again as they walked.

David cocked an eyebrow as he side-eyed his friend. "Now, what are you laughing at?"

"You, dumbass." More chuckles. "This situation. How could you get so far from home and not remember the—" Jessie's foot kicked something as they turned the corner to the front drive. Looking down, he bent to pick up a ring with four keys and a black rabbit's foot dangling from a chain. "I knew it! I knew you were fucking with me this whole time."

David looked at the keyring with astonishment. "Those aren't mine." He held out his hand.

Jessie placed the prize in his friend's grasp. "I don't care whose they are. Will they work?"

"I don't know." David examined the four metal keys with wonder, turning them in all directions in his hand. "I've never seen them before in my life." He grasped the rabbit's foot, pointing it at Jessie. "I'd remember this."

"Are you sure you've even got the right cabin?" Jessie snorted. "It'd be just like your senile ass to go to the wrong place."

David's patience had run out. "I get it. I'm a screwup." He motioned toward the structure without a trace of humor on his face. "This is my dad's cabin. That much I know." He stomped onto the front porch, both to shake off the weather and his frustration. "We can try them, I guess." He pulled at the screen door to gain access to the main one, but it didn't budge. "Are you kidding me?"

"Now what?" Jessie's ire began to rise, the levity of their predicament gone.

"The screen door is locked, too." David shook his head in disbelief as a gust of wind stole his breath. Once the air momentarily calmed, he lowered his arm and fiddled with the keys. "It's worth a shot, I suppose."

A twig snapped in the woods, accompanied by a high squeak. Jessie's face swung in the direction of the sound. "Are there grizzlies around here?" As he looked, a large, lumbering mass of quills bumbled in the distance.

"Sounds more like a porcupine," David answered without looking up. "Vermont only has black bears. They're harmless unless you leave your food out." He settled on one of the smaller keys. "I think this one should unlock the screen at least." He inserted the key into the slot, still muttering. "Come on, lucky rabbit's foot."

"Wasn't so lucky for the rabbit, if you think about it." Jessie began to shiver.

"Ha!" David yowled triumphantly as the screen door popped free. "It worked!" He pulled the set from the socket with a metallic clank. As he fumbled with them again, the happy, hopeful look morphed into curiosity. "Hey Jess, how many keys were on here when you found it?"

"Four, I think. Why?"

Now it was David's turn to laugh. "Where the hell did you learn to count? There are six on here."

"Who gives a shit?" Jessie clamped his arms around himself. "Just get the door open, asshole. I'm freezing."

David meddled with the keys, looking for any of them that might seem familiar or at least look as if they'd fit into the slot of the padlock on the hasp attached to the front door. "This one should do." Another gust of wind convinced him to hasten the pace. The lock didn't budge. "Wrong one. No big—" He looked at the chain once again. "What the hell?"

"What now?" Jessie began to lose his calm, good-humored demeanor with the constant hurdles.

David held up the ring in front of Jessie. "Are you seeing this?" He shook them in front of his friend.

There were eight keys on the ring now.

Another low grunt echoed through the stiff winter air, adding a chill to Jessie's spine. "So you can't count, either. I don't care. Open the door. There's something out there besides the snow."

David glanced toward the edge of the forest, shaking off the thought of the keyring. "Scared of a porcupine. You're so brave. My hero." There were two keys on the metal circle with the word *Master* inscribed upon them, matching the padlock. Pinching both keys, he inserted one into the padlock and twisted. It popped open. David removed the basic, clunky device, tossing it to the floor of the porch. He tried the door, but it refused to open. "It's deadbolted, too." He shuffled through the keys once more and then dropped them as if they were red hot. As he stepped back, the color drained from his face.

Jessie leered at his wide-eyed friend. "Will you get the damned door open?"

David pointed at the ring. "There are ten keys on it now. We started with four."

"Stop screwing around."

"I'm not!" David had forgotten about the weather. Now, it was the keychain, not the harsh elements, that caused his shivers.

"I'm about to break a window." Jessie shoved his friend aside, collecting the ring in his hands. "Give me these." His fingers wavered from the cold as he guided another key into the lock. It refused to budge. "Which one is it?" He tried another one. Same results. "Dammit!" Another one. No luck. His cursing increased with each attempt. After five different keys, Jessie spiked the ring onto the ground like a football player. "Hell with this. I'm going to sit in the truck until you either get us inside or decide to leave." He trundled through the now calf-deep snow to their vehicle. He pulled at the door, but the latch popped out of his hands without opening. "Very funny, you dick. Unlock the truck."

"I didn't lock it." David gawped at his friend. "Remember? We both got our coats. It was unlocked."

"Come on, man. Stop playing around."

"Dude. I..." David felt for his truck keys, but they were no longer in his pocket. Slowly, he looked at the ring his friend had tossed in a huff. The fob for his truck, along with all of his other keys, was now on the same chain. He gathered the collection, pointed his remote at the vehicle, and pressed the *unlock* button.

The Chevy chirped happily, the locks popping. "Finally!" Jessie started to pull the handle. Then the doors clicked once again, refusing him entry. He spun angrily to David. "Knock it off and let me in!"

Without another word, the rotund man pressed again. Once more, the truck taunted them before relocking on its own. The weight of the keychain seemed to increase with each attempt. Examining the contemptuous device, he noticed the spiral of metal the fob was on appeared to be soldered shut. It couldn't be removed.

Jessie began to look around frantically, his lips pursed tight with anger. He bent, picked up a softball-sized oblong rock, and looked at his friend. "Cabin or truck?"

"What?"

"Cabin or truck?" Jessie tossed and caught the rock menacingly. "Which one am I breaking into?" He spoke very slowly, his face red with growing rage. "Cabin? Or truck?"

David thought quickly. "Cabin. We can start a fire in there, at least."

Jessie pointed an accusing finger. "That's the first smart thing you've said. Ever." He stamped onto the porch, stone in hand. "Move." Turning the riprap to gain as much distance between the glass and his frozen flesh, he thrust it at the pane next to the deadbolt. The glass didn't give. The keychain seemed to jump from the excitement. There were now no fewer than two dozen keys on the ring. Jessie smashed the rock into the window again with no results. Once more, the keychain briefly came to life, adding more keys with each attempted blow.

"Dammit!" Jessie turned, slinging the rock at the truck. The impact spiderwebbed the windshield as the stone slid down toward the hood.

"Now look what you did, you—" David's voice trailed off, his eyes growing wide, uncaring of Jessie's glare.

Finally, Jessie turned to see what his friend was gawping at. To their horror, both men watched as the windscreen on the vehicle crackled. The glass was repairing itself.

Jessie's temper exploded. He yanked David by the coat, pulling him nose-to-nose. "What sort of Twilight Zone bullshit did you drag me into?" He shoved his friend backward, nearly making him spill over the handrail and onto the ground below with the force.

David briefly went wide-eyed with fear, rapidly morphing into a red-faced black rage of his own. "I haven't done shit! I didn't ask for this, you prick." He stomped over to Jessie, an accusing finger extended, causing the chef to shrink back. "All you ever do is abuse me and cuss at me. I sit here and take it, day after day, and I still call you a friend. Now I'm starting to think maybe I'm the idiot for sticking around your unbearable ass and trying to show the world that you can be a decent human being. Well, thank you for proving me wrong!"

David bent, snatched up the ring of keys, and began to fumble through them, looking for any that might be familiar, still mumbling obscenities about his companion to himself. Settling on one of the door keys, he slipped it into the lock and twisted. The deadbolt unlatched. He turned the knob, and the door popped open. More importantly, no more keys magically appeared.

"Hey, asshole!" David's tone was cold but calm now. "It's open."

His companion didn't budge, fuming in the furthest corner of the porch, staring out at the worsening blizzard. His shoulders slumped as he leaned against the cabin, his hands stuffed firmly into his coat pockets. David was just about to give up and leave him to his tantrum when Jessie finally spoke in a hushed, defeated voice. "Don't let the door shut. I'm coming."

"Don't let the door shut," repeated something out in the wild in a high-pitched voice, followed by a titter of mischievous laughter.

As he went deep into the cabin, something clicked in David's mind. He quickly glanced at the inside of the front entrance. The deadbolt was two-way; it could only be locked or unlocked with a key. His mind raced. Looking around, he recognized everything. It was indeed his father's cabin. However, there were things added that didn't belong, things that weren't there before.

Is someone inside here screwing with us?

Another bitter gust of wind convinced his still-steaming friend to come inside. David panicked when Jessie habitually shut the door behind him. "No!" It was too late. The bolt snapped into position. "No. Dammit. No!" He twisted at the doorknob, yanking with all of his might, rattling the wood in its hinges. He rapidly shoved the key he'd used into the slot, but it refused to turn. Two more metallic clinks made him realize his fears. The ring was becoming heavier.

"What? What's wrong?" Jessie's face slackened as he witnessed his buddy feverishly attempt to get back out.

"Now we're locked in!" David yowled in rage at the door, attempting key after key to no avail. After a few minutes, he tossed the ever-populating keyring to the ground in disgust with one final yawp of irritation. He threw his back to the wall and withered to the floor, clutching his head in defeat.

The new problem still hadn't settled into Jessie's mind. He approached David with his hand out to help him up. "Come on. We'll figure it out. At least we're not out there right now."

David grunted as his friend assisted him to stand up. He crouched, hands on his knees, taking a few deep breaths to calm his nerves.

As he strolled around the structure, Jessie in tow, his mind couldn't comprehend what it was seeing. Everything, absolutely everything, had a device locking it from use. The kitchen chairs were chained tightly to the table. The living room furniture had strips of spikes across them, held into place with padlocks to prevent anyone from sitting on them. The fireplace had a hinged iron panel across the opening to prevent use. Locked.

"What sort of psycho was your dad?" Jessie muttered as he stared at the cabin's strange interior. "He had to lock everything?"

"I..." David blankly replied, barely able to conceive what his eyes beheld. "I don't think he did this."

They wandered to the kitchen. Every drawer, every single cupboard, even the refrigerator, was locked tight. The taps on the sink had received a measure of child-proofing, the key slot glimmering at them in defiance.

"Are you shitting me?" Jessie chuckled in disbelief, folding his arms across his chest, his head tilting to one side as he looked around.

David's voice became monotone: "We have to figure something out." His breath hung in the air. "We're not going to stay very warm in here without heat."

"Dude, I will break this furniture apart and start a fire on that table if I have to."

"Hmmm," David grunted, now returning his attention to the puzzle of the ring itself.

"What'd you find, sweetheart?"

David raised an eyebrow at the term of endearment from his straight friend.

Jessie sensed that the conversation was about to take an unwanted tangent. "I call you that all the time. Now, what did you discover?"

"Still, it's disturbing coming from you." David breathed deeply. "This ring doesn't have any openings. At all."

"So?"

"So, how did my truck key get on there? Where do the other keys come from?" He glanced at Jessie.

The look of confusion on his face said it all.

David shook his head with a slight chuckle. "If we figure out how this thing works, maybe we can beat it and get outta here."

"Makes sense, I guess." Jessie began looking at the artifact as well. "How do we defeat something neither of us has ever experienced, though?"

"Not sure." The wheels in David's head began turning. "When we found the right key, nothing was added."

"Right."

"When we used the wrong one—"

"Or when we tried to go around using them," Jessie interrupted.

David nodded in agreement. "Two more were added each time."

"So," Jessie contemplated, "we just have to be smarter about which ones we use?"

"Sounds easy, but I'm not convinced it will be." David broke away from his companion, strolling over to the fireplace, a stern look of concentration as he studied the problem. He tugged on the flue cord. It moved freely. He could hear the damper open and close without obstruction. "First things first; we need to get a fire going." He studied the heavy iron plate covering the opening. The locking mechanism had an old-fashioned-looking keyhole: circular at the top, joining a flared, triangular bottom. One by one, he examined the dangling metal. After doing a complete turn on the ring and isolating a few potential subjects, he looked at Jessie. "We have a one-in-three chance to get this open."

Jessie peered at the different-sized choices. "I don't think it's the short one. Seems too stubby for that lock."

David agreed, allowing the shorter one to fall limp.

Jessie's eyes shifted back and forth to the other two, and he shook his head. "I don't know about the others."

David toyed with the final decision. One of them struck him to be freshly made, the metal gleaming and new. The other appeared ancient and weathered, the years charring and etching the material to the point that it seemed brittle. The choice made, he aimed the key at the hole, feeling for any clue prior to insertion. His hand drew back suddenly.

"What's going on? Why didn't you open it?"

"I felt the ring vibrate as my hand got closer. I want to see if it does it again." David switched the hardware and repeated the steps. "Dammit. Same thing. This thing's not going to—" His voice trailed off as a light went on in his mind. "No way." He shifted back to the shorter chunk of metal he'd rejected earlier and tried again. This time, the ring was still.

"I really don't think that will…" Jessie watched as David's face brightened and the lock opened. "Work?" He stood in slack-jawed amazement at the achievement.

David threw open the cast iron door blocking the fireplace and peered up the chimney to check the flue again. "It's open and unlocked. Let's get some heat going."

Both men worked to get a fire raging in the belly of the inlay. David pulled pages from one of his father's many books about Native American culture and other folklore as Jessie gathered a few more tomes. There was a meager pile of firewood staged in an iron bin next to the opening. It would serve to get a good blaze started.

"That won't last very long," David muttered aloud.

"We can burn furniture if we have to." Jessie bent and unloaded a collection of paperbacks. "The kitchen chairs and table are wood. It might stink as the finish burns off, though." He straightened, looking at the carved mantel. The detail was incredible. Finally, his eyes came to rest on the face etched in the center. "Wow," he chuckled. "Your dad was a bit vain, wasn't he?"

David fidgeted as he lit the pile of wadded pages under two of the logs, hiding the nervousness in his gaze. "What makes you say that?"

"This face looks exactly like him." Jessie stood away as the wood caught, unable to peel his eyes from the carving. "Don't get me wrong, it's a beautiful piece. Disturbing but well done. Probably cost him a fortune."

"Oh. That?" David chortled. "Yeah. He did that to himself." His eyes widened briefly as a drop of sweat beaded on his forehead. "Himself. He made that."

Jessie, still concentrating on the elaborate decoration, nodded. "Impressive. I never knew he had it in him."

The fire caught and came to life. Both men stood in silence, hands aimed at the growing blaze. They warmed their bodies there in silence for several minutes.

"It's a bit ironic, you know," Jessie said, finally.

David cocked an eyebrow, tilting his head in curiosity at his friend. "What's ironic?"

"You being a writer." Jessie spun to allow his backside some of the warmth. "And here we are, burning books."

David inhaled and exhaled deeply. "Not my first choice. This act was a matter of survival. This whole trip has been about that."

"What do you mean?"

David drooped his head in shame. "Ever since Dad went missing, Mom and I have gone flat broke. She's retired, and I can't work because of my heart condition. Being an author doesn't pay as well or as fast as people might think. Between her social security and my disability, we're barely scraping by."

Jessie threw an arm around his friend's shoulders. "You're doing your best."

David's shoulders slumped as his chin met his chest. "It doesn't feel like it," he grumbled, glowering at the face blossoming from the center of the hearth. "It doesn't feel right."

Jessie clapped his buddy on the back almost painfully. "You'll get there. I've read your stuff. It's pretty good."

"Thanks, but that's not why we're here." David patted the clock above the fireplace. It was a garish-looking intricate brass design depicting a naked, cherub-like child leaning on the timepiece with a rooster standing sentinel atop it. "This is."

"That ugly-ass thing?"

David nodded. "I was as surprised as you are, especially when I found out what it's worth." David paused for dramatic effect. "Almost seventeen thousand American dollars." He watched as Jessie's jaw dropped.

"In fact, there are several things in this cabin that are worth a lot of money. Mom and I could use that."

"Unreal." Jessie shook his head in disbelief. "That explains the security system around here. Can we even get to any of them?"

"That's just it." David shrugged slightly. "My dad put the locks on the doors and the cages over the windows, sure, but he never did any of this. He certainly didn't install the shatterproof glass. I was trying to beat the storm to at least get to this clock."

"What's the urgency?"

"There's a collector in Hattenburg, just an hour from here." David saw his reflection in the clock's face and felt the need to turn away. "He wanted this thing for his wife's birthday in two days. Now we're trapped and in danger, all because I'm desperate."

Time slowed as the conversation tapered to a standstill, both men taking turns feeding the fire, reluctantly tossing full tomes onto the blaze to prevent its death. Blue-green flames licked at the publications, the blaze devouring them greedily.

"We should think about which doors to unlock next." David dropped a couple of magazines into the stomach of the chimney.

"We'll need food and something to cook in." Jessie contemplated their predicament. "I can improvise on a campfire. We don't wanna wait until we have furniture burning, though. The fumes of the polish might be poisonous and taint our food. The glue from the book bindings is bad enough."

"You're the cook." David gathered the keyring and turned toward the kitchen. "Pantry it is." His eyes brightened as he recalled something. "Dad always kept granola bars and survival rations in case we ever got snowed in like this."

His steps quickened to the long, thin door next to the padlocked refrigerator. *Without power*, David thought to himself as he pondered the lock briefly, *that thing won't do us a bit of good*. He returned his attention to the walk-in pantry and the hasp securing it. He studied it like a scholar. The keyhole on the door itself was almost cliche in shape, not modern in the least. The lock on the hasp, however, looked new, declaring itself *Master*. The ring had no fewer than seven keys with matching brand names to try.

"What's taking you so long?"

David sighed in exasperation. "There are two locks. The ancient one might be easier than the padlock."

Jessie walked over to the dining room table. "You need to do something fast. The books are going up like kindling." He dragged two of the seats from the table over to the fireplace and began breaking them into pieces.

David opted to unlock the easier one first. There were five skeleton-style keys on the ring at that moment. *One wrong move*, he inwardly contemplated as he inventoried the types of keys, *and that could double. The padlock will be even worse*. Carefully sifting through the metal, he took turns aiming them at the mouth of the hole slowly, feeling for the slightest twinge. One by one, he felt his way through them until he narrowed the choices to two. With surgical precision, he made his selection, inserting the key home. It didn't turn, and two more keys appeared on the link.

David emitted a long, low sigh, his arms falling limp to his side. He felt a lump gather in his throat, and his bottom lip quivered. He was tired. A hand landed on his shoulder, giving him another start. Looking up, he saw Jessie's equally exhausted eyes lock with his.

"Let me give it a shot."

Handing what he hoped was the correct latchkey for the lock, David stepped aside to allow Jessie access. The key worked. Now, only the hasp remained. Jessie worked on the Sentry padlock, getting the thing open on his third try. A small sense of hope was restored as light poured into the cabinet. Cans of vegetables, fruit, and potted meats, some appearing dangerously close to their expiration date, filled the space. Jessie gathered a few things, handing them to David. Then, with a grunt of effort, he pulled the door of the pantry off its hinges, splintering the pristine wood.

"What did you do that for?"

Before answering, Jessie leaned the door against the wall, giving it a kick to snap it in half. "We need wood. Besides, do you wanna take a chance on that door locking again?"

They sat next to the fire and ate in silence after popping the lids open with Jessie's Swiss army knife. "Sardines heated over the fire don't taste so bad when you're hungry." The food sat in David's nervous stomach like a ton of bricks. Still, he was happy to have it.

Jessie dipped a finger into his can of deviled ham to get the last bit. Popping the morsel into his mouth, he peered at his friend. "Whatever happened to your old man, anyway? I don't think you ever told me."

The writer pondered the question. "No one knows. He came up here for a weekend and just disappeared. Poof! He was never seen again, and his body was never found. That was long enough ago that we had to have him legally declared dead just to get the insurance."

"Sad. Sorry to hear it, man." Jessie licked his finger again and stood, setting his empty can of green beans to the side. "Better keep the cans in case we need to cook." Stretching his arms high into the air, he wandered around. Then, he began peeling the pads from the kitchen chairs and the cushions from the couches, working around their spiked locks. The fabric tore from the couch pieces, but the padding remained mostly intact.

"What are you doing?"

"If you want to sleep on a hard floor, be my guest." Jessie plopped two cushions down and wadded a couple of the chair seats up into a makeshift pillow. Then he fed half of the cabinet door to the embers in the fireplace. After a few minutes of deep black smoke, the wood caught and sparked alight.

David marveled at his buddy. Then he checked the keyring. Nothing seemed new. "Let me see your knife."

Jessie fumbled in his pocket, fishing the sharp tool free and handing it over. "What's going on?"

"No keys appeared when you took those cushions. I want to try something." He gathered the keys and headed toward the kitchen, straightening the screwdriver attachment to its open position. Placing the ring on the countertop, he studied it as he slowly unscrewed one of the door hinges. The keys remained still; nothing new appeared. Removing the bottom fixture, he pulled the cover free, yanking it down with a triumphant yowl.

His eyes wide with excitement, David began tirelessly detaching each door with renewed vigor. At the bottom of a thin broom closet beside the refrigerator was a canvas tool bag. Inside was a hammer, more screwdrivers, wrenches, and a few other basic household items and implements. Going around the house, David dislodged any door he could by removing the hinge pins and pulling the portals wide, bypassing the locking mechanisms completely.

Jessie saw what was going on and joined his pal in the effort. They worked their way down the hallway, removing any door they could. In the bathroom, they worked to unset the porcelain throne and separate the ring from the cover. The medicine cabinet doors and linen closet yawned wide, their covers gone.

Now, all that was left was the bedroom that once belonged to his parents. David stared at the barrier, internally pleading for it to open on its own as he held the hammer and flat-blade screwdriver. With a trembling hand, he began to reach toward the top pin, but the hammer fell from his sweaty grasp.

"I can't." David collapsed to all fours, tears cresting his eyelids.

Jessie knelt beside him. "It's okay. We have most of the house open now."

David shook his head despondently. "The electrical panel is in their room. If we can get in there, we can remove the cover, turn things on, and have water and heat."

Patting his buddy on the back, Jessie reassured him: "We can survive for now. You did good. If we need to get in there, I can take the door off so you won't have to." He paused, considering their predicament again. "We could do the same thing to the front door if we have to, to get out of here."

David held up the keyring with his truck's fob still on board and shook it. "You forgetting something?"

Jessie strode over to the tool bag, snatched a pair of wire cutters, and snipped the fob free. "Nope. Let's wait this storm out. Then we'll take the front door off and get out of here."

David agreed, getting back to his feet with strained effort.

Both men made their way back to the comfort of the fire, collecting as many blankets from the closets as they could. They broke more of the cabinet doors apart, taking turns tossing them onto the blaze to keep it fed through the night while the other slept. The wind wailed over the flue, the arctic-like breeze tunneling down into the cabin in spite of the fire. Soon, however, both men fell asleep, leaving the tinder to die out on its own.

Shivering, Jessie awoke first. Crimson and orange daylight peeked through the window panes over scattered tufts of cotton in the sky. A blanket of pristine white reflected the morning sun as far as he could see. Gusts wafted clouds of snow into mesmerizing patterns on the surface of the untouched powder. Again, his breath clouded in front of him, sending another quiver of frigid air deep into his bones. Attempting to keep from waking his friend, Jessie grabbed the tools and set off down the hall to the lone remaining barrier.

"To hell with this," Jessie muttered through his chattering teeth. "I'm getting in there and turning on the heat." Removing the hammer and a blade screwdriver, he tapped on the pin on the top hinge. Peering over his shoulder, Jessie listened. David was still in the living room, snoring loudly. "Good. I didn't wake him." A couple more well-timed taps and the piece would be ready for removal once the others were taken out. He worked as quietly as he could, the chilling air in the cabin carrying the sound like a messenger. At last, the final portal was freed.

An awful smell wafted from the opening, sickly and sweet, almost coppery to the senses. A cloud of winter-slowed flies buzzed out in protest, past the chef and out into the main room to seek warmth. Still, David's snoring grew louder. After placing the door with the others, Jessie peered into the room.

"Oh fuck!"

In the middle of the bedroom was a king-sized bed stationed against the wall. It had an ornate brass head and footboards. Their golden luster had turned dull and green through years of neglect. Tied to the footboard were the skeletal remains of a bespectacled man. His flesh, what little still existed, hung in leathery flaps and patches over desolate bones. Even without the eyes still in the deep, empty sockets to tell the truth, Jessie could sense the desperation in the position of the body. His gorge rising, Jessie unleashed what little contents his stomach contained next to the entryway.

David snored even louder behind him as Jessie stepped into the room. The cadaver was clad in a fishing vest and hat, a long-sleeved, green flannel shirt jutting out from the arm holes and collar. He approached the decayed man as if he might come to life, eyes wide in terror. On one of the nightstands, a framed picture of David as a young teen, standing next to his father in this very outfit, stood upright; a reminder of happier times long gone.

Jessie didn't notice that the snoring was now in the same room. As he stood to rush to the living room, David appeared, a sinister grimace on his face.

"Oops. Guess you woke me," David said, swinging a hammer.

Jessie's world went black as he fell to the floor with a resounding thud.

When Jessie awoke, his head still full of cobwebs from the blow, his vision was blurry. He tried to wipe his face, but his arms couldn't move. The sensation of immobility drove the focus back into his mind. He pulled and yanked, but his rope-bound arms barely budged. Across from him sat the remains of David's father, haphazardly placed within eyeshot.

David slipped into view, leaning down with a Cheshire grin, all sanity gone from his eyes. "Ah, good. You're awake."

Jessie struggled in vain. "The hell are you doing? Let me go!" He twisted and contorted until his energy was all but depleted. "Haha. Very funny, Dave. Untie me, and I won't kick your ass too much."

David continued to grin, his glare softening into a faux pitiful gaze. "You don't get it, do you?" He righted himself with a small grunt of effort. "I told you that I'd had enough of your shit." He dug into his pocket, produced the truck's fob, tossed it into the air, and caught it teasingly as he spoke: "I still don't know what's going on with the locks. I didn't lie about that."

"What I did lie about was *this*." He pulled out the keyring with the black rabbit's foot and jangled it in front of his victim. "This is my dad's ring. There was only one set made because he knew I had a gambling habit and that I'd probably pawn his stuff to pay my debts." David paused in his fidgeting with the keys, the truck control in his other hand. "He was always an intuitive one." He sighed, shaking his head as he leaned down and lovingly caressed the cheekbones on his expired father's body. "At least we got to have one last fishing trip together. Right, Dad? Guess you should have noticed when I was taking pictures of things around the cabin." David stood and kicked the carcass, shattering it to pieces. "Then again, paying attention to anything I did was never your strong suit."

The crazed man spun his attention to his prisoner. "I really didn't want it to end like this, but you had to be nosy." David stood over Jessie, a sadistic smile forming from his grin. "Don't worry. You'll die of dehydration before you will of starvation. Maybe I'll leave the front door open so a bear will kill you first."

"Wow," Jessie taunted. "I knew you were psycho. I just had no idea that you were capable of this."

"Maybe if you weren't so busy being hateful while calling it 'friendship,' you might have seen the signs."

"You killed your dad." Jessie wriggled his hands. The knots hadn't been cinched very well, and the ropes were slowly loosening. "Now you're leaving me to die in this fire trap in the middle of nowhere. Some friend."

David stomped over, leaning down nearly nose-to-nose with his captive, white-hot rage flaring through his dilated eyes. "Are we comparing notes on how to treat friends? Is that what we're doing?"

"Oh, suck it up, you pansy." Jessie felt one of the bindings come undone, hoping that David hadn't yet seen. "I treated you like a brother. Better, even, since I hate my own family."

David's eyes softened, his heart hitching in his chest from the excitement. "I... didn't want this. I didn't want any of this." He collapsed to a seated position, his head heavy as he rocked back and forth in despair. "I'm so sorry, Jessie. I really am."

"Me too."

The sudden shift in his friend's tone caused David to peer up, breaking from his self-pity long enough to catch a heavy right hook to the jaw. The force of the blow dropped him flat to his stomach, dazed. The keyring clattered out of his grasp, the truck fob also skittering across the floor like a skipped rock on a still pond. Jessie used the time to undo the other tether and free himself from the footboard. The liberated man sprung to his feet, briefly contemplating the equally appealing notions of whether to finish beating his former buddy to a pulp or escape.

Rushing past a recovering David, Jessie scooped up the truck key and stuffed it into his pocket. Whirling around, he saw David begin to get to all fours, shaking the cobwebs from his head like a prize fighter under the ten count. He scrambled and punted, knocking the wind from both of the less athletic man's lungs before veering quickly toward the wide-open hallway. As he raced to the front door, he saw the pins of the hinges where he had left them. Thinking quickly, he pulled the bedroom door from the pile that leaned in the narrow pathway and angled it back into position.

In the bedroom, David coughed, a spatter of blood spraying from his mouth as he fought to catch his breath. He glanced underneath him in horror as he saw the door being put back into place. His limbs faltered, panic beating his heart into a frenzy as he crawled to prevent being trapped within the confines of the room.

"No! Don't you dare leave me here!" David grunted, his air straining to return. His pleading eyes only met the panel of timber between them.

"Why not? You had no problem doing it to me a minute ago." Jessie yanked the pins from their hinges, struggling to place the door back into its frame. Through the minute cracks as he shifted the wood this way and that, he saw David clambering with one outstretched hand after another. He moved toward the door, creeping nearer and nearer. Finally, the top pin popped into place, pinching a blister on Jessie's finger in the process. "Mother..." It was all he had time to get out before the bottom of the door bulged outward.

David lept at the bottom of the frame, shouldering all of his immense weight into escaping. Wide-eyed, Jessie dropped, spinning to his back and placing his flailing feet against the frame of the opposite opening to gain purchase. Both men groaned and strained against the other—power and muscle versus weight and manic determination. The hefty man got his hands through the side of the door, a feeling of victory bringing an evil chuckle from deep inside of him. Wood cracked and splintered, the metal hardware deforming as the two struggled.

"I'm going to get out there, Jess." David's confidence rose as he began to push through the angle of the plank, squashing and compacting the chef into a ball. "This time, I'm going to win."

"Not even close," Jessie uttered. Those words were followed by a heroic yowl when his feet found a good hold. Shoe leather squealed like tires from within the bedroom as he doubled his efforts, shoving the man back rapidly.

David howled in agony behind the hard wood, blood sputtering up in fountains where his fingers once were. He screamed in terror as his essence spurted before his eyes.

In the hallway, eight digits twitched in protest as Jessie made the bottom hinge whole once more. He threw his back against the wood, casually slipping the middle pin into its slot as the screaming continued on the other side. He panted from effort between gusts of newfound laughter. "Guess you won't be using the keyring. Dick."

"Jessie!" Pleading cries echoed from within. "Don't leave me! I'll bleed out."

Slowly, Jessie picked himself up from the floor, still chortling as he glowered at the disembodied fingers lying in a small crimson pool. "You know, Dave, any time I've said this, I've never meant it. This time, I do. I hate you, and I wish you would die."

To his surprise, when Jessie approached the entrance, the locks all tumbled open on their own, the front door squeaking as it invited him to freedom. He waded through the deep snow, yanking the truck ajar, the oddball latches preventing their earlier escape now gone. Firing the Chevy to life, he gave the cabin one final digit of his own, the still shouting man trapped to his fate in the furthest point within the bowels of the house as he slowly pulled away.

DESECRATION:
THE WET STONES

"Hank Washburn, what in God's name are you doing?" The lovely redheaded woman looked on, horror etched deeply into her pallid complexion and green eyes. Standing next to Greasy Creek, she bore witness as a lanky middle-aged man dressed in bib overalls tossed slabs of stone into the water. She patted the farmer's golden retriever's head mindlessly, a gesture still happily welcomed by the dog. In her other hand, she held a basket filled with a couple dozen farm-fresh eggs for the man.

With a mighty heave, he slung another thick tile into the drink. Spinning on his heels, Hank wiped the sweat from his brow, his thick, sun-bleached brown hair stuck to his forehead from perspiration. "It's my land, Patty. I'll do with it as I please."

"Those were people's headstones!" With her indignation demonstrated by her hands to her hips, she huffed at the farmer. "That's sacrilege to desecrate a grave like that and not move the bodies."

He waved a dismissive hand at her. "Nonsense. Those people have been dead for so long that they don't have living relatives to get in touch with." He grabbed the bridle attached to the brown mare, the bucket of the wagon now emptied of its horrible cargo, and clicked his tongue to prompt the horse back toward the barn.

"Wait!" Patty suddenly recalled why she had come out to begin with, halting the farmer before he could take off. "Don't forget your eggs." She held out the basket with both hands. "Do you have a sickle we could borrow? Papa has some weeds to get rid of."

Hank took the offering, nodding his thanks. He grabbed up a curved blade from the back of the wagon, taking care to hand it to the young woman handle first. "Now, if you'll excuse me," he panted through his exhaustion, "I have a fence to pull and a field to plow. I need that extra acre." He gave a sharp whistle, and the retriever bounded over to the equine transport, trotting off in time as they disappeared over the hill and left the lady behind.

"Oh, Hank," she moaned softly after him, glancing solemnly back into the creek. The water had swallowed the offerings without a trace of the disturbance. "What have you done?"

The sun was beginning to set on the early spring day. The air was sweet with the smell of blossoming clover, which would soon be plowed under to make room for Hank's corn now that the last frost of the winter had hit. The headstones had been clunky and heavy. A good section of the wrought iron fence that surrounded the small graveyard and sectioned his land into two parts had already been pulled up so he could get the farm equipment in for the removal. The scrap lay askew without regard or conscience.

"Arms are sore," he muttered to himself. "I'll finish tearing out the fence tomorrow." He looked to his side and petted the dog, scratching her ears absently. "Come on, Blondie. Let's call it a day."

The dog barked in agreement, slipping off toward the house in front of the farmer, bushy tail wagging at full mast. They disappeared into the small, one-bedroom cabin he'd purchased with the plot of land. It wasn't large, but it was good enough for a confirmed bachelor, especially one married to his work.

Cooking himself a slice of ham, mashed turnips, peas, and diced carrots, he fell asleep halfway through eating the wonderful-smelling sustenance, Blondie happily helping him with the cleanup as soon as she knew the coast was clear.

Hank awoke suddenly, nearly jumping out of his skin, when he heard the sound of a small clunk. With groggy eyes, he scanned the dark room as best he could while shaking off the disorientation of the darkness. Reaching over, he fumbled with a matchbox and lit a table lamp, bringing light to the gloomy room. His dog had passed out at the foot of his shaggy old recliner. Beside her was the dinner plate, licked spotless. In the middle of the floor was the fork he'd used.

Must have been the fork I heard.

"Hope you enjoyed it as much as I did, girl." He pushed himself up from the chair, the dog only licking her chops with a pleasant smile in response as he gathered the utensil and plate. As he entered the kitchen, his socked foot stepped on a small pebble, causing him to hiss and grumble in pain, waking his companion with a curious glance before she returned to her slumber. He bent down, the grimace of pain still lighting his face, and retrieved the nugget.

It was wet. Not just mildly damp but soaking, slobbering wet, almost wringing with water as he examined it.

Did Blondie bring this in? She hasn't chewed on rocks since she was a pup. Must have picked it up when we were by the creek.

Hank shrugged to himself, tossing the stone absently into the slop bucket alongside the turnip peelings. He swung his shoulder in circles to ease some of the tension, grabbing the lamp in the kitchen and dragging himself to the bedroom. "Come on." He patted his leg, waking the sleeping canine. "Let's hit the sack. Big day tomorrow."

That night was everything except restful. Hank was haunted by nightmares he couldn't recall when he woke. Each time, it was the same. He'd sit bolt upright, sweat drenching his head and pillow, heart racing as if he'd just run a marathon. He'd strain his memory, trying to remember what his dream had been about. Blondie would be busy snoring loudly on the rug next to the bed every time. Before morning came, he found himself envying the dog.

The following day, Hank watched impatiently as his coffee percolated into the pot. On mornings like this, it was excruciating to have to wait for the brew. He rubbed the sleep out of his head as best he could, grumbling to himself as Blondie nudged him, whining for attention.

"Dammit, girl! I..." He looked at his companion, unable to be hateful to that goofy face. That was when he saw the water on the floor. He bolted to his feet, kicking the chair back with such force that it fell onto its back. "What the hell?" The puddle was far too large and clear for it to have been one of the dog's accidents. He slowly walked toward the source. It didn't originate at the sink. He could even hear it trickling like a rapidly melting icicle. As he came to the corner in the room where the slop bucket was kept, he saw the tops of the turnips he'd eaten floating on the ground next to the trash bin. It was overflowing with water as if a spring had opened up within its confines.

He gathered the bucket, sloshing stale and vile-smelling water over him as he took the container outside to empty it. The liquid smelled of rot and decay, still multiplying as he upturned it just beyond the front porch. The quarter-sized pebble he'd found last night clunked to the ground in the midst of the flood of rancid water as it clotted into the mud on the ground.

Retrieving the stone, he gawped in wonder as he held it between his thumb and forefinger. It leaked water relentlessly even as he grasped it.

"Dear God." He threw the accursed rock as far as he could, watching in amazement as it spun midair, changing direction toward the field, fanning clear liquid the entire way. It came to rest close to the grounds of the cemetery and rolled uphill to the resting place.

As it hit the freshly violated hallowed ground, he heard another thump, louder this time, come from behind him in the cabin.

He spun, stomping back inside. "You'd better not be getting into that slop, Blondie."

The dog was nowhere near where the sound had originated.

The anger in his voice waned when he saw another stone, this one nearly the size of his hand, in the middle of the wooden floor. Just like its predecessor, it began leaking a rivulet of awful-smelling water. Hank quickly picked it up and heaved it outside. As soon as it touched the ground, it rolled up the slight grade, defying gravity, and headed to the graveyard. Once it reached the disturbed resting spot, another crash came from the living room, accompanied by a frightened yelp. Blondie bolted past him and out the door. She sat beyond the porch, leering at the entrance, tongue lolling as if trying to convince her master to do the same.

The hair on his neck stood on end as he peered past his favorite chair, eyes growing wide with disbelief. A small stream of water burbled from the new, plate-sized, charcoal-colored shale shank that had landed in the center of his living space. The force of the impact had left an indentation on the milled lumber he had installed on the floor over the cold stone foundation, slightly splintering two of the planks. A small rivulet snaked over the ground, stretching out to the door in a single liquid tentacle. When the watery tributary reached the jamb of the entry, it lifted from the floor and appeared to feel the air before plopping back to the ground with a slight splash. Blondie whimpered, retreating from the sight.

Hank felt his ire rise as he reached out for the stone. "Get the hell outta my house!"

Just as his hand made contact, the slab jerked slightly. It felt as if it had come alive in his grasp, attempting to escape. Water poured from every part of it, making his hold treacherous at best. It felt mossy and slick as if it had been at the bottom of Greasy Creek since the dawn of time. The edges were worn smooth from eons of the elements. Still, it appeared to be a part of a larger piece. The letters carved on it couldn't have been more than a century old.

Hank examined the angled tip where the letters were. "E V?" The angle of the ages-old fracture had cut the letters so close that the word was obviously incomplete.

He stomped to the doorway with his hefty load, chucking it outside, barely clearing the stoop of the porch. It shanked into the ground on the carved point, standing upright like a black monolithic tongue poking from the dirt. The grass ripped as gravity pulled at the slate, still leaking rancid water over the thirsty soil. The bulk of it soon thudded to the ground in a muddy sploosh.

"That'll be enough of that." Hank brushed the muck from his hands on the legs of his pants and spat at the stone defiantly.

A shiver crawled up his spine when he witnessed the rock begin to follow the route of its predecessors, not rolling lengthwise but somersaulting end over end to the graveyard, the two letters mocking him with a pause during every tumble. Blondie returned, her hackles at full attention as she locked eyes on the stone, angrily barking. The point dug divots on each downturn before reaching the iron fencing. Crossing the mangled fence, it finally halted, letters right side up one final time before collapsing to the ground as if exhausted from the trip.

Another thunderous smash emanated from within the cabin, this time from the small bedroom. Hank rushed to the source. At the center of a small wooden crater was a smooth, round chunk of red granite the size of his dog's head. Liquid bubbled from the heart of the stone, another stream defying physics as it appeared to reach toward him. Looking up, he saw no entry hole in the roof.

"Where are they coming from?" he wondered, all the while fuming at the strange and inconvenient events.

Crash!

The noise came from the kitchen, accompanied by a tinny clang. Hank's heart raced while he investigated. Petrified, he slowly peered into the room. A bit of sedimentary rock jutted up from the spot on the floor, leaking a liquid trail of its own. The metallic sound he'd heard was the cast iron stove the rock had clipped in its descent. The coffee pot lay on its side, rolling back and forth from the impact. As his morning brew leaked onto the hot stove, a bitter steam rose from the hot belly of the apparatus before it evaporated.

Another boom echoed from the living area, near the foot of the fireplace, the mouth of the disturbing man's face carved into the mantle stretched into a mischievous grin. A mozarkite node roiled water from nowhere, just like the others, vomiting a surprising amount of liquid for its smaller size.

Panic began to overtake Hank. In frustration, he grasped his hair in fistfuls and yelled at the top of his lungs as water pooled at his feet and lapped at his ankles like an attention-starved kitten.

Boom!

"Mother of God!" Hank yelped in surprise, shifting around to see a large egg-shaped quartz geode crack open on impact. Clear, sulfurous-smelling liquid burbled forth like an endless yolk from the sparkling crystals within. A small, black, hair-like worm swam in the drink aimlessly before appearing to catch a whiff of the cabin owner. It lunged like a snake on the strike, causing Hank to pull his foot from the water with a scream. Then, it disappeared into the cracks between the planks.

Wide-eyed and frightened, Hank frantically looked around his feet for the creature to no avail. As fear drilled into his soul, he fell to his knees, weeping and praying. "Lord, forgive me for what I've done." Prostrating himself amid the growing puddle, he yowled his anguish, temporarily forgetting about the whip-like hair he'd witnessed seconds before. "I'll make it right. I'll set things back. Please just stop."

Blondie poked her muzzle through the doorway as her owner lamented, sniffing the air with distrust. With a whimper, she slowly inched her way inside, the escaping water splashing under her paws. The slightest sounds caused her to skitter nervously, but she made her way to Hank, nuzzling herself under his arm. Reluctantly, she sat on the damp floor, continuing to press her weight into her human in a gesture of comfort. Finally, the man broke his wailing and hugged her closely.

"Come on, girl," he sniffled, standing. "We've got work to do."

Hank headed out to the barn, happily followed by the retriever. Strapping the cart back onto the horse, he led them to the creek. "Damned thing is cold, even in the summer," he muttered, staring at Greasy Creek balefully. "Snow melt will have the water freezing."

He steeled himself as he stripped down to his long johns and waded into the stream. He winced as it reached his crotch, sucking in air through gritted and chattering teeth.

The constant movement of the creek made locating most of the stones difficult. Thankfully, that portion of the waterway wasn't deeper than his chest. Still, he nearly drowned as he gathered some of the larger headstones. One of them, a white granite slab, had cracked on its initial impact in the creek bed. As he hoisted it, it fell into two pieces, part of it slipping from his grasp and landing firmly on his left foot. Hank howled in pain as a small crimson blossom streamed from his injured body.

"Something broke." He pulled his foot free, still carrying half of the marker. He limped from where the other half assaulted him and returned to shore. His lips were turning blue, his skin pallid from the frigid stream.

"Dammit. I was almost done. I can't do no more. I'll die if I get back in there like this."

He stripped off his wet underwear and briefly stood naked before struggling into his dry overalls. His foot throbbed with each movement. A couple of his toes had already turned an unhealthy shade of purple from the icy drink in which they had been submerged. His body uncontrollably shivered as he fought to regain heat. Even the bright sun hadn't helped much on the early spring day.

"Blondie!" Hank watched as the dog yipped her excitement at her name. He patted her lovingly as she came to his side. With his energy sapped from the ordeal, he looked at his companion dead in the eyes. "I need help. Go get Patty. Go on, girl. Go get her!"

The bushy tail flopped back and forth as the dog woofed her way down the road to the neighbor's house. Hank picked himself up, still unable to put weight on the foot. Grabbing the reins, he guided the horse to the cemetery while sitting in the wagon. Each bump in the path started his agony anew, and white flashes of electricity popped behind his eyes.

"I'll get this done even if it kills me." He glanced over his shoulder at the cabin. "You win," he shouted to the structure. "Do you hear me?" Then his rage melted away, fading into a barely audible mumble: "You... win."

Weakly, he gathered the smallest of the headstones, hobbling it back to where he thought it had been. It would have been a jigsaw puzzle under the best of circumstances—figuring out whose stone went where. Now, in his weakened state, it was a near impossibility. Locating a patch of disturbed earth that seemed to match the size and shape of the rock, he gently placed it on the ground, nearly pitching himself to the dirt with it.

"Where's that damn dog?"

Patty was hanging her wash on the clothesline to dry when she saw Blondie come bounding toward her, barking and raising a fuss. The retriever spun in a circle, woofing at the woman, then faced the direction from which she'd come. Patty watched the canine for a few seconds before realization struck her. Her hand went to her mouth in a gasp. Dropping her chore, she rushed into her house. She had a party line, the only one for several miles, so her neighbors would ask to use it once in a while.

Snatching the phone from the receiver, she spun the dial. She heard a pair of voices chatting on the line, unable to recognize them in her panic. "I hate to interrupt."

The voices on the line went dead silent.

"I have an emergency. Can I use the line?"

The others agreed to hang up, and Patty dialed.

"Anderson residence. This is Margaret speaking." The woman on the other end sounded as though she'd been interrupted.

"Margaret, this is Patty O'Toole. I think something might've happened to Hank at the Washburn place. Can you send Doc Anderson?"

There came a gasp. Those who had been conversing had continued to listen in.

The older lady tisked her disgust at the lack of privacy. "Sure, sweetie. I'll gather him around right now."

"Okay. Thank you." Patty felt a bit of relief. "I'm gonna head up there to check on him now. Tell the Doc I'll meet him there." After receiving a confirmation, she hung up the phone, never minding the chatter that had started up once the eavesdroppers thought the coast was clear. Spinning to the door, she leaped off of her front stoop to follow the dog back to its master.

Patty's heart raced as much from fear as the exercise of the four-mile-long jaunt to Hank's land, Blondie leading her by several paces. As she approached the cabin, she caught a glimpse of the cart and horse.

Blondie barked from the top of the hill. Ignoring the stitch in her side from her rather athletic and unplanned sprint, Patty rushed to the wagon. Hank lay facedown on the ground, barely moving or breathing, his arm outstretched toward the hauled cargo. A few of the headstones remained, drying in the vernal sun in the back. One was split into two pieces, but the second part was nowhere to be found. Blood soaked his left foot and pants leg.

"Hank!" She hastened to his side, kneeling and turning his head to her. "Hank! What happened? Speak to me."

The farmer weakly opened his eyes, speaking shakily from his still-purple lips. "Must... put... stones... back."

Patty slowly turned the man onto his back. She lay his head on the ground and shifted herself to his foot to take a look. *He's lost a lot of blood*, she thought to herself. Tearing off a strip from her dress, she applied a tourniquet to his leg. His foot was mangled. A couple of his toes looked to be in bad shape, too.

"Please," Hank moaned breathlessly, "put the stones back, Patty."

The young lady looked from him to the wagon and back. She shook her head, the tears in her eyes streaming onto him.

"Patty, please!"

She didn't want to leave his side, but the urgency in his voice caused her to act. Picking up the smallest of the remaining markers, a thin cross made of two-inch-thick slate, she hefted it between her legs, wobbling almost comically as she carried it through the wrecked fence. She rested it on the ground as she scanned the yard for a hole in the grass that resembled the base of the stone. Finally locating a promising prospect, she shook her head.

"Of course, it's in the back." With a deep breath, she hobbled it to its original area.

She repeated the trip, first matching the bottom of the gravestones with what she believed to be their spots in the cemetery before huffing and hefting them into place. All that was left was half a white granite tombstone that had split down its length. The other part was missing. Her arms and back aching from the task, she set the half marker in place and returned to the farmer.

"They're all in place, Hank, but one is still missing a piece." She kneeled beside her neighbor, cupping his head in her hand.

Hank smiled meekly, his face flushed of color from the ordeal and blood loss. Slowly, he pointed a weakened finger toward Greasy Creek. "Other. Half."

The sound of approaching hooves sent Blondie into a fit of excitement. The black two-horse carriage kicked up a small cloud of dust as it drew nearer. Patty was unable to tell who the passengers were, but she prayed it was the town doctor. Her heart leapt with glee as it rounded the corner and up the driveway. She bolted upright, absently spilling the farmer out of her grasp. He let out a weak groan while the redhead waved frantically to the approaching transport.

"Over here!" Patty hopped up and down, fanning the air feverishly. "Doc Anderson, he's right here! Come quick!"

The carriage pulled to a stop at the bottom of the hill, and a middle-aged, bespectacled, and balding man dismounted, carrying a black leather bag. He motioned for the driver to accompany him and was quickly obeyed. The men scrambled to the scene.

"Let's get him inside. Come on, Hank." Scooping the farmer up and onto their shoulders, they assisted him into his water-soaked cabin, Patty close behind, wringing her hands. They all gaped at the spectacle, the liquid seeming to flow from nowhere and out the door like a fresh spring. Stones of all sizes and shapes plopped and splashed into the drink, appearing from thin air as they looked around.

The men waded through the inches-deep flood and into the bedroom, carefully laying the patient on his bed. The water level was already halfway up to the mattress. The doctor examined the farmer quickly, testing his breathing and sight.

"Creek," Hank muttered. "Last stone."

Patty whirled around, not giving it a second thought. She left the men to tend to the wounded and made a beeline for the creek. She traced the wagon's wheel marks to the place where she had only a day ago witnessed her neighbor heaving the markers. Without hesitation, she dove into the cold, flowing water and located the other half of the heavy slab. She struggled to breathe as she carried the cursed puzzle piece, water sloshing into her mouth with each step.

At last, she managed to bring the thing to shore, collapsing next to it from the effort. Gazing upside-down, she considered the long trek to the cemetery with hateful regard. She heaved a determined breath and went back to the task at hand, pulling and dragging the half-marker as quickly as her tired limbs would allow.

Back in the cabin, the doctor and the carriage driver were doing their best to make Hank comfortable and satisfactorily wrap his foot. The rain of stones and pebbles had become an indoor hail storm. As various rocks of size and shape plipped and plopped into the growing tide of water around them, they worked to mend the farmer.

Without warning, the pelting ceased completely. The bewildered men scanned their surroundings, unsure of what to make of the already strange circumstance or its sudden stop. As the waters receded, they witnessed the floor of the cabin littered with various river rocks worn smooth by time and tide, some even covered in algae.

"It's done!" a breathless Patty called from the entryway, leaning on the jamb to catch her breath. She gaped at the floor, dumbstruck. It had been nearly covered in damp rubble. Her own feet had been cut open from her chore, but she paid it no mind as she slowly stepped inside. Blondie shook some of the water off, trotting over to the redhead with a happy woof. As the neighbor made her way to the bedroom, she knelt briefly, patting and hugging the dog. "You're such a good girl."

The doctor and his assistant returned from the room before she could make it inside. "I believe he'll be okay," the physician reassured them. "He just needs to be kept warm and on bed rest." The carriage driver made a beeline for the door, not wishing to stay another second in the odd cabin. "I'll be right there," he called to the horseman.

"I'll stay with him overnight," Patty volunteered. "Would you be so kind as to tell my father where I'm at on your way back to town?"

The doc nodded solemnly. He bent and gathered a few of the stones in his hand, examining them. "Strangest thing I've ever seen."

Patty's lips were tightly pursed as she held her tongue about her theories on why it happened. "I'll clean things up around here. Thank you again for your quick work, Doc Anderson."

The physician gently grabbed her hands and patted them in appreciation. "I'll be back in the morning to check on you both." Without another word, he glanced around one last time, shook his head in wonder, and left.

By the time night fell, Patty had removed most of the debris that had fallen from nowhere, and the floor of the house had begun to dry. She started a small fire in the stove and was working on one in the fireplace to assist in taking the moisture from the cabin. As she lit the flames to life, she glanced at the mantle. The carving of the haggard mountain man, his face frozen in a silent scream in the center of the piece, gave her an unshakable case of the heebie-jeebies. The eyes appeared to be aimed toward the bedroom, yet somehow still followed her to the rocking chair.

She fell into an uneasy slumber, her dreams haunted by an odd young man with raven black hair and a smile that sent a shiver down her spine. She started awake when the rooster crowed at sunrise. Checking her surroundings, a brief bout of disorientation set in as she caught her bearings. It had almost felt as if the sound of the rooster outside had shaken her awake.

A mournful bay emanated from the bedroom.

"Blondie?" The neighbor scrambled to her feet, nearly upending the chair in her haste. She shot to the door where the farmer lay, glancing at the retriever as she huffed her sorrow, nudging the man in a futile attempt to wake him. She whimpered and whined as Patty closed in, her hand going to her mouth in speechless shock.

Two more stones had fallen in the night, each apparently a portion of a headstone she'd removed from the house the day before but couldn't find a spot for in the cemetery. They had smashed the unfortunate farmer's head in his sleep. Each of the new pieces of intruding mineral matter had a single letter inscribed upon them: *I* and *L*.

Patty sat on the front porch, sobbing for hours and hugging the dog, and was still there when the doctor's carriage came down the drive.

From the look of the caretaker, the medical man already knew the status of his patient prior to entering the house for confirmation. His face went white as he peered into the room, eyes locking on the crisscrossed slabs. Slowly, he retreated to where he'd left the weeping woman. His eye caught the now-dead fire under the mantle. When he glanced up, his blood turned to ice at the carving. It bore an uncanny resemblance to Hank.

THE SOUVENIR

"Mommy, can I have a toy?"

Sylvia grimaced slightly, almost reflexively, as her son's words pierced her mind, her headache reminding her that the whole camping trip was nearly over. She slowly turned toward the child as he pleaded again. His sandy brown mop of hair, barely tamed from waking up so early in the morning, waggled in strands that stood at full attention as he glossed over the selection of hand-carved souvenirs on display, circling the table with a predator's hunger in his eyes. His brown puppy dog eyes met her green eyes, and her heart overtook her brain's stubborn refusal. Walking over to him and brushing his hair down with her hand, she took in the display of crafted buildings with a hint of disapproval.

She kneeled to straighten the collar on his white shirt. "Look at you," she tisked. "You're a mess." She discreetly zipped the fly on his pants, a task his six-year-old brain hadn't quite grasped, whether getting dressed or relieving himself. "Those aren't toys, Levi; they're decorations."

Tears of rejection began to well up in the boy's eyes. His lips trembled as he spoke: "You promised. I was a good boy."

A well-dressed man in his mid-fifties approached the two. Sylvia knew it was her new husband, Malcolm, but she didn't bother to look at him when he came into her peripheral awareness. The only thing she despised more than the great outdoors was the man who'd taken her and her son to the Smoky Mountain Campground in the first place.

He studied the small relics—replicas of the buildings painstakingly fashioned to resemble the cabins that lined the grounds. The hinged roofs on all of the items opened to reveal the detail whittled into each piece. "They look sturdy enough to me. I think he can handle one." He ruffled the boy's hair. "You think you can be careful with it if we let you pick one, sport?"

The waterworks immediately evaporated from Levi's eyes as he nodded with feverish enthusiasm. "I'll be careful with it. I promise!"

Sylvia rolled her eyes and shook her head slightly, breathing an exasperated sigh as she stood. She flattened out her riding pants and sweater. "Malcolm, you'll spoil him," she whispered, an edge to her voice.

"It's fine. It'll keep him occupied for the long drive home." He shot her an authoritative glance before returning a loving gaze to the child. "Okay. Pick one. But just one."

If it weren't for your bank account, I never would've married you.

"Fine," she relented. "If it gets us away from this bug-infested hellhole."

The boy squealed with delight as he did another lap around the display, his eyes darting from one structure to the next with indecision. Finally, they came to rest on a cabin that very closely resembled the store in which they stood, complete with the fireplace, expertly carved and hand-painted to look like stone. He popped open the roof and examined the inside. It wasn't laid out like the store and seemed a bit smaller, but it had the eerie mantle just like the one by the register, though the face in the center was different.

"I want this one."

Malcolm smiled despite the cold shiver that ran down his spine upon looking at the miniature. *Uncanny*, he thought as he glanced over the boy's shoulder inside. "All right. Let's go pay for it."

Levi skipped over to the counter.

A weathered old man, gray-haired, balding, and bespectacled, sat behind the register. He peered up from his workshop desk, gently setting down another piece in progress as he painfully stood and hobbled to the checkout, his back hunched from a lifetime of hard labor even into his golden years. "What'd you find there, young man?"

The boy placed the cabin on the counter, practically vibrating with excitement, much to the clerk's amusement.

He picked up the piece, turning it this way and that to get a closer look. "Funny," he remarked. "I don't remember carving this one." He chuckled, straightening his glasses from the tip of his nose. "Of course, my memory won't even let me recall what I had for breakfast half the time."

"How much for it?" snorted Sylvia impatiently.

The shopkeeper, clearly unimpressed with her tone, tilted his head toward the kitchen, where an equally elderly woman stood at the iron stove, tending to a pot of coffee. "How much are the cabins, Ma?"

Without turning her sweet face to the man, she responded matter-of-factly: "Forty dollars. You put a lot of work into those things."

The clerk smiled at the couple and the young boy. The woman exhibited sticker shock at the price. Hope instantly drained from the boy's face. The old man didn't really appear fazed. He leaned on the counter with both elbows and stared into the boy's innocent brown eyes.

"You promise to take real good care of it?"

Again, Levi couldn't contain his happiness, his hopefulness returning by degrees.

The old man looked at Malcolm. "Tell you what. I'll let it go for thirty since this little guy wants it so much. Whaddaya say?"

Malcolm glanced down at Levi, the boy's eyes glistening with silent pleas. He produced a fat wallet from his back pocket, his face becoming momentarily serious as he spoke to his stepchild. "You promise not to break it? It's a very expensive toy." He laughed as the child's enthusiasm only grew in spades. Smiling at the elderly woodworker, he plopped a fifty-dollar bill on the counter. "Take the forty. It'll be worth it."

The shopkeeper took the money and hesitated before handing Malcolm back a ten-dollar bill. "You sure? I'm happy to sell it for thirty."

"I appreciate the work artists put into their creations." The stepfather paused, looking closely at the toy cabin. "What did you carve it from?"

The carver readjusted his glasses again as the wheels in his mind did their best to search for the answer. "Well, if it's anything like the others, I made it from the wood of a wall we tore down. So, whatever the original wood of the cabin was. Pine, most likely." He looked at Levi with a soft smile. "You want a bag for that, young man?"

Levi shook his head, practically squealing with delight as the merchant handed the souvenir to him. He hugged it tight to his chest, taking care not to crush the precious item. "Thank you!" The boy spun around and raced toward the door, turning around long enough to wave at the elderly couple one last time before climbing into the back of their Mercedes-Benz for the long drive home.

"I still think you're spoiling him," Sylvia huffed, walking casually behind her son.

Malcolm ignored the jab, looking at the shopkeeper one last time. "I'll make sure he takes good care of it." Placing the key to their cabin on the checkout counter and smiling, he spoke as he slipped out. "Thank you for a wonderful stay."

After the lovely family had left behind nothing but memories and a trail of dust from the gravel road, the elderly woman approached her husband. "Maybe you should think about making actual toys with that wood, too. They might sell a little better."

"That's just the thing, Ma," he answered. "For the life of me, I can't remember making that one."

As their white-walled tires finally hit the pavement once more, Levi settled in the back seat, soaking in every tiny little detail of his new plaything. Spinning it this way and that, he memorized every scratch of the chisel, the smooth surface of the bottom with a name he couldn't read inscribed on it, the expertly shaped stones of the fireplace, inside and out. Even the inside was meticulously detailed. The hinged roof had rafters that were practically carbon copies of the ones in the shop, right down to the knots in the beams. The inner part housed furniture, all carved in place, unmovable. There was a stove, much like the one on which the old lady had been making coffee, a table with spindle legs and chairs, and even a bed with pillows. Every part of the trinket appeared to be painted in such a realistic fashion that Levi felt as though he could climb in and take a nap on the bed. As the motion of the car began to take its usual effect on him, that's exactly what his imagination did while he drifted to sleep.

"Hey, sweetie."

Levi's mom's soft voice slowly stirred him from his slumber.

"We're stopping for gas. Why don't you come with me to use the restroom?"

Slowly, the boy awoke, rubbing his knuckles into his eyes.

She watched a look of panicked horror shoot to his face when he suddenly realized his new toy was missing. He patted himself, his head darting this way and that, searching frantically.

"It's on the floorboard."

Relief overcame Levi as he stretched down to gather it, hoping that it hadn't broken when it tumbled under his mother's seat. He struggled with it, his heart breaking with each unsuccessful tug, trying to dislodge it from the seat. "It's stuck." Another wave of panic overtook him. "Mommy! It's stuck. I can't get it." One last cautious yank, and the cabin freed from its prison, none the worse for wear. Levi stuck his head down to peer under the seat as if trying to see why the mean device wanted his toy so badly. Under the place where his mother had been sitting was a small package of brown paper. He began to reach for it, his curiosity piqued.

"Let's go," ordered Sylvia impatiently, pulling her son away from the seat. "We don't have much time." She forced Levi out of the car, turning to the attendant who was pumping their gas and checking their oil and wipers. "Which way to the bathrooms?"

"Just inside on the left, ma'am."

"Thank you." She began to lead her son away. "Your toy will be fine, honey. We won't be gone long."

Still, Levi never took his eyes off the car until they disappeared into the gas station. A few minutes later, they exited, and he pulled himself free from his mother's grip, rushing to get back into the car to check on his cabin. Levi plopped into the back seat, examining the souvenir with scrutiny to make sure no damage had been done. Sylvia shook her head as she returned the seat to its normal position and climbed in.

"It worries me," she started, glancing at her son and then her husband, "how much attention he's giving that thing."

"Are you worried," Malcolm retorted with a playful smirk, "or jealous?" He paused, watching the kid appreciate his obsession. "It's just new. It'll wear off in time. Then, we'll put it up for safekeeping until he's older." He cocked his head to peer at the rearview mirror. "You ready, sport?" His gaze was met with a slight nod. "Home, here we come."

The car pulled away from the waving attendant and back onto the highway. Levi studied the miniature cabin, a smile on his face. Sylvia glanced back at her son. He giggled as he looked and waved at the toy, greeting something only he could see. A shiver danced down Sylvia's spine.

During the rest of the ride home, she heard Levi chattering to his replica, having a one-way conversation with a new imaginary friend. By the time they pulled into their home driveway, she had become worried about her child's new obsession. As soon as the door was unlocked, Levi rushed into the house and up the grand wooden staircase to his room, unintentionally slamming the door behind him.

"Oh, I wouldn't be too concerned," Malcolm soothed as he heaved their luggage from the trunk. "He's six. A lot of kids have imaginary friends at their age. Just let him be a child, for God's sake."

She hadn't expected Malcolm's last statement to sting the way it did. It deepened her loathing for her husband. It didn't matter that he was right. He usually was. That wasn't why she despised him.

She guessed Malcolm might have meant it when he said, "I do." But, for her, their marriage was one of convenience, a necessity after Levi's father went off to Europe to fight in that awful war. As soon as she got the telegram that her love wouldn't be returning, her mind panicked, worrying about her child not having a male role model in his life. Sylvia practically latched on like a tick when the owner of the bag manufacturing plant she worked for took a sudden interest in her after her brief mourning period. As soon as she graduated from secretary to wife, she quit to prevent dealing with the ever-churning rumor mill. She would finally be able to raise her son without having to punch a time clock.

"You coming?"

The sound of her spouse snapped Sylvia back from her daydream.

He was standing at the door to their house, bags in tow. "It looks like it may start really coming down."

Sylvia felt the distinct plop of a raindrop on her face. "I'll be in in a minute." She waited for Malcolm to disappear into their abode before reaching under her seat to retrieve the brown paper bag that her son had almost brought to her husband's attention. Opening the neatly folded seal of the container, the woody smell of the mushrooms she had found during their stay in that godforsaken campground. The red, rust-colored caps of the fungus practically glowed from within the darkness of the bag. The research she had done at the library prior to their excursion explained that these and other fungi closely resembled each other. One was poisonous; the other was a delicacy.

A soft smile settled on her face. "I hope I got the right ones." She desperately wanted to surprise Malcolm with what she'd found, knowing his love for mushrooms of all sorts. Folding the bag closed once more, Sylvia pondered which recipes she could use to give her husband the best culinary experience possible once her findings were dried enough to use.

As she popped through the elaborately carved front door of the mansion-like house they called home, Sylvia had to quickly hide the paper bag behind her back as Malcolm raced past her, carrying a happily giggling Levi and his awful toy around on his shoulders. Her blood boiled at him as they did laps in the ample foyer area.

"Malcolm, be careful!" The edge in her tone brought a rapid halt to the fun and games as the man lowered a disappointed boy from his perch.

The flash of brown caught Malcolm's eye, the suspicious action, the quick, guilty look on his wife's face even more so. It was the same surprised expression Levi had any time he was caught doing something he wasn't supposed to be doing. Sylvia was concealing something behind her back and was almost hilariously horrible at covering it up.

"Go upstairs and play." Malcolm ruffled Levi's hair next to the grand redwood staircase leading to the bedrooms. "We can play later." He patted the boy on the backside as he slowly climbed the stairs, the rail in one hand, his cabin in the other. After Levi had drifted into the playroom, Malcolm approached his beloved, a wry look on his face. "What's behind your back?"

She had been caught. Her mind raced for an explanation, settling on a partial truth: "I found some mushrooms on one of our hikes. I was going to surprise you with them."

Malcolm clapped his hands and rubbed them together, hunger in his eyes. "Ooh. Mushrooms, huh? Give them to the cook. She knows which ones are good and how to prepare them." He pulled Sylvia close and kissed her passionately.

Sylvia returned a guarded smooch, breaking away from him as soon as she could and keeping the bag well away from his prying grasp.

Ugh. He kisses like a fish. I hate that.

"I'd better get these to Rosie as soon as I can. Who knows how long they'll last?"

With a hint of disappointment at their brief liplock, Malcolm yelled after her, watching as she disappeared toward the kitchen. "I can't wait to try them."

She had already gone.

As Sylvia darted through the double doors leading to the immense cooking area, she planted herself against the frame with a sigh of relief. Her heartbeat began to calm after a few deep breaths. *He's right*, she practically thought aloud. *Rosie will know the difference between a good one and a poisonous one. I'd better not let her see them.* She went into the walk-in pantry and found a nice dark corner of the potato bin where she could stash them to dry.

With her deed complete, Sylvia headed upstairs to lie down for a bit. *Between the car ride and almost being caught*, her mind pondered, *I think I need a nap.* Passing by Levi's playroom, she heard her son talking to someone. The conversation seemed very one-sided as she pressed her ear against the door to listen.

"Yeah." There was a serious tone to her son's voice. "I know." A long pause. "She can be mean sometimes. I think she misses my real daddy."

Slowly, Sylvia spun the knob and cracked the door to peek in. Levi was lying on his stomach on the floor, happily drawing on a piece of paper in front of him, his little legs kicking in the air behind him. In front of the paper was the little cabin. For a brief second, she could have sworn that she saw a light on in one of the windows. She also thought she spied a small shadow scooting past the illuminated window just before the light went out. But that was impossible. Wasn't it?

"I think she just needs a nap, too." The tone in Levi's voice wasn't one of fact but one of agreement.

She stepped fully into the room, her eyes locked on the souvenir. "Who are you talking to, honey?"

Without looking up from his scribbling, her son answered: "My friend. He lives in the cabin." The boy stopped his scrawling and listened to the air before nodding and returning to his creation. "He says that you shouldn't do it."

Sylvia's heart leaped to her throat as she slowly approached her occupied son. She could feel her pulse behind her ears as she stared wide-eyed at the toy. "Shouldn't do what, sweetie?"

Levi paused again, looking at the cabin in front of him, his face scrunched in severity. "What mushrooms?" He cocked a curious glance at his mother. "What are mushrooms, mommy? He says you shouldn't use them. Use them for what, mommy?"

Sylvia swallowed the panic building in her screaming mind as she hovered over her son. "They're for cooking. Rosie will know if they're good or not."

Levi slowly tilted to his side as he appeared to listen to the cabin once more. "He says you didn't give 'em to Rosie. You hid 'em."

As his body cleared the scribble on the page, the pounding in her chest increased. A large building had been roughly sketched with three petrified stick figures flailing hopelessly in the windows: a man, a woman, and a boy, as best she could discern from her six-year-old's artwork. At the base of the structure appeared scratches of red, yellow, and orange spiking upward like flames.

All of the blood drained from her face, her knees weakening beneath her. "I think…" Sylvia slurred. "I think mommy needs to lie down." Without another word, she turned and exited the room, her gaze never leaving the toy cabin.

Levi watched with confusion and concern as his mother left.

"Are you okay?" Malcolm's voice was the last thing Sylvia heard after a prolonged shriek and before her husband caught her to prevent her from collapsing to the floor in a heap.

When she came to, a doctor was hovering over her and waving a broken vial of smelling salts under her nose. Sylvia slowly opened her eyes, the blur resolving in sight along with the fogginess in her mind.

She sat bolt upright with a scream, scrambling backward and rattling her headboard against the wall. Malcolm and the doctor rushed to comfort and restrain her. Sylvia spotted her teary-eyed and concerned son. He carried that accursed cabin. And she began flailing and yowling in fright.

"Sylvia! It's okay. You're safe at home." Malcolm tried his best to be soothing, but his wife did not calm down.

"That…" the woman pointed an accusing finger at her child's toy, "thing! That Thing is evil. Get it away. Destroy it, Malcolm. There's something… someone inside! Lights came on. I saw him. He's in there!"

Levi began to bawl, experiencing a combination of fear of his mom and the possessiveness of his cabin.

Rosie, the cook, who had assisted when the mistress had first fainted into the man's arms, ushered the bawling child out of the room as his mother continued her hysterics. The doctor quickly rifled through his bag, filling a syringe with a clear liquid and injecting it into Sylvia's arm. Soon, the frantic woman began to relax, slipping into a deep sleep.

After she'd been settled into bed, Malcolm and the doctor emerged from the room, the physician wiping his brow with a handkerchief. "That should help her sleep." He looked solemnly at Malcolm. "Has she had these delusions long?"

"No. We just bought the little cabin for Levi this weekend." Malcolm choked back his concern. "I've never seen her act like this before."

The doctor nodded slowly. "Perhaps she just had a small nervous breakdown." He produced a vial of pills, his own nerves on edge from the encounter and causing the bottle to rattle like an infant's toy. "Give her one of these at night, or whenever she starts to act"—he paused to choose his words with surgical precision—"restless. Let me know if her condition gets worse." The smaller, older gentleman gathered his bag and began to descend the staircase. Two steps in, he turned his back. "It may be a good idea to keep that toy away from her for now."

Malcolm allowed the physician some space before following him downstairs to see him out. After they reached the landing on the main floor, the physician turned and gave the man of the house a hopeful smile. "I think she'll be fine after some good rest. Give her time. I've seen things like this quite a lot since the war."

The men wrapped up their conversation, and the doctor went on his way. Malcolm secured the door and went to look for Levi and Rosie when he heard some rattling in the kitchen. Following the sound, he peeked through one of the windows in the double doors. His stepson was perched on the counter, clutching his toy tightly, tears drying into a crust on his cheeks. Rosie began singing an Irish hymn that seemed to calm the boy down while she banged about for what she was looking for. Finally, she held up a small pot.

"Here we are. You've been hidin' from me, have ye? Ye bad thing, you."

Her conversing with the cookware made Levi giggle.

She took the boy off of the counter and stood him on the ground. "I'll brew you up some hot cocoa. How about that?" Her offer gained an enthusiastic nod from the child.

Malcolm slowly popped through the door.

"Would you like some as well, sir?" Rosie asked.

"If you don't mind, Rosie." Malcolm strolled over to Levi and knelt to his level. "May I see your toy for a second, son?"

A fresh wave of fear and waterworks started. "No! You'll take it away!" Levi began to fuss over his possession.

Malcolm soothed as best he could. "I promise I'll give it right back. I'm not going to take it away. I just want to look at it."

With suspicion embedded deep in his eyes, Levi reluctantly handed over the cabin. The stepdad slowly studied the carving before popping the latch to flip the top open and look inside. There was nothing there aside from the carved furniture. There certainly wasn't a man living in there. Nor was there a source of light. It was simply a carved display and nothing more. *I don't see anything*, he thought, returning the cabin to the boy as the smell of boiling milk began to fill the air.

Levi snatched the toy from his stepdad in a way that almost startled the man. He hugged it tightly. Then, he began to listen to something only he could hear. "Yeah. I like him too," he said to the unusual souvenir.

Malcolm stood, patting the boy on the head. "Why don't you go play? I'll call you when Rosie has our hot chocolate ready. Just be quiet so you don't disturb your mother, okay?"

Levi smiled brightly and skipped away, the double doors swinging back and forth like saloon wings behind him.

Once the boy was out of earshot, Malcolm looked at the cook. "My family's falling apart, Rosie."

"Blarney, Mr. Steed. Absolute rubbish." She stirred the pot as she finished the concoction. "Many a wee lad and lass have pretend friends, sir. And the missus... she's just had a bad day. Happens to the best of us, sir."

"I hope you're right, Rosie."

"Aye. It'll blow over. You just wait." She tapped the wooden spoon on the rim of the pan. "I'll get it poured and add some marshmallows. You go fetch the lad, would ye? Should be cool enough in a few minutes." She smiled at the homeowner as he began to exit the workspace. "I'll bring it to you in the playroom." Malcolm nodded, lips pursed with worry, and left.

"You've got your hands full, you do, sir," Rosie whispered, crossing herself when she knew he was no longer watching. She divided the drink into three cups, keeping hers separate to add in a little something stronger. "Lord help you all."

Sylvia awoke just as the sun was setting, disoriented from her unscheduled nap, her head still foggy from the sedation. Her clothes had wrinkled from being slept in. Slowly, she rose from the bed, her feet a bit unsteady beneath her. Finally, she gained her bearings and headed down the hallway. Levi's bedroom door was open wide, as it usually was when he was put to bed. Wiping the grogginess from her eyes, she peeked in on him, her eyes adjusting to the darkness of his room. Stepping up to his bedside, she leaned down to kiss him goodnight on the forehead, causing him to turn onto his back. She peeled the covers away to reveal that infernal toy. He had taken it to bed with him and slept with it as if it were a stuffed animal.

Hatred boiled inside of her. Carefully, Sylvia removed the cabin from her son's grasp, doing her best not to disturb his slumber. She held the keepsake to her face, sneering daggers into its interior. It looked ordinary enough from every angle, but she knew better. She hated the thing ever since she first laid eyes on it.

"I'm going to break you into a million pieces," she whispered, anger seething in her hushed voice.

Levi moaned, tossing around a bit more. Worried that he might awaken and see her attempting to steal away his most beloved possession, Sylvia hesitantly returned the offending thing to her son's side.

"Next time." Sylvia turned and walked out of her boy's room, heading down the stairs for a bite to eat. In her medically induced nap, she had missed dinner. Her stomach impatiently growled as She rounded the first few steps on the staircase.

She was nearly halfway down when she looked up for the briefest second, failing to see the obstacle under her next footstep. Losing her balance, she screamed and tumbled the rest of the way to the landing of the first floor. She lay there, moaning and dazed. Her left elbow felt like it was on fire, as was her right ankle, the one that had found the object.

The thing she'd tripped on clattered down the steps behind her, coming to rest upright beside her head. It was the damn cabin. Her eyes went wide. A light came on in one of the windows, followed by the silhouette of a younger man. Her face paled, stretching into a horrified glower. A scream rose in her throat. She could almost see the apparition clearly. In a fit of panic, she pulled herself away from the thing and against the front door, yowling in terror.

Rosie rushed in from the kitchen, wiping her hand on a filthy apron. Malcolm emerged from the opposite direction, likely from his study, where he often smoked a pipe and read for an hour or so before retiring for the night. The cook rushed to the shrieking, downed woman, trying her best to both soothe and restrain her. Malcolm closed in quickly to assist. Carefully, they brought her to a standing position, but she was unable to put weight on her right leg.

"That cabin tried to kill me!" Sylvia pointed to where the toy had struck the floor beside her. But it was gone. A crazed look befell her eyes as she frantically searched for the little carved structure.

"There's nothing there, Syl." Malcolm took the brunt of her weight to guide her to a nearby high-backed blue chair. After sitting her down, he looked at the cook. "Go get her medicine, please. It's on her nightstand."

Sylvia shoved him away. "I don't need—"

"What's going on, mommy?" Levi rubbed the sleep from his eyes as he ventured to the top of the stairs to see what was happening. In his arms was the cabin.

"That's... That's impossible!" Sylvia's eye began to twitch, and her lips trembled as sweat blossomed on her forehead. It was all she could do to keep from going into hysterics once more. She could see the worry and disbelief in Malcolm's eyes. "I'm telling you, that thing was on the stairs," she growled through gritted teeth. "It tripped me and made me fall."

Speechless, Malcolm's mouth rose and fell without a word, his heart breaking for his wife's plight, both real and imagined.

Rosie reached the top of the stairs and guided the boy back to his bedroom. "Go one, now. Yer mother's not well, and you don't need to be seeing it."

"It has to go!" Sylvia roared. "Malcolm, either that cabin goes, or I do." She studied her husband's reaction for a few seconds. "Fine," she grunted, standing up on her good leg. Hobbling over to the hall table, she snagged her purse, slinging it over her shoulder in a huff before limping out the front door and slamming it resoundingly behind her.

Sylvia slid into the driver's seat of her luxury sedan and started the engine. She wanted to put as much distance between her and that godforsaken souvenir as possible. A backfire shot her pulse through the roof as she put the car in reverse, backed out of the driveway, and started down the winding road heading east. As she put feet and then miles between her and the house, she began to relax. Before, the adrenaline was enough for her foot to work the gas pedal. Now that the excitement was wearing off, the pain was kicking in.

Seeing a short straightaway she knew well, Sylvia eased her pained foot off of the gas pedal. Rather than lose momentum, the engine revved higher, gaining speed. Her eyes flew wide, her heart returning to her throat, and she gripped the wheel with white-knuckled intensity. During a quick, panicked glance in the rearview mirror, she could have sworn she saw a young, dark-haired man dressed in clothes from another era. Her mouth became a silent scream as the straight stretch of highway began to wind up ahead. Attempting to slow down, she stomped on the brake pedal. It didn't budge. It was as if—

Peering down, she shrieked at what she saw: the cabin had appeared beneath the pedals, wedging itself there to keep the gas to the floor and the brakes useless. A dangerous curve lurked ahead, one that she wouldn't dare take at such a high speed, even at her angriest. The cliff on the other side of the meager guardrail was sheer and ended in jagged rocks that had, over the years, claimed many a haphazard traveler.

Thinking quickly, she stomped on the clutch and popped the transmission into neutral, but the inertia was still faster than her reflexes were capable of maneuvering. Her irises shrank, sweat pouring over her forehead as the curve closed in.

I'm going to die!

Her chest tightened as the highway flashed by, imminent death increasingly near. The right side of the road was lined with trees, their bark skinned bare by others in similar circumstances. Suddenly, she swerved into the forest.

A tree is better than a freefall.

The sedan bucked from the shift, leaning on two wheels as the vehicle veered to the passenger side. But it was too much, and the car began to tumble madly like an Olympic gymnast. Inside, Sylvia was tossed like a ragdoll, the shattered windshield raining glass on her, cutting her in a million places. The metal surrounding her bent like a tin can. She blacked out as the car came to its final jarring stop on its side against a sturdy cedar. The tires spun like a top, pointed at angles unintended for function.

A trucker, who had been a few yards behind the woman and witnessed the accident, slowed his rig to a complete stop and shambled out of the cab as quickly as his arthritic knees would allow. He followed the broken path cleared by the car's display of unintentional tumbling to where Sylvia drooped from her seatbelt like a limp toy, blood dripping from multiple wounds. Crimson-soaked hair marked the shed essence of its wounded host, debris entangled in the matted mess. The smell of leaking gas caused the man to quickly use a knife he had strapped to his side to free the stranger from her binds. Carefully catching her as best he could and lowering her to the ground, he dragged her out of the mangled car and a safer distance away just before a spark lit the wreckage into an inferno.

A passing family stopped to gawk, the mother protectively covering her children's eyes as the father rushed to assist.

Black smoke billowed upward, catching the eyes of nearby highway patrol and approaching traffic alike. Soon, sirens closed in on the scene, wailing their approach to the growing throng on the asphalt. Using the oncoming lanes to get to the site, the men in the firetruck and the sheriff's car gaped before they flew into action. The officer called for an ambulance as the others worked to douse the flames before it turned into a wildfire.

Sylvia's pulse had weakened dangerously by the time the paramedics arrived and tended to her. Her eyes barely fluttered during the trip to the hospital as the glass was picked from her tangled hair like crimson berries.

When Sylvia awoke in the hospital with a screech of terror, the staff rushed in. Malcolm had been sitting in a rather uncomfortable chair by her bed, Levi playing with his cabin on the floor and chattering absently to his imaginary friend. The sudden snapping of the silence sent the boy into bawling hysterics as his mother pointed at her son's favorite possession in a prolonged yowl of terror.

"That thing tried to kill me!" Her breathing quickened as her heart drummed against her ribcage. The flailing of her arms sent the IV tubes into a gnarled dance as the mother clutched her head in a fit of madness. "Get it away! Burn it."

Tears flowed from mother and son alike as Malcolm ushered the child out of the room to calm the situation while nurses and orderlies invaded the space to restrain and sedate the terrified patient. Sylvia slowly relapsed into a medically induced slumber. Levi, however, was inconsolable, shaking traumatically in his stepfather's consoling embrace.

"Mommy hates me." The boy sniffled, his trembling lips and cracking voice edging from the shock of his mother's rejection. Pooled brown eyes pleaded to Malcolm, tugging at his ability to remain rock-steady for the boy's sake. "Why does my mommy hate me?"

"Oh, Levi," the man soothed, hugging the child tighter to fight back waterworks of his own. "Your mother's sick. She doesn't mean it." He broke the hug, holding the boy at arm's length and locking eyes. "She isn't well. She loves you very much. She's just having a very bad time because of the car crash." The lies caught in his throat, scratching like barbed wire as they came out. "I think we just need to keep your toy away from her from now on, okay?"

Levi nodded, turning his gaze down to the floor and then to the souvenir. Solemnly, with a tone of finality in his little hushed voice, he looked at the little cabin, a gleam of newfound hate in his eyes: "Shut up!" The boy slung the model, sending it skittering across the tile floor with a loud clatter. The toy crashed against the wall, the hinged roof separating from the main carving with a resounding snap, both pieces parting ways.

The sudden display of hostility toward the prized keepsake caught the stepfather and the staff off guard. The child grabbed his father figure in a deep embrace. "I want my mommy."

Malcolm gripped the child and stood. "She's sleeping, but we'll go back in for a bit. Okay?"

It wasn't long before Levi climbed into the bed with his mother, curled up, and fell asleep by her side, his thumb in his mouth as he nestled.

Several months passed, and Sylvia's injuries healed. Her relationship with her son deepened, and her intense hatred of her husband waned to nothingness. They sat around the dinner table, enjoying some of the beef stew Rosie had prepared. After the meal had finished, Sylvia, now a changed woman, took in the empty bowls to offer her compliments to their talented help.

"That was absolutely wonderful, Rosie. The mushrooms were a delectable touch."

The bowls clattered to the floor, shattering on impact. Spoons clanked, and scraps of the stew splattered against the linoleum. Sylvia's eyes grew huge as she leered at the shelf above the counter. The cabin that Levi held in such high regard was perched just above where the meal had been dished out.

The cook turned from the soapy sink, a confused look on her face. "What mushrooms, dearie?"

HAUNTED MEMORIES

I'm not exactly sure where to begin. Although I have what some might call a checkered past, I wish I could remember it. At the very least, I'd like to know what got me here. My name is Marvin Lathrop, and I escaped from Leavenworth Correctional Facility this morning. A piece of information I possess already isn't an easy one to carry: I've been labeled a dangerous criminal for the murders of my wife and child. But I had to get out of there, out of that prison. After serving seven years, I still can't recall the events leading to my incarceration.

I remember the trial, of course. Neither the judge nor the jury believed my amnesia defense. Even the doctor's testimony to my condition wasn't enough to earn me my freedom. "Transient global amnesia," he had called it. The prosecution argued, quite convincingly, that since there was evidence of neither brain damage nor a history of epilepsy or stroke, it was a condition manufactured to keep a killer free. They gave me a double life sentence.

I pull from my overalls the single possession I'd taken with me from my cell and look at it: a beautiful picture of my lovely brunette wife in sunglasses and a wide-brimmed hat she had to constantly hold down to keep the beach wind from claiming. Beside her is my five-year-old son, thin as a rail and tanned darker than both of us combined. His sun-bleached, mid-length hair flops over his energetic and striking blue eyes. I stand behind them, turning as red as a lobster in the early morning sun as the waves crash and gulls call in the background. I had asked a passing beachcomber to take the photo so we could all be in it.

A tear falls on the picture. I wipe the glossy surface dry and put it away. Not a single day of my sentence went by that I didn't think of them. My boy would have just become a teenager this month. I need to find out what happened. I need to figure out why I can't remember.

The wail of the sirens yanks me back to the present. I look conspicuous and need to get out of this jumpsuit. I unzip the outerwear and leave it in a heap behind me, along with my government-issued shoes and socks. It would be far easier to explain being half-naked than wearing an orange billboard declaring me *PROPERTY OF LCF*. I encounter a creek and follow it upstream, crossing anywhere I can, back and forth, to distribute my scent across the wild landscape. They'll be after me soon and likely have tracking dogs with them. I go as fast as my legs will carry me through overgrown woods and the outskirts of the small town of Tonganoxie. I pilfer some clothes hanging out to dry in the summer breeze. They're slightly baggy on me, but they're better than nothing. It's almost three o'clock, and the sun is turning up the heat. So, I rest up by sleeping near Lawrence, under a bridge that crosses the Kansas River on I-70. Traveling at night would be better, certainly more comfortable. Besides, I'm less likely to be discovered under the cover of the stars.

I wonder if my son would've become a Jayhawk.

I shamble around the college town, keeping as far away from houses as I can to avoid being spotted. I finally arrive at Clinton State Park, and it's their busy season. Tourists and campers picnic and play in the sun. I purloin some fishing gear and rubber waders to disguise myself as a fisherman. Then I burn my hand slightly when I steal a hot dog from someone's grill while their back is turned. I don't stick around the crowded campground for long. The last thing I need is attention. I figure if I stick close to the water, I can make a getaway if necessary.

Strolling around the enormous lake, I come to a clearing with a cabin overlooking a peninsula. It's perfect. The more I look at it, the more sense it seems to make. Any road once leading to the structure has long since been overgrown with weeds and hasn't looked traveled in years. I can barely even make out the tire paths. The building appears sound, though the roof is littered with several seasons of rotting vegetation. Tree seeds have sprouted in the gutters. The temptation to clean them out is overwhelming, a carry-over from being a homeowner in my own right, I suppose. I know such actions would give away the fact that someone is here. No. Things must remain the same.

The inside is musty and unkempt, and the floorboards creak under my weight in protest. There's a fireplace, but I know I shouldn't use it. The smoke would give away my position for sure. It's summertime, after all, so the need to stay warm isn't as pressing as it might be during a different season. Cooking food, however, will undoubtedly prove problematic. I can't keep pilfering food from the campers. Eventually, that will see me caught. A large cast iron kettle hangs like a museum display at the center of the flue.

As I pass the fireplace, I catch my reflection, the image captured by a rose-tinted mirror hanging above the mantle. The sight gives my blood pressure an unnecessary jump start. My time behind bars wasn't kind to me. I look haggard, unshaven, desperate, and destitute. None of those observations is far from the truth. I avert my gaze and continue.

There isn't much I can do about my finances without stealing or making a mistake, even if I try to earn it honestly. I don't want to go back to Leavenworth—that much I know. Prisons aren't meant to be resorts, but there was a definite caste system in place there, and I didn't fit the bill. At times, I deliberately got myself put in solitary confinement just to escape potential threats to my life. It never worked, though. One thing convicts have is good memories.

I had to escape when I did. Otherwise, it was a guarantee that I'd never find out who killed my family.

I'm not even sure who helped me get out. I received a specific set of instructions to follow. And once I got out, I was on my own.

The directions came in a series of unaddressed letters. They looked harmless at first—an anonymous person writing pen pal letters to lift my spirits or some baloney like that. I read the first one until I practically had it memorized. It wasn't until I had a dream that night that I discovered I hadn't actually read it at all. Encoded within was a very detailed step-by-step process.

Over that year, the mail came, and I added them to my pile of keepsakes. In time, it revealed a plan that went off without a hitch. I don't want to say what it was in case I need to use it again. Whoever gave me the information knew the ins and outs of that place like clockwork. I never even thought to question it.

All that matters is that it worked. Maybe once I solve my little mystery, I'll leave the States and start again in another country. Canada or Mexico, perhaps. I hear Argentina is lovely.

The grumble in my stomach reminds me that I need to figure out the food problem. Fishing would be the easiest, but without cooking, it could be risky. I walked the perimeter of the cabin. Someone had left a small hibachi in a pile of uncollected and strewn garbage. The grills are rusty, but a hot fire could remove most of it. I find an old steel wool pad and some expired cooking oil in the cabinet. Not my first choice, but I have to use what's here.

Placing the hibachi in the fireplace, I light a small fire with twigs and branches in the rusting body of the grill, hoping the smoke doesn't attract too much attention. That helps me season and sanitize the grates. Night will arrive soon. I can catch some fish, and the darkness will hide my fire if I keep it small. I gather more wood to cook my food and boil some water later.

A knock on the door prompts me to stand in an instant. I can't see anyone out the windows. I crouch down, being very careful to move slowly and prevent the floorboards from giving my position away. Creeping over to the kitchen, I collect a large, rust-pocked knife and put my back against the cabinets facing away from the door. That's when another knock sounds. My heart races. Sweat drips from me in torrents.

"There's no way anyone knows I'm here."

A third knock sends my adrenaline into overdrive. Cautiously, I make my way to the windows, peek out, and see absolutely no one. I slide to the door, slowly turning the knob and cracking it open. The porch is empty except for a small brown sack. Still wondering who might have seen me, I poke my head out and snatch the bag before snapping the door closed and bolting it.

I open the bag and reach inside. Whatever's there is fluffy and feels like a stuffed animal. My face scrunches as I detect a dried stain of some sort. Yanking it free, I drop it on sight, my eyes wide in disbelief. It's my son's powder-blue teddy bear, the one my mother gave him when he was born. Slowly, I kneel and retrieve the bear, my eyes filling as I relive every moment that thing has experienced.

"Just look at you!' my mother cooed at him in the hospital room, shaking the bear this way and that. His head shifted randomly, and his eyes never focused on the source of the voice, but he paid attention to the strange person making funny noises.

One morning, when he was three, he woke us up screaming after a nightmare. We both rushed into his room, frantic and concerned. He had been so frightened by whatever haunted him that he had wet the bed. After he calmed down, he told us about his dream.

"There was a bad man. Hims had a knife." James scrubbed at his eyes with the sleeve of his pajamas.

"I should check the house," I said and proceeded to look everywhere in his room.

"Let's get you changed and cleaned up," my wife comforted. She unzipped his pjs and got him naked for a quick bath.

She sang to him as she bathed him.

After my patrol, I fetched a new set of sheets from the linen closet and a new bed liner. Changing the bedclothes, I listened with a contented smile on my face. By the time they returned, with James wrapped in nothing but a towel, his hair still damp and mussed, the room was ready for him.

Carol dressed him anew.

Then, he crawled into bed. "What if the bad man comes back?"

I knelt as she tucked him in, holding his favorite blue teddy bear. "Teddy will keep you safe in your dreams, okay?"

James let out a long yawn, indicating that he was calm enough to sleep on his own once again. "How, Diddy?"

It always brought a smile to my face when he called me "Diddy."

"Teddy here is magical," I explained, making the bear hop and stroll up the bed toward James with a massive grin on my face. "He'll protect you by being there in your dreams. All you have to do is love him and believe in him." I snuggled the toy into James's face, eliciting a giggle as he snatched his bear from me. "Remember. If the bad man comes again, Teddy will save you."

We both kissed his forehead as he yawned once more. We stayed near, watching over him while he fell back into a deep sleep, his stuffed toy clutched tightly. It wasn't the last time he had a bad dream, but it had become a rare thing for him to wake up from one in a panic.

That bear would become his avatar, his security blanket of sorts, going everywhere he did at all times. It took an act of God or great timing to peel it away from him long enough for my wife to send it through the washer.

You would have thought the world was coming to an end when it reappeared sans one of its button eyes. He looked at his mother as if she were a superhero when she sewed it back on. It was a little low and crooked, but I think that made James love the bear even more. Through stitched seams and bad dreams, that bear kept my son company.

The stains I felt were blood. His blood. I'm sure of it.

I look at the dried, coagulated stain, tracing it with my finger as tears slightly blur my vision. My knees give out, and I collapse to the ground, clutching the toy to my chest as I weep. James is gone, taken before his life could even begin. My broken heart throbs at the strain of his memory.

I rear back, threatening to launch the stuffed animal across the cabin, but I stop and bring it back close to my heart as I stand, still weeping. Another knock comes from the front stoop. I set the toy down gingerly on an end table, stomping angrily to the door. I unlock it and yank it open.

"I don't know who you are, but if you think fucking with me like this is funny, you'd better stay in the shadows! I will fucking kill—"

My feet kick something—a clear plastic bag. Through the opaque evidence label, I see a delicate golden chain peeking at me, taunting. My heart sinks again. My legs become rubber once more as I clasp the sack, studying the contents. It was a gift I had given Carol for our anniversary: a locket that opens to reveal minuscule photos displayed inside. The jewelry and bag alike sport crimson reminders of that fateful night.

Opening the bag, I reach inside. The blood still feels fresh! How can that be? After seven years, it still seems slick. With my eyes wide in disbelief, I examine my hands, lightly rubbing the fingers together to make sure what I sense is real, spreading a red stain on my digits. My mind goes into panic mode as I urgently remove the locket. More memories flash through me, rending my soul.

It was an anniversary gift. My arms reached over my wife as she held her long hair out of the way, and I clasped the ends of the chain together behind her neck. The gold glinted at me as I gently kissed the nape of her neck. She leaned into my love with a slight purr. Wrapping my arms around her pregnant belly, I gently pulled her to me and hugged her close.

"Once the baby is born," I cooed, "we can put a picture of him—"

"Her," she corrected. "I want a little girl." She twisted the locket on its chain to peer at the shrunken photo of us kissing on our wedding day.

"Her." I smooched her neck some more, swaying us both to unheard music. "We can put a picture of her in there beside us." I paused, accentuating it with another light peck. "Or him." We made love that night ever so carefully, affirming our dedication to each other.

As I cradle the jewelry in my hand, its delicate gold chain shifts in my grasp, and another recollection occurs.

As another contraction hit her, she clasped my hand. Hard. She had surprising strength while she fought through the agony of childbirth. I bit my lip to stifle the wringing she was giving my knuckles and slid my free hand into my pocket, where I had to place the locket, caressing it nervously. She was afraid to wear it during the birth for fear of snapping the chain.

"Come on, Mrs. Lathrop. One. More. Push!" The doctor sat at the stirrups, his hands under the hospital gown. "He's almost here!"

Carol complied with another mighty yawp that seemed to shake the lights with its intensity. A few seconds later, we heard his first cries.

A nurse wrapped our son in a white towel, holding him out to show us. He was purplish in hue but fading to a redder color, and his skull appeared a bit misshapen from the birth canal. He was covered in blood, but we didn't care. He was perfect. "It's a boy," she declared triumphantly. "I'll get him cleaned up, and then you can have him back."

My wife looked heartbroken that they took him away, almost as if she'd never see him again. Then, the pain of the placenta coming out distracted her with another mighty grunt of effort. The nurses cut his cord, cleaned him up, and the doctor circumcised him per our request. Finally, our crying newborn came back to us as they placed his naked body onto hers for the first time. His wailing stopped almost immediately as she held him, bawling with happiness. My tears flowed, too, as I watched mother and son bond. It would feel like an eternity before I would get to hold him, but I was content to savor my family and its newest addition. Our love made life. It was real. He was real.

My mind returns to the present with an audible snap that nearly knocks me to my back. I'm dizzy from reliving those moments. I pedal backward on my butt through the door and slam it shut with my foot. My heart races, drumming my ribcage so hard that I think it might explode. Hell, part of me wishes it would just so I can see them again, if even for an instant, before eternity falls on my soul. I wail loudly, clutching the locket to my chest, rocking back and forth as I grieve like I never have before.

As the initial wave subsides, I collect the bear and sit on the recliner in the living room. Tears blinding me, I wrap the chain around the stuffed toy's neck and work the clasp. It dangles loosely, even double-banded, from the small toy, but I hold the joined mementos to me like a treasure.

I contemplate lighting something: a lantern, a flashlight, anything. This cabin is secluded enough that it would be safe, yet someone knows I'm here. I never heard footsteps, though. The floorboards on the porch didn't protest their weight as they had mine, yet someone knows. What's worse, they know *me*. They know my past.

The shadows of the cabin take on a life of their own. I desperately want them gone, banished by anything I can find. Every movement, every sound sends my heart into my throat. The wind from the lake seeps in through the windows, billowing the curtains in a way my mind takes as threatening. I tightly shut all of the panes I cracked open earlier. The atmosphere in the cabin grows heavy and stale, a palpable malice in my head. My eyes flit this way and that, my neck snapping in any direction where I think I perceive movement. My chest drums steadily, nerves on edge, even as my eyes adjust in the darkness to which I've resigned myself.

I'm beginning to hate this place. Parking myself on the floor, my back to the wall between the front door and the window next to it, I sit clutching the bear and locket, rocking back and forth, wide-eyed. My flight instincts are kicking into high gear. Nodding to myself, I stand and gather any evidence of my presence here, stuffing it all into the brown sack in which the teddy bear had appeared. Just as I reach for the knob, another knock comes, this time at the rear entrance.

Stomping over, I fling the screen door ajar, checking everywhere for the slightest sign of movement, a grimace of fury on my face. I step out only to have my feet slide from under me, sending me careening to the floor with a resounding thud.

As the stars of the impact fade, I slowly sit upright, half in and half out of my supposedly secluded hiding spot. I examine my traitorous feet with ire before I locate another evidence bag. It's what caused my legs to fly out.

I snatch it from the stoop recklessly, and something inside pokes through the thick plastic, stabbing deeply into my palm, all the way through my hand. I can't suppress the yowl of agony before it escapes my lips and echoes through the still, quiet night.

I glare at the thing dangling from my right hand with a mix of rage and horror—a bag draped over the blade of a large, blood-soaked butcher knife.

"Who are you?" I think I've only said it internally until it comes back to me in the rebound. "What do you want from me?"

Nothing. No response.

I slam the doors, latching them as securely as they allow, wincing in pain with each movement of my hand. Slowly, I pull the knife in the bag free from my hand, blood pouring from the wound in torrents.

Visions begin popping to life in my head. They don't feel real to me, like they aren't even mine. Yet I look on as if I'm the one controlling the thoughts. Hands flash in front of me, drenched in a fresh, crimson essence. The knife they hold is equally blood-soaked, imbued not just with blood but with memories.

My mind rewinds the scene, taking me back to before her throat was cut. She and I had made love after tucking James in for the night. Afterward, I wandered to the kitchen for one of the famous post-coitus snacks she perpetually joked with me about. As I mapped the contents of the fridge, looking for just the right thing, I felt my mind shift in a way I had never felt. Still conscious, control of my body was no longer mine.

I heard someone else speak to me: "I'll take it from here, brother."

The mysterious voice rattled in my noggin. It was familiar, yet I couldn't place it to save my life. Taking on a life of their own, my hands yanked a butcher knife from its block. I felt helpless as my traitorous feet ambled back up the stairs to the bedroom I'd come from. My beautiful wife lay on her side of the bed in that lovely state of half-sleep from our conjoining mere moments ago.

"Who are you? What do you want?"

I could feel the maliciousness overtake me.

"Your happiness," the voice echoed throughout my skull. "I'm going to take everything from you now."

She turned her slumber-addled head to me and must have seen the intent in my eyes. Her gaze grew into a panicked fear. She raised her arm as my arm flew into a swing that cut her deeply.

"No!" I screamed, but it never left my mouth. All I could feel was a maniacal grin. "Run, Carol! I can't stop myself!"

She didn't hear me. A scream pealed from deep within her as she shuffled away from my advances, hitting the floor with a resounding thud, still trying to make her escape. "What are you doing, Marvin? Why are you hurting me?"

She pleaded for her life as I stalked her around the room, slashing when I got close, sometimes missing, other times, gashing her open.

Tears streamed down my cheeks as my body refused to cooperate with my demands.

"What's going on, Mommy?" a slumber-filled voice chimed from behind as I cornered her against the footboard.

"James! Run! Hide!" My wife let out one final scream as I slowly turned my head toward the little voice and slit her throat, that grimace of hate still on my face.

I stood, looking at the viscera-soaked digits in a distant haze, a garbled scream to my left. Peering over, my wife, the woman I knew I loved beyond compare, lay half-upright against the footboard of our bed, still holding her neck as it fountained her essence onto the carpet. She held her other hand out to me, not in a gesture of need but of defense. She bled profusely from gashes in her guarding arm, a ghastly look of terror etched on her face. Soon, she wilted to the floor in one final gargle. It sounded as if she had said something, but the memory was too unsettling for it to be clearly discerned. Or perhaps I hadn't wanted to hear what she had uttered with her final breath.

The boy, now wide awake in horror, spun on his heels and thundered down the hall, slamming his door behind him. I took one final glance at my expired beloved and gave an uncontrolled chase.

"No!" I pleaded with whoever was guiding my tirade. "Please. Not him, too."

"It's your fault, brother," uttered the thing driving my body. "You were born a killer."

The venom in that voice was palpable.

"You denied me my life," it continued, "my own chance at happiness. Now I'm taking yours."

Still unable to place the sound to a face, I fought against my actions to no avail.

"You knew this day was coming. You may have forgotten about me, but I've never forgiven you."

Betrayed by my limbs, I made my way to my son's sanctuary.

"If you can remember who I am, I'll spare him."

I heard James's screams from beyond his bedroom door, frightened and frantic. The bloody digits wrapped around a locked door and rattled it angrily. I could hear my son's pleas as clear as day, yet my voice was garbled and distorted. Still, I felt the putrid hate in the sound as those hands tested the door. My strong shoulders forced it open in a shower of wooden splinters, listing the door off of its hinges.

Stepping onto a toy-littered carpet, I listened with those stranger's ears. I felt a stab of pain as I peered down. A pile of Legos beneath my bare feet caused a mumbled curse to escape. The hallucination had me hunting my precious child. We had played hide-and-seek many times. I knew all of his favorite spots. That muffled voice called to him, enticing him to show himself. Red hot flashes of anger flared behind my eyes as I stooped, sweeping the bed covers aside to an empty floor. The closet. I stalked to the folding door as that odd, gargling sound oozed from my throat. I felt my ears press against the angled slats of the closet, listening intently. My voice cooed at the petrified child, probably trying to convince him that everything would be fine if he just came out.

I felt each of the cool, neutral slats as my face slid to the floor. A small pin pricked my right cheek, probably a sliver of wood from the door. No sound came from within the space, yet my bloody fingers grasped the wood curtain and peeled it back. Those hands stabbed at piles of shoes and toys, hoping to find purchase.

A whimper came from behind me, and I shot upright. The toy box. Of course! I spun to the sound and lurched forward. I could smell him now. He had wet himself in fear. It grew stronger with each step toward the container, a wooden treasure chest the size of a steamer trunk I'd made with the very hands that were now preying upon him. The lid was shut, a clear indicator that he had thought it would keep him safe.

I could feel the concept of latching the hasp cross my mind, leaving the child to starve and dehydrate amongst his possessions. Instead, the hands elected to yank the lid wide and reach inside. They wrapped around his young neck, pulling him, frightened and fighting, from the box. The hand with the weapon raised as he let out a final yowling plea for me to stop.

The memory ends with me screaming 264hunderrous denial. Just as quickly as it arrived, it vacated my mind, leaving more questions than answers. I don't understand why this vision, these thoughts, haunted my mind. I never would have harmed a hair on his beautiful head. I loved him. I cherished my family. I soaked the bear with emotion, holding it tightly as I rocked back and forth on my knees. I buried my face into the toy and howled my anguish. My boy was gone. That couldn't be undone.

My heart races as I return to the present, sweat pouring from me almost as fast as the blood from my wound. My hands fly to my face as I weep in despair. It's no wonder the jury convicted me. I had, in fact, slaughtered my family, or at least my body had. Against my wishes or not, they had perished by my own hands. Nothing could bring them back or undo what had transpired.

I lament there in the shadows of the cabin for what feels like an eternity, my back against the rear door.

The door vibrates with another set of raps, pulling me slowly from my pool of self-pity. Defeated and forlorn, I slide away to allow the door to drag in its worn groove on the floor. Someone has left another present on the stoop. This time, it's a length of thick hemp rope and what looks like an envelope. Hands trembling, I collect the items and shut the door behind me. Scrawled on the front of the carrier are the words *Join your family*. I flip it over and pull the tucked flap out, revealing a picture.

I barely have the photograph halfway out when I recognize the setting. It's the last Memorial Day before we moved to Kansas from our native New Mexico. I grew up there, met Carol, and then got a job offer I couldn't refuse near the college town of Lawrence. We went to my parents' grave sites to lay one final wreath before relocating several hours away. Their marker, a double headstone of maroon granite, still shone in the sunlight, though a few years of weather had removed a bit of the luster. Beside their slabs was an older granite carving. A petrified child lay peacefully sleeping atop a small stone column. The inscription on the pillar read *Melvin Lathrop, we never knew you, but we loved you.*

I knot the rope to match my stomach, tossing it over the rafter spanning between the living room and the kitchen, a skill I'd picked up in prison. I'd contemplated it plenty of times in my tenure wearing orange. I almost succeeded a couple of times, too. But I was discovered by a guard or my cellmate before the job was finished. Each instance left me in a progressively deeper pit of emotion that no amount of medication or psychological therapy could remedy.

That was until the letters began to arrive. They proclaimed my innocence, that if I found my way out of containment, all of my questions would be answered. The letters gave me instructions on how to decode the writings, and I deciphered the encrypted directions on how to escape from prison. I followed the step-by-step instructions religiously. For the first time since my incarceration, I had hope. I lied to the shrinks, telling them that their therapy was helping and the medicine was doing its job. Still, there was a notable renewed vigor in my stride. The promise of innocence and answers had filled me with hope.

I no longer feel that hope. All I feel now is a longing to carry out the final instructions on the outside of the envelope.

I line up a chair under the noose as if foolishly preparing to hang a light without the use of a ladder, positioning it just so. Snaking the rope around the weight-bearing post dividing the two halves of the cabin, I knot the opposite end tightly, constricting it around itself with a silent, definitive nod, confident of the mechanics of my creation.

Mounting the recliner, I slide the hitch over my head. My tears have cried themselves dry, my heart only desiring the relief of the oblivion that awaits me. With one foot on the seat and the other on the top of the back, I rock the furniture under me until it falls out and away, removing the slack with a jerk. My limbs involuntarily twitch and fight, clawing at the snare in spite of my innermost wants. Air escapes from me, never to return, as I feel my head swell with trapped blood.

"You deserve this, brother."

He appears in front of me, the owner of the voice I heard on that fateful night. He resembles me to the point—

Now I recognize him! He's my twin, Melvin. My mother told me about him on her deathbed. He was stillborn, with my umbilical cord wrapped around his neck. In her final breath, she blamed me for his fatality, claiming that he had told her of the actions that happened within her womb.

How is he here? How is he grown?

Questions flutter through my throbbing brain in the final, eternal nanoseconds of my life.

"I was jealous of you even before we were born. I knew you would be the dominant one. That's why you eliminated the competition. Wasn't it, dearest brother?"

There's that bile-filled hate again, the same I experienced when my family was killed. It oozes from his voice, thick and bitter.

"Now you can join me in Hell."

My body sways from the rope, and my will grows weaker with each pendulating swing. As I dangle toward the end table next to the rocker, I feel a fuzzy hand give me a weapon. The knife. Gravity spins me to see the benefactor. The blue bear is in a different position from the one in which I'd left it, the locket still shuddering from unseen momentum.

Melvin witnesses the transaction. I can see it in his eyes. They hold a mixture of disbelief and righteous indignation, and his lips curl in a sneer of rage. Then, as the world begins to fade from me, it morphs into a grin.

"You could cut yourself free," he growls, "but I'll be there every time you feel even the slightest bit of happiness. I'll be there to make you drown in it as I turn it on its ear."

"Then we'll be reunited." I make one final sway, clamping my arms around the specter of my sibling in one final embrace. The knife falls from my hand, clattering in a metallic clang to the floor. "In Hell."

He yowls his hate as we become entwined once again, the Lake of Fire's flames licking at our souls forevermore.

FERAL

I read *Tarzan* many times as a child. The legend surrounding the ape-man had permeated pop culture for decades. *The Jungle Book's* Mowgli was just as indelible a character, but they were both works of fiction. There was absolutely no way a human child could survive in the wild. As infants, we are far too helpless and dependent upon others for our well-being. When you stop and think about it, it's amazing that we even rose to the top of the food chain at all. Was it our opposable thumbs? Our ability to use tools and fire? Or was it something just a bit more? These existential questions would only come to mind when, under the influence of some serious ganja, I relaxed with my close high school friends.

My name is Thomas Everett, and my life has never been anything noteworthy. As a man in my thirties who works in a print shop bindery, I perform menial and repetitive tasks every day to bring junk mail and magazines to everyone's doorstep. I make enough money to pay my bills, and that's pretty much it. If my job has a particularly good spring, by the time the slow summer season kicks in, I might have enough overtime money saved to spend a week camping. I'm okay with that. I love the great outdoors. Anything that gets me away from the clackety-clack of a folder, the whine of a cutter blade, and the hustle and bustle of the city is right up my alley. While I don't mind the crowded campgrounds around the lakes, it's hardly the seclusion I prefer. No. I have a cousin who owns thirty acres of Tennessee woodland on the edge of the Great Smoky Mountains near the Cumberland Plateau. They discovered a cabin right smack in the middle of it, did some minor repairs, added some furniture… the whole nine yards. All I have to do is bring, catch, or hunt for my food and keep the place clean. No tent required. And it's less than a hundred and fifty miles from Nashville, where I live.

What does one have to do with the other? Come on. Surely, you've guessed it by now. It shouldn't really be surprising, not if you've ever driven through the state of Tennessee. Most of the people residing outside the bigger cities are dirt poor, and it shows. It's heart-wrenching to witness. I feel like a damned king "slumming it" through the farmer's market in disguise. Kids with matted hair, who look like they haven't bathed in years, clutch parents who are just as unkempt. Even the homeless in Nashville don't look that bad. After driving through one ramshackle town after another to reach my cousin's land, I feel like complete shit just for having the audacity to crave vacation from my life.

When I pull up to his house, even my cousin has a disheveled appearance. He peers out from under the hood of his 1957 Ford, a pet project that has taken almost as long as he's been alive. It took much of that time just to get the engine block back into the car. He wipes oily dirt from his hand before extending it in my direction as I close my car door, still studying the insides of the auto.

"You still haven't got that thing running?" I laugh.

He returns his free hand to the wrench, emits a muttered curse, and ducks out from under the hood. "Nah. Still waiting on parts." He smiles a checkered grin, his missing teeth making him look almost cartoonish. Wiping his hands on a towel that looks like it could have made the trip on the Mayflower and absorbed every speck of dirt along the way, he gives me a side hug before I light up a filterless cigarette.

"You've been waiting on parts for this thing ever since it came off of the assembly line, you old bastard." I jab him in the ribs gently with my elbow.

"Respect your elders, boy." He tosses the rag so that it drapes over the car's fender.

"Elder, my ass," I continue the banter. "You're only one minute older than me, Dale." We both chuckle before falling silent for a moment. "How have you been?" I ask, finally.

"Been keeping it together."

The sadness in his eyes gives me a pang of shame for even remotely looking down on him. An infant begins to cry inside the trailer. The screen door does very little to stifle the sound. "Is that little Abby?"

His forlorn state remains, yet it now mixes with a bit of bright pride. "Come on in and meet her."

I follow my cousin into his trailer. Despite an exterior marked by prolonged disrepair, the inside is kept tidy, if not a touch cluttered. Pictures of him and his wife are everywhere. I look around as he disappears into the back bedroom. Next to the television, a framed photo of Ariel, her baby bump nearly in full bloom, stands front and center, with Dale lovingly embracing her from behind. They look happy and hopeful, and Ariel is absolutely glowing. I pick the image up for a closer look but quickly return it to its place when I hear him approaching.

"Here she is." The comment is directed at me yet aimed at Abigail, cooing to her and rocking her gently as she smiles at him, slobbering on her fist. "Sorry it took a bit. She needed to be changed." He bounces her gently in his arms. "Yes, she did."

He continues making noises and faces at her as I lean in for a better look. "She's beautiful, cuz."

"She looks a lot like her momma already." He brims with pride and happiness while holding her. "Can you take her for a few seconds? I need to make her a bottle."

I comply happily, scooping her from him carefully, mimicking his motions to keep her calm. He peers at me with those big baby-blue eyes and smiles, but it doesn't last long. Her face begins to contort into a wail. I increase my bouncing a little and gently shush her. "It's gonna be okay. Daddy's making you something to eat right now."

Dale finishes mixing the formula and sits in his recliner, holding his arms out for his daughter. As soon as I pass her off and the bottle is in her mouth, her crying is placated. "There you go." He silently rocks back and forth as she greedily consumes the contents.

"I know you said you're getting by"—I search for the words with care so I don't offend him— "but do you need anything? Anything at all?"

He smiles uncertainly at me, the sadness returning to his eyes. "Nothing you can give me, cuz. I miss her momma. Beyond that, I'm doing my best."

"I know you are, Dale. Just know that I'll help in any way I can. "

"You and your family helped with Ariel's funeral. That was more help than I can ever repay." As Abby finishes her bottle, he switches her position and stands to burp her over a towel on his shoulder.

I can feel that I'm treading close to his pride. "That was family helping family, and we would all do it again without a second thought. Just know that if you ever need something, don't be afraid to ask."

"I got this, Tommy." He bounces and pats Abigail's back. Soon, she emits a belch that would make a barfly proud.

I smile reassuringly, laughing at the baby as she sends me a satisfied smile. "I can see that." I use the towel to wipe up some spittle running down from the baby's mouth. She coos and smiles over her daddy's shoulder at me. I make silly faces, which she seems to like. "You really are a good daddy."

"I wanted this more than anything." Soon, with her father's coaxing, little Abby's eyes droop once again.

"Give me a few minutes to get her asleep again, then we can visit some more."

I step outside to light up a cigarette. As I look around and see car parts and junk littering the yard, I shake my head at the contrast between the inside and out. I can envision the litter of the lawn morphing from sharp, rusted metal to plastic toys, a sandbox, doll heads, and a baby pool. As I prepare to snuff out my cancer stick, I nearly jump out of my skin when a hand lands on my shoulder.

"Sorry, cuz. Didn't mean to give you a fright." His gaze shifts from me to my bad habit and back again. "Those things will kill ya one day."

I raise my eyebrow accusingly. "Didn't you used to smoke?" I pull out a flask of whiskey and take a pull from it, offering it to my family.

"Almost two packs a day. Gave it up for the baby's sake three months before she was born."

He pats my back, forcing out a belch before I can stop it. "You do have the magic touch."

We both laugh heartily, and he swigs from the metal container before returning it to me. "You want some shine for your camping trip?"

I accept a mason jar of pale yellow liquid. "Looks like piss water."

"Let me know if you like it. I'm trying to add flavors to the concoction. This one is apple pie." He pauses for a while, taking a slug from a jar of his own, but his eyes are fixed on the horizon in the direction of the cabin. "I want you to be careful out there, Tommy."

The tone in his voice makes my brow furrow. "Why? What's going on?"

"Don't rightly know, but I've had chickens come up missing; calves mangled, and one of my dogs got himself dead from something out there."

"Maybe a coyote or wolf?" I suddenly feel the urge to crack open the jar he gave me. I sniff the container just to be sure that he isn't tricking me. The scent of hard liquor clears my sinuses with a whiff. "Wow! That's some serious hooch."

"Could've been one of those," he continues, without his distant expression changing. "But whatever took out Zeus had to be powerful. Not much got past him. Smart, too. I've laid bear traps and went back to see them snapped with a tree limb and the bait gone." He takes another hit from his jar, and I follow suit. "It covers its tracks, so I can't tell what it is. Strange noises at night, too."

"I'll be fine. Just gonna do some fishing and play a lot of solitaire." I take another sip, this time without wincing. "Goes down smoother the more you drink it." I spin the lid back in place and walk it over to my truck. "I've got enough food to keep me indoors all week if need be."

"Just be careful. That's all I'm askin'." Dale capped his jar. "You packing?"

I show him my hunting rifle. "Never come down without it. Besides, I might get in the mood for rabbit or squirrel."

"Tree rats are good, but you ought to avoid rabbits. It won't frost for another couple of months." He puts a hand on my shoulder. "Hope you enjoy yourself, cuz. Come by if you need anything."

I laugh heartily at his concern. "I'm not going into the next state, Dale. I'm just gonna be over yonder."

We hug more like brothers than distant cousins, and I climb into the cab of my truck. I still can't unsee that haunted look in his eyes as I pull out of his driveway and toward the rough, overgrown road leading to the cabin in the middle of his land. It almost has a look of finality in it, like he's seeing me for the last time.

I should visit him a lot while I'm here. Something's not right.

The road practically gives me whiplash as I head to my destination. Pulling into a clearing in the middle of a thick, sun-deprived forest, I hear the crunch of gravel as my tires come to a halt near the structure in which I'd be spending the week. I sigh contentedly, my realization of the reflex only occurring to me a few seconds later. Jumping out of the vehicle, I grab what I can and spin to look at the cabin.

"Huh. Looks like Dale's done some work."

I step onto a brand-new covered porch, complete with a swing. I can't see the spring-fed creek of the lake from this angle, but I can hear the light trickle of the water. The tops of the trees wave in the wind as if greeting me. Woodpeckers drum for their lunch as I snap the lock open on the hasp with a key.

"I'm telling you, this place is heaven."

I nod appreciatively, taking it in one last time before cracking the door wide. The inside is pristine, just as Dale's trailer was. On top of the dining table are a few small brown paper bags. One contains fresh farmer's market peaches; another, tomatoes. Between them is another bottle of moonshine. "He really rolled out the figurative red carpet for me."

Still a bit of a musty smell to the place, but that'll go away once I open a few windows.

Walking into the bedroom, I take a peek outside. The underbrush rustles at the edge of the clearing. I watch that area for a while but never catch a glimpse of what's there. I shrug. "Probably a coon or possum."

I finish unloading my gear, dropping off my pole and tackle box by the door. The stream always has trout, bass, and bluegill in the deeper parts. I can catch dinner one day.

I hear a thunk coming from my truck. Spinning and racing back outside, my heartbeat quickens as my vehicle rocks back and forth. I still can't see what's there.

I see a flash of thick, matted, black hair and... flesh?

"Is that a naked person rummaging through my truck?"

My whisper is loud enough to give whatever's rocking my vehicle pause. I can see that disheveled crown of black tilt itself in my direction as if listening.

"Hey!"

The thing jolts. Its nerves are obviously on edge.

Slowly, I watch as it peers over the bed in my direction. Striking blue eyes leer at me with a mixture of absolute fear, hate, and no sense of what passes for civility in the modern world. As it slowly rises, the creature grunts through a shredded pack of hot dogs crammed into its mouth.

"A boy?" I wonder at the naked, filthy child in front of me. "Hey! Wait!" I take a step toward him. He flinches, bolting toward the tailgate and away from me. I slow my approach, attempting not to spook him. Holding an arm out, I comfort him. "I won't hurt you, kiddo. You like hot dogs? I can—"

Another step is all it takes to send the kid fully into flight mode. He growls at me territorially, snatching as much of my food as he can before leaping from my truck and disappearing into the thick underbrush. I freeze in place, not knowing if I should give chase or remain at the cabin. By the time my brain makes its decision, it's too late. The boy is gone.

I marvel at the event that just transpired. "Damn, he moves fast."

Walking over to my truck to assess the damage, I shake my head, my mouth still agape in disbelief. My cooler lays on its side with the contents spilled unceremoniously over the scratched paint of my well-worn bed. The eggs are all broken… the few that are left, at any rate. The ice melts in the sun, splayed out in a fan from the toppled container. The hot dogs aren't the only thing he made off with. Every type of meat I had is gone, save for the bologna.

It's over thirty miles to the nearest store, and the light of day will be fading soon. I scoop what I can back into the cooler, righting it. I can live on bologna and crushed bread for a night, but I know I need to get back to my cousin's trailer quickly to let him know what I've seen.

I hastily lock up the cabin and head to Dale's. My truck feels like it can fall to pieces as I drive fast down the potholed dirt path. About halfway to his house, I catch the brush beside the road rustling. Fearing that whatever it is might bolt out in front of me, I slow to a crawl. I'm fairly certain it's the boy, but the weeds are so tall that all I can see are flashes of movement. Coming to a complete stop,

I throw the transmission into the park position and roll down my windows.

"Is that you? Are you playing games with me?"

My questions are answered with a titter of laughter, both innocent and ominous. The brush moves from my side. I catch a brief glimpse of the black mane and dirty, deeply tanned skin as it crosses to the passenger side. My mind races as I attempt to decipher his games.

Is he playing, or does he simply not know better? It's not like there's tons of traffic around here to teach him the dangers of cars.

Leaning over the console to the other seat, I cautiously attempt a glimpse. Hearing a low guttural growl just outside of my line of sight beside the vehicle, I place my hand on the sill and peer further. Suddenly, he pops up like a jack-in-the-box, a mix of playfulness and insanity in his eyes, and scratches my hand deeply with his long nails. I yowl in pain and surprise. Another chirp of giggles, and he shoots off into the forest once more.

My left hand begins to bleed from four deep gashes. I frantically search my cab for anything to wrap it in, finding some unused fast-food napkins in the glove compartment. I roll the windows back up most of the way, cursing at myself for being naïve and trusting. Wincing in pain, I put the truck in drive and complete the trek to Dale's house.

Heated by urgency and anger, I feel my face change colors as my tires slide to a stop outside of the trailer. "I hope to hell he has some disinfectant." I kill the engine and throw the door open.

"Dale!" I holler at the top of my lungs as I step from the cab. When I note the volume of my voice, I almost clap my good hand over my mouth, recalling that he might have a sleeping infant inside.

After a few seconds, my bewildered cousin peeks out the door. He quickly scans me up and down, seeing that I'm clutching my left hand. "The hell?" He disappears into the trailer for a short eternity, reappearing shirtless and buttoning his pants. "What happened to you?"

I feel my face blush. "Did I interrupt something?"

"I was taking a nap. You gonna tell me what happened, or do I have to guess?" He rushes over to look at my hand. Some of the napkins dried into my coagulated blood. Removing them was painful, reopening parts of the wound. His face loses all color as he lifts away the makeshift bandages. "What the.." he censors himself, whispering through gritted teeth. "What did *that*?"

"You need to take all of your traps up." Dale looks at me as if I've just informed him that I'm the emperor of fantasyland, but I continue: "I know what's been terrorizing you. It's a boy."

He still looks as if he either doesn't believe me or doesn't want to.

"I know it sounds crazy," I admit. "If I hadn't seen the kid myself, I wouldn't have believed it either."

I proceed to tell him about my encounter. I can still see doubt on his face, but he listens. After I finish, he stays quiet for some time. "He's completely wild?" he asks at last.

"Sure seems that way." I hold up my hand to accentuate the statement. "I think he was trying to play, but he doesn't seem to know how."

Dale nods slowly. Abigail starts crying behind us in the trailer. His attention divides before he finally speaks:

"Well, I can't do nothin' about the traps right now. Sun's about down. Let's get you patched up for now. Gotta get those scratches done up. Humans are filthy animals." He leads me back into his trailer, where I see the frozen image of an adult film on his television. I grin at him and chuckle. He turns beet red and smiles coyly. "I don't get a lot of *me* time. I was taking advantage of Abby being down for a nap."

"Speaking of filthy animals..." I nudge him playfully but then wince when a sharp pain shoots up my arm from my hand.

"Lemme get Abby taken care of real quick-like. She probably needs changing and a bottle."

I marvel at how fluidly he changed the subject. "Do you have peroxide? I can do this while you get your girl taken care of."

"Bathroom cabinet," Dale utters before disappearing into the main bedroom toward the sound of his wailing infant.

I hear him coo at her, followed by the rip of the strips fastening her diaper in place. Reaching into the cabinet, I remove the dark brown bottle of peroxide. I see some gauze and waterproof medical tape. Half a bottle of the liquid and nearly the entire roll of gauze later, my hand throbs but feels better. I reappear from the lavatory to see my cousin cradling his daughter and feeding her.

"I owe you bandages and peroxide," I inform him. "I'll get some at the store tomorrow when I go to town. If you need anything before then, let me know. I'll get it for you while I'm there."

"Don't fret about it. I bang my hand working on cars all of the time." He paces and rocks as he speaks. "Come by in the morning. If you're sure, I'll make up a list. I gotta call Darlene and see if she'll look after Abby for an hour or two."

I go to my family members and softly touch the baby's cheek, a wide smile on my face. She's nearly back to sleep in her daddy's arms after her formula. "Will do," I whisper.

I head out of the trailer with a hurried wave behind me and climb into my truck. Dusk paints the clouds shades of orange, pink, and red, the purple of twilight chasing behind as twinkling stars begin to fill the night sky. I always forget just how many are visible when I'm away from the bright lights and noise of the city. As I drive back to the cabin, I go slow with my high beams on. Even then, the countryside seems incredibly dark.

Who knows what will pop out in front of me?

The next morning, I wake up, and the sun is already sending serene beams through the windows. Reaching over to the nightstand, I grab my watch, look at the time, and see that it's nearly ten o'clock. "Must've slept longer than I thought."

After a good stretch on the edge of the bed, I step into my jeans and sniff my shirt to see if I should switch it out.

"I'm camping. No one's with me to care if I smell a little bit." I shake the preposterous thought from my head. "I still need to go to town to resupply what the local wild child took off with."

Caving, I decide to shower. I head over to the utility closet, kneel, and check for the blue flame. "Good. I don't have to wait an hour." I stand, collect my change of clothes and a towel, and start my day.

After my shower, I seek breakfast items in the fridge, forgetting that the carton of eggs had been ransacked. Slumping in defeat, I shut the door and finish dressing for a long haul to the nearest town. The rumble in my stomach makes me hurry the process along. Once clothed, I climb into my truck and make the bumpy drive to my cousin's trailer.

I pull up just as he tosses a rifle into an unfamiliar Jeep. He must have sensed my confusion at the sight. "It's Darlene's," he explains. "She's gonna let me take it into the woods while she watches Abby."

"Don't shoot the kid." I search his face for his reaction, but he remains stoic. "Be careful. The boy's eaten too many raw squirrels." I hold up my freshly bandaged hand for proof.

Dale smiles and nods. "I don't aim to shoot the kid, but if I have to scare him away, that'll do 'er."

"You got that list for me?"

"Oh!" Dale reaches into his pocket, pulls out a folded envelope with several items scrawled on the back in barely legible chicken scratch, and hands it to me. "You need money?"

"Nah. Keep it. You're family, and you're letting me stay in the cabin." I look over the requests, making sure I know what each of them is. I refold and pocket the envelope in my pants. "Once I'm back, I'll help you out." With a hurried wave, I throw my truck into drive and marvel at the smooth wonders of a paved road into town.

I finish my supply run, stopping at the trailer to unload Dale's groceries. Darlene pops into the doorway with

Abby cradled in her arms. The baby is contentedly nursing a bottle.

"You must be Dale's cousin," she says, pausing to recall my name. "Um… Tommy?"

I chuckle a bit. "You can call me Tommy or Tom." Loading my arms with sack after sack, I squeeze past her and plop them down on the counters. "If you'll tell me where everything goes, I'll put them up. Seems you've got a handful." I bolt out for the last load and return.

As I rifle through the haul, loading the fridge with the more obvious items he asked for, I empty the rest and put them away according to Darlene's instructions. "Dale still in the field?" I ask.

"Yeah. Haven't seen or heard from him in a few hours."

I nod, folding the last paper sack down. "I'll get my things put away at the cabin and go look for him. Any idea where he might be?"

She indicates the general direction he went. I say my farewells to her and Abby and head off down whiplash road to the cabin, where I make short work of unloading my supplies. I then grab my shotgun and head off toward the southwestern corner of the forest. Driving slowly, I keep a close eye on the brush next to the truck. The tall grass is nearly up to my cab windows and ready for the hay farmer to harvest. For now, I have to rely on flattened patches to see where Dale might have driven. Coming to a fork in the path, I choose the one that looks fresher, hoping that might be where he's gone.

My diligence is rewarded. Darlene's Jeep is parked in a clearing at the edge of the thickest part of the forest.

"Dale!" My voice echoes into the blackness of the underbrush. Letting him know I'm here will hopefully keep him from shooting me. After a few seconds, I get no answer.

Guess I'd better track him.

My father took me hunting as a kid. Quite often, in fact. I had actually gotten pretty good at tracking game, but I'm hardly an expert. It's always a bit more difficult if the ground isn't wet from a fresh rainfall, and it hasn't rained here for at least a week. Still, I know the signs to look for: trampled weeds, broken branches, blood (indicating injury or worse), or, in this case, boot tracks.

"Dale?" I call out again as I spy the tracks leading into the dense growth. Still no answer. "Dale! If you can hear me, speak up." I start to worry that he's potentially hurt himself.

Thirty acres is a lot of land, but it's not so huge that he couldn't have heard or answered me.

My heart flutters nervously, but I'm determined. "Come on, Dale. Where are you?"

I search for any signs I can find, but once I get under the umbrella of the thick canopy above, I know that finding clues will become increasingly difficult. Slinging the rifle over my shoulder by the strap, I kneel to check the prints for direction. Thankfully, there's only one set of fresh tracks, but I have no idea where all of his traps are. Hell, I barely know the lay of the land. I do know there's a stream that runs through the dense growth, and his tracks point in that direction. I decide to follow, but I first locate a large branch and use it to punch the ground in front of me as I walk. The last thing I need is to trigger a forgotten trap. Now that the thought appears in my head, my mind spins with worry.

What if he's done that very thing? What if he got caught in his own trap and bled out?

With a quickened pace and eyes to the ground, I feel along with the branch and move as fast as I can safely go. Then, at last, I see Dale off in the distance, standing in one spot, unmoving.

"Dale!" Still trudging through the carpet of rotting leaves and forest debris, I hasten to him.

Is he in a trance or something?

"Dale! Cousin?" I reach him and grab his shoulder. "You okay?"

He screams and jumps away from me, sprinkling me with his urine. I jump back at the same time, both in surprise and disgust.

Dale yanks the earbuds from his ears, his eyes so wide that they practically bulge from their sockets until he sees it's me. "Dammit, Tommy! What the hell are you doing, sneaking up on me like that? I could have shot you."

A laugh escapes me as I peer down. "Looks like you did." Shaking my head, I add, "You oughta know better than to wear those when you're out here alone. Something could have snuck up on you."

"Yeah? Well, it's a good thing I was already pissing." My cousin zips up, his breath returning to normal.

"Did you get all of your traps?"

He nodded in another direction. Following his gaze, I see a canvas duffle bag with several rusty, dirty traps jutting out. "All but one," he says. "Seems to be missing."

"You probably just forgot where you put it."

"Nope." He shakes his head insistently. "I know right where they all were, and one of them is gone."

"Any blood around where it was?" I feel a pang of concern, worrying that the boy might have caught himself and pulled it free.

"Clean as a whistle. Stake is pulled, too." Dale pauses for a few seconds. "Do you suppose that, if he knows what they do, he'll use them for hisself?"

"It's possible. He wasn't born in the woods."

"How do you know?" Dale pulled a wad of chewing tobacco from between his gums and lips, tossing it on the ground.

I begin to speak, but an odd howl echoing through the woods interrupts me. We turn our heads in unison toward the sound.

"That weren't no kind of dog," Dale remarks. "Or wolf."

Another wail pierces the forest. This time, it sounds pained, injured. Our eyes go wide at the sound as we pinpoint the direction from which it came. There's a desperation in its tone. It emanates from the deepest part of the forest, the part where very little sunlight can break through the thick leaves. As the yowls continue, we quicken our pace to a near jog, yet the scraggly saplings, bramble bushes, and fallen branches prevent us from a full-out sprint.

"You don't s'pose," Dale breaths between wide arching bounds matching mine, "he hurt hisself?"

"Maybe." I huff alongside my cousin, dodging trees. "He coulda seen how you did it but caught himself trying."

The bellows draw closer as we near the gaping maw of a cavern on his property. The blackness of the small opening, only big enough for a man to crawl through, seems to belch a sinister aura to me. I catch a glint of eyes hiding behind the blanket of shadow.

"Dale! Wait!"

I reach out to my cousin, but it's too late. Now it's Dale's turn to howl in agony after the metallic trap spring sounds. He falls to the ground, his left ankle painting the nearby forest floor crimson. I rush to him and try to pry the jaws of the bear trap open. I forgot how difficult these things can be once triggered. My hands slip, causing the teeth of the trap to go deeper. He screeches anew as the trap snaps bone.

"Sorry!"

Thinking quickly, I unload my rifle's chamber to prevent firing and use the gun as a pry bar to help unclench the mouth of the device. The agony in my cousin's screams echoes across the wild landscape.

"Got it! Pull your leg—"

I look over and see that he's passed out from the shock. Putting my foot on the bottom of the trap as I hold it agape, I spin my weapon around and jam the butt into the jaws close enough to the hinge that I can snake my cousin's foot free. Blood spurts out at a slow pace.

I need to get him tied up, or he'll bleed out.

I hadn't been paying any attention to the cave or the low, guttural growl blossoming from the darkness within. I doff my belt, tying it around his leg above the deep laceration. Dale yells as I apply the makeshift tourniquet, his only conscious action in the last few minutes.

"Stay with me, cuz."

The growl grows deeper, the acoustics of the cave magnifying it like a megaphone. "Mine."

I freeze in terror, slowly turning my gaze as I attempt to pull Dale to his feet.

"My," roared the voice from within the bowels of the earth with a deep yet childish pang of possessiveness, "food!"

Without thinking, I yank my gun free of the trap, gouging the wooden butt deeply as it snaps with an empty metallic clank. I lower the weapon's barrel at the eyes in the recesses of the cavern's mouth.

"He's not food!" I tell the presence, aiming at the rocky opening. Pulling the trigger, I attempt a warning shot. But I'd forgotten that I'd disarmed it only minutes prior. The hollow click of the trigger mechanism emboldens the thing in the cave.

The eyes draw closer, the shadows of the shelter giving way to the limited sunlight as a cherubic face glares at me with the intensity of a higher predator. The matted black mane clears the entrance, followed by the boy's sinewy chest. Crawling like a panther on the prowl, he circles me, stalking me. I spin in an attempt to keep him in my sights, not an easy task with a barely conscious, full-grown man hanging on one shoulder.

The boy's voice thunders another growl: "My food." His eyes meet mine, and I see that anything human within him is gone. All that remains is savagery and hunger. He rocks back and forth, almost like a cat readying to pounce, tucking under himself for the leap. As I watch intently, his muscles release as he springs.

Though I clumsily swing the rifle, I land a solid blow to his temple with the tip of the barrel.

The boy yelps, dropping to the ground. He skitters away, feeling the fresh wound on his head with every other step, but he never turns his back to me. The red on his hand enrages him further, his lips curling back in a grimace of hate. He belts out a roar that would reduce a tiger into submission, my legs becoming noodles under me, the rifle clunking to the ground in a small cloud of dirt. He readies himself for another charge. I throw my arms up as a shield, bracing myself while covering Dale as best I can, but the impact never comes. Instead, hot, rancid breath blankets my face in a reverberating trill. Slowly, I crack my eyes open, meeting the boy's dark, feral gaze as he straddles me, swiveling back and forth, clawed hands extended and ready to strike.

Contemplating my next move, I slowly lower my arms, locking eyes with the boy. Standing up in slow, unthreatening movements, I keep visual contact with the wild child. I pull my cousin to me to try and stand him back up, but the boy yanks him out of my grasp with unfathomable strength.

"My food," he reiterates between grunting, pubescent, crackling tones.

I pull Dale back in a desperate tug-of-war, growling back at the child in as authoritative a voice as I can muster. All the while, my heart hammers against my ribcage. "Not food. Friend."

The boy begins to quake, his gaze fixed on my fallen family member. The hunger on his face is refreshed, his tongue licking at his teeth involuntarily.

I've seen these types of convulsions before in cannibal movies. I don't think this is the first time he's eaten a human.

I make a sudden rush to the weapon on the ground. The boy answers in kind, raking his overgrown fingernails down the length of my forearm. Instinctively, I pull away, coddling the fresh wound and sucking in air through gritted teeth as blood trickles.

"You're making it awful hard to like you, boy." The phrase escapes me before I can even stop it.

He grabs hold of Dale and starts dragging him toward the earthen maw from which he sprouted with alarming speed. Just before he can duck into the cavern and take my cousin to a god-awful fate, I stop his advance by wrapping my legs around a tree and fiercely holding on to Dale's arms.

"Fuck. You. Kid." Straining against the boy's demonic might, I pull back, freeing, if temporarily, my cousin from his clutches.

The boy bolts at me once again. This time, I swing wide with my leg, catching him in that tender place between his. He collapses in a heap, cradling his exposed parts, trying to regain his breath with an excruciated groan.

I stagger to my feet, a bloodied smile on my face. "Yep. That's the universal language right there." Stumbling over to the rifle, I grasp it and examine the gouge marks and the bent barrel from trying to free my cousin. "Might not be able to shoot with it"—the steel feels like vindication in my hands—"but I can damn sure put a rabid dog down with it."

Still, I have to look away when I bring the butt of the gun down with a wet crunch.

It takes the better part of a year for Dale to regain full use of his foot, even if all of the feeling never returns.

Doctors say that's due to the length of time between injury and surgery. Dale doesn't care. "A limp is better than nothin'," he says.

Abby is running around the yard now, pestering the chickens and sheepdog as much as they'll permit.

In spite of the haunting memory of that visit, I still come by at least twice a year to see my cousin and his family. Darlene has moved in, and now there's talk of marriage and a baby brother for Abby.

I can't shake the sound that boy made when he lured us in, the roars he emitted when I took my family back. I don't sleep well in this cabin anymore. We buried the kid in a grave in the middle of the forest, yet I can feel his animal eyes on me, hungry, injured, vengeful. I keep my new rifle loaded and at arm's reach. Just in case.

Some nights, even in my own bed, I can still hear his howl.

ABOUT THE AUTHOR

Dan B. Fierce lives in his hometown of Kansas City, Missouri, with his husband of twenty-plus years and his family. He loves horror, comedy, and many things in between.

He has contributed short stories to many anthologies, all of which can be found in your favorite online bookstores in both digital and physical formats. Please see the "Other Stories By" page for a comprehensive list.

This book is his third solo publication.

OTHER STORIES BY DAN B. FIERCE:

"Warning Shot," "Mistaken," and "Revenge" — *The 2020 Indie Authors' Short Story Anthology,* edited and curated by Mustang Patty (Heathory Press)

"Abandoned Bikes" — *Clues and Culprits: An Anthology By the Indie Author's Group*, edited and curated by Mustang Patty (Heathory Press)

"El Cangrejo" — *HorrorScope (Volume 1),* edited by H. Everend

"Take Me to Church" — *We're Here: An Anthology of LGBTQ+ Horror*, edited by James G. Carlson (Gloom House Publishing)

"Hobo Nickel" — *Cursed Items Anthology*, edited and curated by Alisha McAdoo (Aye Alba Anthologies)

"The Void Screams Back" — *Crazy from the Heat*, edited and curated by Christopher Pelton (Psychotoxin Press)

Roadkill King by Dan B. Fierce (Fierce Imagination)

"Jamie Dice" — *Winding Paths*, Edited by Frances Pai Ippolito and Ken Hueler

"The Fledgling" — *That Old House – The Bathroom Part Two*, edited by Voices from the Mausoleum

"Accessorize" — *Spectral Spectrum*, Wicked House Press

Father Figure: Suspenseful Tales of Fatherhood by Dan B. Fierce (Fierce Imagination)